The Anniversary

*Forty years later the secret is
revealed, will it heal or hurt*

Sarah Stirling

Tellwell Talent
www.tellwell.ca

ISBN
978-1-77941-771-8 (Hardcover)
978-1-77941-770-1 (Paperback)
978-1-77941-772-5 (eBook)

This book is dedicated to my
two children, Dax and Amy
Always in love,
Mum

Prologue

She was lying on top of her bed, dressed for work: pale green wool skirt, soft yellow sweater, sheer nylons, painted toenails, pink. Her make-up had been applied perfectly, although I could see she was chalk white underneath, clown like. She wouldn't have liked that. Everything went still. Dark, freezing, blackness, my head large and hollow like I'd lost my mind. My eyes darted around the room. What happened? Clues painted a story in a fraction of a second — the empty pill bottle, her Bible on the bedside table — although my thirteen-year-old mind had no comprehension of earth time. I was in a world unknown, a black hole with no edges, no rules, no guidelines. I placed my fingertips lightly on her breastbone as if my touch might arouse her.

"Mum?" My voice echoed in my head.

The phone rang, blasting electric shocks through me. My bones melted and I dropped to the floor, curling up small to contain remnants of who I was just a minute ago, before. The phone rang and rang. The sound of a tortured animal came from somewhere, it scared me.

No, this is not happening, not happening. This is a dream. Wake up!

Time passed. *Did I sleep?*

Reluctant to move, I stayed curled on the carpet. I'd never noticed the brilliant blue and green looping threads in my parents' bedroom carpet, even though I had spent many nights sleeping on it. Each loop consisted of four to five shiny threads, the green at right angles to the blue. Thousands of them, all the same, this way and that in perfect unison to produce this dark turquoise carpet. Something about the perfect pattern comforted me.

The carpet became the sky as I flew back to the tragic nightmare I so desperately wanted to escape. My mother lay perfectly still above me. I dragged my weighty body to its knees, bringing myself to prayer position.

Empty pill bottle

Green skirt

Yellow sweater

Still chest

This was now my mother, but not my mother. Who was she now?

Gingerly, I touched her hand. Cold, but not like a winter cold where the slightest sensation of life can be felt in the veins. My mother's hand was dead cold. I felt nauseous, my mouth filled with thick slime. My large, hollow head spun and I swallowed hard.

Then spotted the journal.

Chapter 1

All in a Day

Phillip entered the room with a gust of assertiveness and opened the curtains like a servant might do in the eighteen century.

"Are you awake?"

He didn't sound as obliging as a servant. I groaned and rolled over; I had not slept well. He dotted my forehead with a familiar peck. I disliked pecks but was afraid to tell him in case all forms of affection ceased. We were nudging that stage in married life when the boys no longer occupied our constant attention. Our heads popped out of the gofer hole now and then to take a sniffy look at each other, but we kept our observations to ourselves unless they were complimentary.

For all intents and purposes, his side of the family looked the picture of function, but there were stories under the rugs if one were to lift the corners. You could see them in the strain nestled in the deep lines on my mother-in-law's face. Fiona and Dave were barely surviving the affair Dave had with a co-worker

— an outrageous occurrence for a Brit and the CFO of a successful law firm. He was sentenced to a life of somber guilt, which he wore like a double chin.

Fiona had taken on a persona reminiscent of a small, bubbling volcano camouflaged in flora and fauna. Her smile was planted on her face as if she were constantly posing for a picture. The kind of smile that warned onlookers there was something terribly vulnerable about this woman. She fluttered like a trapped bird, laughing too easily at nothing funny. Being around her for long periods of time exhausted me, but once in a while at the family cottage when the boys were out fishing, we'd find our footing.

Last summer, while sitting in oversized Adirondack chairs on the dock in the lazy afternoon sun, Fiona said, as if already in the middle of a conversation, "I still want to kill her you know."

She kept her gaze straight as we sipped our favourite orange cranberry punch. I quickly caught the drift.

"Don't blame you, Fi. She betrayed her gender," I said, straightening my shirt with righteous indignation.

"I've been told I blame her because I avoid holding Dave responsible."

"They're both responsible."

"You're right," she said with a weary sigh.

Her cheeks had been kissed by the sun and the lake glistened in her eyes.

"Your hair looks cute like that Fi, just thrown back in a pony. You look youthful and relaxed."

"Oh gosh, my hair, it's a mess. I never know what to do with it at the lake," she said, fussing with the ponytail.

Damn. Why did I shift the conversation?

"Here you go," I said topping up our glasses. I gave her a minute.

"I wonder if he ever loved me."

Why wouldn't she wonder? Deception has jagged corners that cut and bite.

"So what if he tells me he loves me? He told *her* he loved *her* too. For a year. How am I even to know if *she* was the only one?" She shot me a sideways glance, then sighed. "You have no idea how sick I am of this, of ruminating on the same thing every single day. I just cannot let this go. I'm driving myself mad."

"You're still seeing your counsellor, right?"

Why did I say that? I hate it when people ask me that.

"Yup, still seeing my therapist, still on medication, still doing the same thing and feeling the same way."

"Sorry Fi, I know you're doing all the right things."

I slid my butt forward, slouching in my chair, and put my feet up on the heavy wooden coffee table in an attempt to elicit a *chill-out* mood. Fiona sat straight up in her chair and leaned over the arm towards me as if to tell me a secret.

"I'm scheduled for ten hypnotherapy sessions; my first one is Thursday morning. Don't tell me what you think unless you're in agreement."

She turned back to the lake and took a sip.

"Hypnotherapy — mmmm, well … Why not?"

"Really? You think I'm not doing something dangerous or stupid?" She said in an excited voice.

I hesitated. Didn't know much about hypnotherapy, but I didn't want to discourage her.

"No, not at all. How did you find a hypnotherapist? I think there's a few around, and I guess my only concern would be how reputable they are, ya know?"

"Here she is," she said, pulling a flyer out of her pocket. "I like the sounds of her approach. I read about others, but she stood out to me; I've had my consultation with her already." She slowed her speech, "I like her and her office space. It's kind of spa like," her fingers on her left-hand making quotations. "But she's not flaky at all. I'm doing it."

She turned to the lake again as I read the flyer.

"Looks okay to me. Do you need a ride?" A little skepticism lingered.

"Oh no, I'll be fine," she said, lightly patting my hand. "Maybe emotional but not groggy. I'll let you know how it goes."

She put her feet up on the coffee table. A rare moment of *chillin'* with Fiona. Often just sharing an experience gives strength to the wounded. She now had me in her corner. I couldn't help but wonder if Dave might prefer a frightened, victimized Fiona. Once his "cheated on wife" came through the knothole, she just might blow the house down. As I sipped the last of my drink, I quizzically gazed at her as she held her smiling face to the sun. She was no pushover. A giggle played hopscotch in my belly. *Dave would be wise to educate himself on the powers of a woman scorned*, I thought.

Fiona Wright and Dave Hughes had met later in life. Well, in those days meeting at twenty-eight and marrying at thirty-three was considered late. Both the same age, both accountants, both hoping to have a family. They met at a conference in Kelowna, BC, but there was no eye flirting between them from across the room. Their meeting was one of circumstance, their name tags had been placed beside each other in the dining hall.

Fiona fell in love with Dave immediately. The jury's still out on Dave's love for Fiona, hence the five-year courtship which ended with an ultimatum: "Marry me or I'm leaving you." He owed it to her, after all; she'd stuck around for five years.

Along with getting a good education, I've also instilled in my boys to not rush into marriage. Fiona's worked damn hard all her married life to make sure Dave believes he did the right thing by marrying her. Of course he did the right thing, but what a power trip for him to keep this "you owe me" game going. The subtleties of communication between a couple are only known by them. Eggshells can crack and break under foot as each avoids the truth of a situation. Fiona and Dave were ticking time bombs.

. . .

Phillip is the eldest of two boys. After realizing he'd never play professional hockey, he became an airline pilot and is now a bona fide workaholic for Air Canada, although, I have to say our family holidays — perks that come with his career — have been fabulous. He'd whisk the boys and me around the world, each vacation a new adventure, rich in experience. We worked well as a family on vacation.

He was already a commercial pilot when I met him on the pediatric ward of VGH where I was a nurse. Of course that would be my profession; I'm a born mother. He and his brother Peter were visiting Peter's son, Dave Jr., sweetly referred to as DJ; Phillip was Uncle Lip, short for Phillip. It occurred to me that he resembled a prince from a Disney film, almost too good looking. As it happened, he was equally charming. Using the resource of my name tag, he looked into my eyes and said, "Maggie, I would like to date you."

"You're at least two inches taller than me, so I accept your offer," I said with a coy smile.

That was that. We've been together ever since. With no discussion about future plans, we dated quickly, had sex far too soon, married in a speedy fashion, bought a home and had three boys, Brian, James and Jeffery. The years flew by that fast — bing, bang, boom!

Though our third pregnancy was unplanned, we treated it as our last attempt for a girl. In all honesty, I was relieved when I spotted that familiar male protrusion at the base of Jeffery's belly as he entered the world. At thirty-seven, I wasn't entirely sure I was up for parenting a girl. My role model hadn't been all that helpful. Phillip was fabulous with his boys, and Jeffery slid nicely into the family fold.

Our marriage is not typical. We've used words like "divorce" and "I'm leaving!" to threaten and accuse as the emotional effects of my mother's suicide uncontrollably reared their ugly heads in me. Numerous sessions of couples counselling over the years had little effect as Phillip is excused by default; my past out traumatizes his.

I've come to dislike the term soulmate; it's stressful. When Phillip and I were engaged, we were on an elevator leaving a club. I was intensely aware of being admired by a young man standing adjacent to me. As if willing me to look at him, I did. He first smiled, pleased that he had achieved his goal of getting my attention. I sheepishly smiled back, intensely aware of not only feeling desirable sensations but also an unexplainable comfort, like home. We shared a life's story in each other's eyes in less than five seconds. *You're the one*, I thought. He shrugged his shoulders with a look of both resignation and hope. It was up to me. Would I drop the arm of the man I was with and move to him? Who would do such a thing? Instead, I gripped Phillip's arm tighter as if to say, *Don't let me go.*

It's unfortunate, and maybe juvenile, but when I hear the term soulmate I first think of the guy on the elevator. Then I rationalize that people have many soulmates in their lives, and Phillip is one of mine. And that guy might have been a real jerk, but I don't think so.

Phillip's a good man. He's like an old shoe, a good-looking old shoe. Which isn't a bad thing. Although, he's not a great communicator, there's something wonderful and reliable about him. In his line of work, it would be easy to have affairs, a girl in every port. Admittedly, I've spent too much time looking for evidence of such. Only once did I ask him, a few weeks after his father's affair was revealed.

"Do you think differently about your dad? You've been … quiet."

"I'm disappointed," he said, folding a heap of laundry on the bed so we had a place to sleep. "He hurt Mum. She's keeping a brave face, but she can't fool me; she's hurt."

"You must know pilots that have affairs?"

"One, but I never did like the guy. Are you worried I would?" he asked, stopping to look at me.

"Well …" I said, clearing my throat, eyes downcast. "I can't deny it has crossed my mind … if opportunity presented itself. Which I'm sure it does …."

"Ya, it's presented itself." His voice softened while he folded his socks. I could almost see the woman in his mind. "But no, I've never had an affair, and I never would. It's just not me, damn it!" he said, lightening the mood and reaching out to tickle me.

After our shared giggle I said, "Thank you, Phil. That means a lot to me. I married a good one."

He winked at me, and I never looked for evidence again.

Even though I was considered a natural beauty when younger, aging has not been kind. Taking after my dad's Swedish side, I have height, which I've maintained for the most part. However, my once blonde hair is now white, my once bright, sparkling blue eyes are less so and instead of a slim body on a big frame I'm now rather square from my shoulders down. My fair skin had a natural hue at one time, but now, well, it doesn't. If I'd ever had to wear make-up when I was young, I'd know how to put it on, but I never learned and now it's too late. Other than a bit of lip gloss, I can't be bothered.

"Bye, I'm going now. Are you up?" Phillip called from downstairs.

"Yes, I'm up! Bye, have a good trip!"

I put a sock over my eyes, willing sleep. Instead, I floated in that unique dreamy space between conscious and unconscious. I am in a strange house, only I know it to be my home. I walk down a hallway with trepidation, as if on a roller coaster that's slowly climbing up and up, clicking and clacking as the chain grabs the track pulling me closer and closer to the inevitable fall. Something is terribly wrong. I enter a room to find my sister Grace dead on her bed. Even though I'm only a teenager in my dream, Grace is in her forties. I touch her chest as I had done to my mother, and she opens her eyes and says, "See? See what you've done to me?"

Chapter 2

A Secret Life

Right after finding my mother dead, I phoned my father at work. He sold tires, or, more accurately, he owned a tire shop. It took forever for him to come to the phone. I imagined him buried under a pile of tires getting high on the smell of rubber and gasoline.

"'LOW — JACK'S TIRES.'"

He always answered the phone as if he was on the twenty-sixth mile of a marathon and you were going to be the reason he failed to complete it. My mouth opened but no words came out. I thought I might be sick. I slid down the wall to the floor.

"HELLO?" Dad yelled in frustration.

"Don't hang up, Dad," I squeaked out.

"Maggie, is that you? What's the matter?"

"Mum's dead," I whispered.

I have no recollection of what was said after that. Time had its own agenda. I felt much older than my thirteen years. I always had, really. But now there was no option to be young should I choose to be. That was gone.

The house was dark and damp, I remained on the floor, motionless, acutely aware of my mother lying dead in the room above me. A type of paralysis crept into my body. The phone rang. *Curious, Mum would call from work about this time.* My heart skipped. *It was a bad dream! She's alive.* No, she wasn't. I crawled to the phone and gingerly placed the receiver to my ear as if it would scald me.

"Hello?"

"What's wrong?"

Grace had keen intuition.

"Nothing, nothing. Was just choking on toast," I said, pulling myself together. I felt dizzy and leaned my head against the wall.

"I've been invited to stay at Joanie's for dinner. Can you tell Mum? Mr. Lake will drive me home — is that okay?"

"Ya, I'll tell Mum, it'll be okay," I said, relieved.

"OK. You sound weird, are you sick?"

"I might be — maybe. I'll tell Mum."

"OK, bye," she said, sounding concerned.

This was not uncommon communication between my younger sister and me. We shared a silent agreement that we'd stick together and do the best we could given the parents we had. It was a minefield we'd navigate together.

Dad came slamming through the door as if he might still have time to save his wife. He shot a look at me, sitting on the floor in darkness. Was it disgust? He flew up the stairs. I imagined him staring at my mother in her green skirt and yellow sweater. How pretty she'd look. He'd look for signs of breathing but find none. Pick up the empty pill bottle, shake his head, confused, somehow responsible. He'd take her lifeless cold hand towards his lips but then stop and lay it gently back down beside her. He would ask himself what he was supposed to do now, with two daughters coming of age. Tears would rest on his lower eyelid, he'd blink and feel them roll down his cheeks. I'd never seen my father cry. I imagined his blue eyes glistening like the ocean. He'd kneel beside the bed as if praying, like I had done, and begin to sob, like I had done.

I crawled to the sofa and smothered my ears between cushions to drown out the sound of his crying. I must have fallen asleep because the next thing I remember is Dad lifting the cushion off me. He said nothing, but I suppose he wondered if I'd smothered myself. A blur of phone calls were made and lights turned on in the dark house. Various authorities came and went, including police. Our yard was wrapped in yellow police tape like on TV. It was surreal — I hadn't killed her!

My mother was pronounced dead at 16:52. That would mean she would have still been alive when I got home, it made no sense. I parked myself in front of the TV, pulling a cushion to my belly and chest. The familiar characters moved their mouths and hands. How strange that they carried on as if nothing had happened. The doorbell rang again. Dad was upstairs with the coroner.

"Maggie, answer the door."

Those were his first words to me. I wasn't cold, but I trembled inside deep down and my hands shook. The doorbell rang again.

"Maggie!" Dad yelled.

I'd not been on my feet since walking out of my parents' bedroom. With the cushion clutched to me, I pushed myself to standing with the other hand. My legs continued to shake. I could not get a handle on my body; it simply trembled at its own will. I opened the door, it was raining. Two men in identical black suits stood at attention. The collars of their tattletale gray shirts were flipped up to prevent rain from dripping down their necks, thin black ties wound tightly at their Adam's apple. Rain bounced off their shiny black shoes. They solemnly grinned at me and said they were here to "pick up the body." My mother had lost her name along with her life; she was now "the body." I left the door open, pointed upstairs and went back to the TV.

Our family doctor came a few minutes later. Although exhausted, I managed another trip to the door.

"Hello Margret," the old guy said as he pushed his way into the house and out of the rain; he never did get my name right. "How are you, dear?"

"Marget," I mumbled.

"Yes, I understand. Where's your father?"

"Upstairs with Thing One and Thing Two."

He stared at me, puzzled. I stared right back at him, empty. He backed away and slunk up the stairs. I felt sorry for him; I was rude and made him feel bad.

My mother was carried in a body bag out to a rain-soaked gurney sitting in our walkway. I half hid behind the sheer as they slid the gurney into the black hearse. I pictured her dressed for work, toenails painted, make-up on, zipped into a thick plastic bag. *She'll be cold with no coat.*

Dad stood out in the rain to watch the hearse turn the corner, out of sight. The regard he displayed for my mother's well-being was redundant; he was too late. I once again returned to the TV and turned up the volume. He stood inside the doorway, dripping.

"Where's Grace?"

"At a friend's." I didn't look at him.

"Are you hungry?" he panted.

"No," I answered. *How could I eat food as if Mum was alive?*

"Maggie?" He softened and I looked at him. "I'm going to have a shower and then I'll make us some supper."

I turned back to the TV and silently wept for my old doctor whom I had hurt.

"Mags, supper's ready. Come have something to eat."

Have I slept again?

"Come on into the kitchen," he said, standing over me.

"I'm not hungry."

I didn't really know if I was hungry or not. It just didn't seem right to eat with Mum dead.

"I'm not either, so we don't need to eat much, just a little."

"Fine," I said, relieved he persisted.

Surprisingly, I managed to choke down some canned beans and toast. The sugar in the beans appealed, and toast is always good.

"I don't know how to tell Grace," Dad said, shaking his lowered head in disbelief.

"I'm telling Grace," I said, coming to attention. "I'll tell her, you don't have to say anything, okay?"

He sighed and nodded, resigned and relieved.

. . .

Jack Holm might have been mistaken for simple, but I saw the complexity of my father from a young age. He was born in Visby, a tiny village on the island of Gotland, Sweden, in 1930, the only child of Eric and Ebba Holm, both in their mid-forties. They ran Eric's inherited family berry farm just outside Visby, and the berries they sold in the short, cool summer months yielded enough funds to sustain them through the long, frigid, dark winter. A lonely existence for my father no doubt, although he never said so himself. In 1950, he married Elsa, his sweetheart he had known and loved all his life; they were both twenty. Keeping with tradition and simplicity, they chose to stay on Gotland, although by Ebba and Eric's standards they may as well have moved to the moon when they bought property in Sundre, an extremely small community at the southern tip of the island. It was the farthest from home they'd ever ventured.

They lived in a three-room house and rented out the two small cottages on the property in the summer months for those looking for complete solitude and maybe a bit of bird watching. Jack always had a supply of gas on the property for lost travellers. He posted a sign by the side of the road that read: "Gas, Sweets and Lodging Available." This gave worried travellers incentive to stop and chat, which then led to viewing the Holms' charming cottages, often ending with rental income for the couple.

Typically, they would not rent their cottages in winter. No tourists for one thing, and with only a small wood-burning stove, the cottages were too cold and difficult to heat. During their third winter in Sundre, a lone traveller who wanted to rent a cottage for the winter to write his book found his way to them. Elsa, like all other Gotlanders, was a hard-working, generous host. While the tenant took his morning walk, Elsa cleaned and restocked his cottage and always left warm, fresh baked goods for breakfast upon his return.

In an attempt to keep the small cottage warm one exceptionally cold morning, she overloaded the wood-burning stove, causing the wall behind the smokestack to ignite. The fire took hold like a hellish tornado, claiming Elsa's life and Jack's soul.

The desolation of Sundre was the perfect place for Jack to mourn himself into alcoholic oblivion. A year after he lost his beloved Elsa, he pressed pause on this drunken behaviour long enough to pack up and head westward to Nova Scotia, Canada, only meeting his parents at the Visby ferry for what would be considered by most, a formal goodbye. Indeed, a curious thing when a mother and her only child have so little to say to each other.

It seemed a very big deal in our home when Dad returned to Gotland for his father's funeral. Mum wanted to join him, but Dad was having none of that. His former life, before Nova Scotia, was out of reach to all he knew.

Eric died in 1967 from what we now know to be Alzheimer's; he was sixty-two. He was buried on the family farm alongside his parents and grandparents. In 1997, Dad received news that his mother had died at the age of ninety-one. He did not return to Gotland for her funeral. He did not view Ebba lowered into the ground in the spot reserved for her beside Eric.

There were a few family photos in our home growing up, but only one from Dad's side. It lived on our whatnot on a shelf all its own. Dad's twelve years old. It's a black-and-white photo, but I can see his light crystal-blue eyes, the same as his father's. He's tall and slender, wearing grey earmuffs, no hat. A sweep of hair lays slick across his forehead. His hands look red with cold, as do his cheeks. He has on a black wool jacket, baggy pants and old lace-up boots. Eric and Ebba are on either side of him looking equally as cold. They're not touching each other, and no one is smiling, maybe because of the cold. Ebba's wearing a fitted black hat that covers half her face, and I need to strain to see her eyes under that hat. She and Eric wear long wool coats almost to their feet. I wonder why Dad doesn't have a long coat as well; didn't he need one to stay warm? I want so much for it to be different. I want to see a hint of touching, maybe Ebba's hand on her son's back, but her hands are firmly tucked in her pockets. It's a cold picture to look at.

At the age of twenty-three, Dad had established himself in a boarding house in Halifax, Canada. Grace and I loved to hear stories of this boarding house. Not so much because we loved the stories — to be truthful, we didn't understand them. It was because Dad came alive telling them. It was a rare occasion to hear him talk about himself at all, let alone talk about himself being happy. I'd picture him as a younger man, handsome, full of fun. A time before me.

While living at the boarding house, he enrolled in a business program where he met my mother's cousin, Bob. Bob invited Dad to join him in Lund Harbour for the summer break. Laurie was a young girl of sixteen, Jack, twenty-three. Their three-year courtship, from what I gather, was full of strife.

"We were passionate; we loved with passion and we fought with passion," Mum would say as if they had the kind of relationship people envied.

Lund Harbour is a small village founded by my ancestors down the south shore of Nova Scotia. The family tree on Mum's side is a small forest. Laurie and Joyce Lund were the daughters of Elizabeth and Stewart Lund, my grandparents. Elizabeth had two sisters, our great-aunts, Marget, whom I'm named after, and Rose. At one time this small village had a thriving fishing industry. Husbands and fathers were fishermen. Wives and mothers gutted and filleted cod at the Main Street Fish Plant. Children lost fathers at sea as if it were tradition. The fish plant closed down before I was born, and Lund Harbour is now a charming tourist destination.

Dad loved the quaintness of Lund Harbour as it was similar to Gotland in ways. He tried to convince his new bride to stay and raise a family there, but my mother had been busting to vacate that one-horse town and salivated at the thought of living in the city. Marrying Dad was her way out. Mum said the row they had on their wedding night after Dad said he wanted to stay in Lund Harbour was one for the record books. She'd always cynically laugh when telling that story. I detested that story.

Dad was no match for the likes of Laurie Lund, and they were city bound the very next day. They rented one side of a duplex on the east side of Halifax and started their unusual life together. When my mother described herself as the "happiest she'd ever been, living in that duplex," I knew her unhappiness was because of me. *If only I wasn't born, my mother would still be happy living in the duplex in Halifax*, I thought. Out of the mouths of babes.

Chapter 3

Just One Lie

Even though Grace was still in the land of before, her antenna went up as she came through the door. I watched as she quickly assessed the goings on in her home. She looked toward the den: Dad, drinking — check; living room, TV on, sister sitting at attention — check. I placed the cushion I'd been clutching beside me and turned the TV off.

"Where's Mum?" she said anxiously.

"I have something to tell you," I said, patting the sofa for her to sit beside me.

"What?" she said with frustration as if she could scare away her own fear. She sat on the edge of the sofa, head cocked to one side looking at me, wide-eyed. "You've been crying. What's wrong? Where's Mum? Is she having quiet time?"

When we were children, Dad would say, "She's having quiet time," as the answer to Mum's need for days upon days of sleep. And there better be blood if we disturbed her quiet time. But that was then when we were children. My gaze dropped.

"No, not quiet time."

Her face changed, like flat light, expressionless, feeling nothing, as if she already knew but dared not go there. I'd not make her ask.

"Mum had a heart attack and died."

"What"? she said barely audible.

Unable to say the words again, I nodded that she had heard correctly. Her face contorted, balancing between the land of before and after. One cannot stay in this place, but the resistance to move to the land of after is strong.

She whispered, "Mum's dead," needing to feel the sensation of the words.

"She had a heart attack. I found her — dead."

It flowed off my tongue like silk. I met her gaze, her dark eyes just like Mum's. I told her a story out of nowhere. It went on and on until the words stopped falling out of the sky into my head. It was easy really, what needed to be done. When had I ever lied to my sister? When had I ever lied at all? I guess every time I told her, "Everything will be okay," I was lying. This, though, was the ultimate lie. This was the bombshell lie. But it was the best I could do to make everything okay.

Dad heard us crying and stuck his blurry-eyed head out the den door. I shook my head *No,* he retreated. If my mother had known the ultimate chaos and destruction she would cause with her final action, I wonder if she'd have followed through.

"Is Mum … in the hospital?" Grace asked.

"Kind of, but not to get better. She's just … there."

In a morgue on a cold slab. I had seen enough detective movies to know this is where bodies were kept.

"I'll never see her again?"

The totality of it all washed over her. Only a few hours ago, I'd felt the same thing. It seemed so long ago now. I held her as she cried. It was like we were drowning. We hung onto each other like life rafts, not daring to let go for fear of sinking into the dark, foreboding ocean. I stroked her head as she buried it into my chest. She wanted to sleep, the escape kind of sleep. I placed her head on a cushion and gently draped the throw over her. I could not stop stroking her head. The head I'd been stroking all my life to reassure her it would be all right, that I was right here.

The lie sat in the pit of my stomach like a boulder. It sat in my lungs like pleurisy. Dad said it was fine that Grace thought Mum died of a heart attack. He actually told me I made it easier for her. *Had I?*

This lie has run my life for forty years. Even though I've been rehearsing how to tell Grace the truth, I've come up empty. How do I start, avoid pain, hurt, betrayal, misconception? And who can I blame? It went on and on in my head ad nauseam. I've learned how to hide the truth in layers of lies, like hot lasagna. Lies bond together in pathological insanity. And even though I can change this course at any time, I do not and have not. People make wrong choices in the name of good intentions, but at some point, one must confess to the wrong choice or live a burdened life, which has been my choice.

Until today.

Chapter 4

What Had She Said to Me?

The sock over my eyes had failed to supply reprieve, so I pulled it off with a sigh of exasperation and stomped to the bathroom. Phillip had drained the hot water tank with one of his twenty-minute showers, so the tepid water running down my back only justified my misery.

Tension between Grace and me had escalated recently. I couldn't remember what the issue was, but it didn't matter because it had nothing to do with the truth. Like drapes clawed by a scared cat, our sisterly bond had been shredded over the years, thread by painful thread.

Our last conversation irked me right from the beginning.

"And how are we today?" she said in that ridiculous little-girl voice.

I swallowed hard, didn't want to take the bait.

"Good, good, all good," I responded, trying to convince both of us. "And how are you?" I said in my adult voice, addressing her singularly.

"Ah — okay, I guess. You know."

At least her voice had dropped an octave. She wanted to talk about her ailments, but I just couldn't do it. After a long, tense pause, she realized I wasn't going to inquire.

"So what's up, what can I do you for?"

A phrase we used as kids, turning the words around. Why couldn't I have fun with that? It was harmless.

"Hope you can join us for dinner Sunday. We're celebrating James's birthday."

"Well I don't know Maggie. I've not been well; I just don't know what shape I'll be in." She said curtly.

"OK, no commitment, it's just the family. Usual time, six; no need to bring anything. Let me know Sunday if you're coming." My own voice was now high and squeaky.

"Right! Got it! I'll be sure to let you know Sunday — talk then."

Click.

"Bye," I said sarcastically to no one. *Now whose fault was that?*

. . .

My mind was filled with jumbled words that I just *had* to sort. Was I rehearsing or ruminating?

"Grace, I have something to tell you."

"Yeah?" she would say absentmindedly.

"Well, you know how I told you Mum died of a heart attack?"

"Yes?" Eyes ablaze.

This is where it all falls apart. I don a clown's costume, red nose and all.

"Well, I made that up. She actually killed herself! Ta-DA!"

I used to get much further, dragging Dad and Aunt Joyce into my heady dialogue.

"They were adults, they should have told you the truth!"

The little counselling I did participate in, clarified that I couldn't control what anyone else did or didn't do. The question was and still is – What am "I" going to do? This never seemed fair.

Sunlight streamed into the bedroom, and despite my cranky self, I smiled as I stuck my head out the window and pulled crisp, cool air deep into my lungs. Steam rose off the rooftops as night's mist evaporated. Summer flowers were coming to an end. *Could I not just spend the day in the garden, snipping, digging and pulling until my fingernails were gone?* I shut the window and dressed for work.

Today I felt compelled to pick up the infamous journal that was nestled in my sock drawer. The very journal I spotted lying beside my dead mother, the journal I'd hope would explain her actions and express love.

Just the night before, Mum told me she bought it on her lunch break. It was evening, dinner dishes done. I was on my way upstairs to my room and saw her sitting in the living room, her exquisite face illuminated by the lamp light. Curious to see what she had in her lap, I leaned over the back of the chair, so close to her. I think I was touching her hair. I could have touched her cheek. I remember thinking I'd like to but didn't want to spoil the moment. Her soft white blouse loosely draped to show just the hint of fleshy breasts, a thin gold chain obediently followed down, out of sight.

"What's that?" I quietly asked.

"It's called a journal; it's like a diary — but different."

I leaned farther over her shoulder, smelled her shampoo.

"What are you going to write in it?"

She opened the cover and slowly wiped the first page with her hand as if to clean the slate.

"Oh, anything that comes to mind," she dreamily said as if the possibilities were endless.

Something about me? I felt excited.

My mother's name lay timeless, as did her last words. She was once a real person. Laurie Marie Holm was written in perfect print on the front cover. I ran my fingertips over her name, feeling for something. I opened the journal; her last thought lay starkly on the page in her best cursive penmanship:

I can't take it any longer, this day, Sept 23rd, 1974.

How many times had I read those words, imagined her writing them, placing the pen down, lifting up the pill bottle, unscrewing the lid, dumping them all into her one hand, putting one at a time in her mouth with a swig of water, each time shaking her head back to coax the pill down her throat, stretching out on her bed, pristine like, straightening her skirt, methodically deciding where to rest her hands. On her chest? Arms bent or straight beside her body? She decided straight, on either side of her body, neatly tucking herself in. She'd wait. How long? Did she ever for a split-second think, *What have I done? No, Grace, Maggie, oh no.* But then it would be too late.

My car was wintry cold locked up in our concrete garage. Good thing I got up when Phillip left; I wouldn't need to speed to work. After retiring from a lengthy hospital career, I secured a school nursing position with Josh, a special needs young man. A lad of great stature, he stood 6'1" and was built like a man. He struggled with a combination of Autism and seizure disorder. His heart was gentle and his mind determined, and he followed his mind most of the time.

Almost smug about being early, I slowly pulled into the parking lot. Children filled the playground as they enjoyed the last few days of summer. I parked the car, now toasty warm. I closed my eyes to quell the burning under the lids, a hangover from my restless night. In seconds, the playground noises faded and I again drifted between that heavenly space of awake and asleep where dreams come easily. A radiant vision of my mother appeared looking beautiful, surrounded in light, draped in layers of flowing white cotton. She smiled peacefully and then bent down and whispered in my ear. The cotton brushed my face and arms. Her fragrance filled my nose. I reached out, grasping for the flowing cotton to keep her with me. She continued to speak to me, but I couldn't hear her. She turned, looked over her shoulder smiling and was gone.

With that, a ball hit the side of my car, jolting me into consciousness. My eyelids felt lead heavy as if I were in a drunken stupor. Three little boys stood at guilty attention waiting to be dismissed with their ball. I waived them on and staggered into the school. I felt both shaken and elated by the vision of my mum. I'd never had a vision before; even when I begged for one. But what had she said to me?

Chapter 5

Ornament of Love

The school smelled of fresh paint from summer maintenance. It was the familiar green that was destined to be applied to the walls of all institutions. A note was stuck in my mailbox letting me know Josh was home sick today. Being that I worked for the health authority and not the school board, I had the day off. *Was this a gift from Mum?* Gift and Mum in the same sentence seemed an oxymoron.

Memories of my childhood birthdays run together as one burdened, lacklustre event, except my eighth. Mum was feeling well. I guess the accurate way of wording it would be to say she was not in a depressive state, which, in fact, meant she was in a manic state, so not exactly "well." She participated wholeheartedly in my celebration, throwing me a party. It was at this party that Penny and I established our "best friend" relationship. Penny thought Mum was beautiful and way more fun than her mum.

There was a great ta-do about the gift opening. We formed a circle on the living room floor around a colourful variety of boxes adorned with curly ribbons. I had attended other birthday parties so this wasn't the first time I had seen a delicious display of gifts, but it was the first time such a display was for me.

It was curious that my mother included her gift in with the mix on the floor; it made me uncomfortable, although it was indeed a beautiful box. I unwrapped it first and instinctively held it up for all to admire, as she would have wanted. It was a white ceramic statue of a loving mother tenderly holding her baby. This was meant to be *my* mother holding *me*. The kids moved in close to see this beautiful little sculpture while my loving mother sat on the arm of a chair smiling sweetly. No one could possibly guess she'd spent the last three weeks in bed, unbathed, barely eating. She was beautiful, easy to forgive.

I imagined Mum seeing the sculpture on the store shelf, thinking of me, being moved by feelings of love for me. She'd pick it up with me in mind, the perfect gift for her darling daughter that she loved so deeply. I saw it clearly and was moved to hug her. Of course, I had many tangible gifts from my mum but none like the ornament of love, as I call it.

. . .

Having a weekday off with absolutely nothing planned was a rarity, I felt adrift. Gardening no longer appealed, so I headed west toward the beach and sea wall that was nestled under the copper-yellow-and red-splashed North Shore mountains. Beautiful yes, but nothing like the Atlantic fall colours. The trees there display a painter's palette of gold, crimson and magenta. Comparing the west and east coasts of Canada has been a lifelong game of mine. Making the east far superior to the west bolstered my dissatisfaction with life. Fortunately for my own sanity, I no longer do this. One only has to listen to the country's weather reports to know the good fortune of living in the west.

As our family grew, it became evident we needed more space. Ice skates, skis, rollerblades, hockey sticks, balls of every size, bikes, golf clubs, and all the paraphernalia that goes with sports and three active boys — four counting Phillip — meant we needed to move. The North Shore made sense as the mountains would be in our backyard for skiing and biking; everyone would be happy.

I found a spot in the sand and wriggled my butt east, west, north and south to form a seat. Holding my face to the sun, I looked to the heavens, willing Mum's return to whisper in my ear. The ocean was composed; gentle flaps of water pretended to be waves. Salty sea air was so deeply ingrained in my cells it was like the amniotic fluid in which I was formed. I breathed deep into my belly, exhaling the tension and fear that had its tentacles wrapped around me. Stretching out on my back, I closed my eyes to listen. Gulls and children screeched as they soared and played.

The inside of my eyelids looked orange from the penetrating sun. *Mum, come to me,* I willed. I waited. *Please, Mum, what did you say? I couldn't hear you.* I waited. Nothing, no sign of her. *Give it up, Maggie. Can't force these things.* I headed to my car for water. As I flipped the sunscreen mirror down to apply lip gloss, I saw her in my reflection. But like a magic trick, she was gone just like that. *Now you see her, now you don't.* But it was there, a hint of Mum around my mouth and chin. The rest of me was Scandinavian, tall angular, white blonde hair, light-blue eyes, all Dad. Grace, on the other hand, was all Lund. Eyes a mixture of sultry sorrow and sexiness, fleshy body in all the right places, full, lustrous auburn hair and a smile that filled the room. And yet, people could still tell we were sisters. We loved that.

Chapter 6

My Mother's Laugh

It rained for a week after Mum died. I remember this because Grace and I were held captive in the house, missing a week of school. Dad spent his time in the den imbibing and talking on the phone. Every day he talked to Mum's sister Joyce, who lived in Toronto with her husband Brian and their four kids, our cousins. Typically we saw them once a year in Lund Harbour, so it was unusual to see her alone at this time of year. Nothing made sense.

Grace and I lived on cereal and mac and cheese. We watched copious amounts of TV, slept together in our clothes in a single bed where we cried ourselves to sleep. Grace wanted to talk about Mum, but I was hesitant, fearful of losing track of the lie. Aunt Joyce would tell her the truth. She'd explain it in a way that excused me for lying. I could hardly wait till she arrived. I liked everything about my aunt. She paid attention to her children as if she enjoyed them. Like characters in a romantic movie, she and Uncle Brian talked and smiled and touched each other, saying,

"Thank you, dear" when being handed a cup of tea. She had a way of talking to me that made me feel smart.

While Dad picked her up from the airport, I prepared Grace's room for her visit. When I opened the linen closet door to retrieve clean sheets, my mother's scent escaped as if it had been locked up. I scooped towels and sheets into my arms and buried my face in them, inhaling her deeply. Just as quickly as her scent was there, it was gone; I simply could not keep hold of her.

"It's time to have a bath and wash our hair," I said. "They'll be home soon."

"Okay, you go first," Grace said groggily as she woke from a daytime sleep.

My first bath in a week felt divine. Warm and soothing. I caressed my legs, they felt skinny. My belly, empty; my chest, numb. Sliding my head under the water, I wondered what it felt like to drown. *Just open your mouth and breathe in.* I sat up quickly. *No, I would never.* I was stunned.

"No, I will never." I said like a vow.

The tub seemed smaller as I could no longer stretch out. Nothing, not even my body, remained as it once was. *What about my soul?* It wasn't tangible so how could it be assessed for damage? Does a soul remain innocent no matter what? Is my mother's soul innocent? It wasn't her soul that took the pills, it was her body in a green skirt and yellow sweater, lying dead. Tears dripped into the water, and with the sound of each tender splash, I cried harder, lost in a nightmare. Grace knocked on the door,

"Are you okay?"

I sat up straight, this new, unfamiliar self stuck together with tape and bubble gum.

"Yup, I'm just washing my hair. Be out in a minute."

I dunked under as if being baptized clean. *Water, wash it away.*

It did feel good to have clean hair hanging loose around my face. A part of me resisted feeling the slightest bit better; I didn't want to give Mum the satisfaction of that. Clothes I wore in the world of before looked dated, so deciding what to wear was tedious.

"I have nothing to wear," I said.

Grace looked at me as if I had lost my mind. "What do you mean? You have all your clothes — right here," she said, pointing to my full closet.

We started to laugh.

"Well, I mean, what do you call this?" She held up my sweater and we laughed louder.

"We shouldn't be laughing," I said as I collapsed on the bed, laughing harder than I ever remember.

Grace flopped beside me laughing equally as hard. "Why are we laughing?" she said, with a snort.

"I don't know!" I said, as my laughter flipped to crying.

I held in a loud sob, didn't want to scare her. I sat up, bewildered by how quickly I went from hysterically laughing to hysterically crying, as if the two belonged together. Grace sat up too.

"Laughing like that was weird; nothing's funny."

I reached for my little sister's hand and said, "It was funny, that's good, it made us laugh. Laughing's okay," I said to reassure her we weren't monsters. I was relieved she hadn't noticed me crying.

The front door opened and Dad yelled up the stairs, "Aunt Joyce is here girls, come and say hello!"

"Okay, be down in a minute!" I yelled. "Grace, hop in the tub, have a quick bath. Never mind washing your hair, it takes too long to dry. Just wear your bathrobe, it'll be fine."

I threw on a black sweater I'd not worn in a while, and blue jeans, good and baggy. The laughing and crying gave me energy. For the first time in a week I sensed blood running through my veins. I applied lip gloss that I'd bought at Woolworths for $1.29. At the time I wondered if Mum would approve. The conversation asking her for permission was no longer an option, but there was no relief in that. Strange how her saying a firm "No" would now be welcome. I applied another coat, my lips were blindingly shiny.

Halfway down the stairs I froze as my mum's laugh wafted from the kitchen, around the corner and up the stairs like ribbons into my ears. A lyrical, full, contagious sound that went to the deepest places of my heart. My knees buckled, I sat on a step, closed my eyes, put a hand over my mouth to keep in a gasp and listened to my mother in her sister. Dad came around the corner shouting, "Girls ..."

but tapered off when he saw me sitting on the step. "Maggie, what are you doing? Come and see your aunt Joyce." He turned back into the kitchen.

Tears were welling up before I even entered the room. Aunt Joyce looked more like Mum than I remembered. She walked to me with outstretched arms.

"Goodness you've changed so much in two months. I can't keep up."

I fell into her embrace and inhaled her. She didn't smell like Mum. I gave her a squeeze and reached for tissue, my tears always so close to the surface.

"Dad, did you tell her about what I told Grace?" I asked in an urgent, low voice.

Aunt Joyce sat at the table, took a sip of water, pursed her lips and nodded. Dad didn't look at me as he had busied himself making tea.

"Yes dear, your father told me everything and we think it best to just leave it this way," she whispered. "I mean, why bother upsetting her more? It just seems cruel to change the story now."

She wouldn't look at me. My mouth dropped open and I looked at Dad in disbelief. I wanted to protest, but he shot a tight-jawed look at me that said, *Leave it alone*. Aunt Joyce sighed and dabbed away tears. I aggressively wiped my lips clean with the sleeve of my sweater, leaving my mouth bruised and my sleeve shiny with pink grease. This was only the start of their scheming.

"Grace, you've grown too," Aunt Joyce said, standing up and rushing around the table to greet her youngest niece.

They hugged and began crying.

"Don't you worry dear. Everything will be all right."

Grace had put her pajamas on, and I wished I had too. No longer was my mother visible in her sister. It was as if a sea had parted, enticing me to enter the path between two giant walls of water. With no choice, I stepped in, so small against the mountains of deep blue on either side. There was no other way. Even though I was meant to trust that I would not be swallowed by the unpredictable sea, I didn't. I had no faith in the path that lay before me.

Another pot of tea was made. It was all my aunt drank, gallons of it. She was like a chain-smoker, one after the other, sip sip sip. Grace and I sat quietly, listening to the adults talk about Mum.

"She was so beautiful — so much promise. She struggled so ... unnecessarily — She loved her daughters, though — And she was a good mother, sister, wife — Her favourite flowers were nasturtiums, we must get some for the service — But where are we going to find nasturtiums this time of year?"

The sea parted and I was seduced into the terrifying void. As the hot tea touched my raw, burning lips, I surrendered.

Chapter 7

Out of My Hands

The first funeral I ever attended was my mother's. We knelt in prayer, heads bowed. I took a sideways glance at Grace. Her hands were clasped tight in prayer mode, eyes shut equally as tight, barely breathing. *What was she praying for? Mum to magically appear? What else was there to pray for? Surely not the forgiveness of our sins.* I opted not to view Mum in her casket. Seeing her dead once was enough. She would be cremated, her ashes returned to us in a container to be buried.

Aunt Joyce cleared her throat and blew her nose before she started the eulogy.

"For those of you that don't know me, I'm Joyce, Laurie's sister. Laurie and I grew up in Lund Harbour, down the south shore. The Big House, as we now call it, was our family home, and I'm happy to say it is still in our family. The grand living room is the size of an apartment. Our Christmas trees were enormous, ten feet tall with long, willowy branches covered in magical ornaments, lights and garland. We had visitors coming and going year-round.

 Mother used to keep a brick of stinky cheese on our kitchen table in an attempt to keep Laurie and me away from the cookie jar, but my clever sister would take a big breath, hold her nose, run in, grab a handful of cookies and we'd run off with our stash.

We had a wonderful upbringing; meadows and beaches a stone's throw away. As we got older, our shenanigans became more daring. We'd sneak out to meet up with friends on the outskirts of town. One night we smoked cigarettes and both ended up holding each other's hair while we were sick.

Even though we married and went our separate ways, we made a point of rendezvousing in the Big House every summer, and now our own children have fond memories of Lund Harbour. Laurie and I loved those times together …"

She started to cry, so did most of those listening.

"I'll miss them," she said, dabbing her nose with her tissue. She lifted her head as if talking to an angel above and said, "I love you, Lo."

Only my aunt called Mum Lo; Mum called her Jo. My aunt would say, "Would you like some tea, Lo?" Mum would answer, "I'd love some tea, Jo," followed by lyrics of laughter.

As my aunt spoke, I thought about the fun-loving preparation for our summer holidays. Conversations started weeks before school ended. Mum's funky winter blues cracked like a calving iceberg as phone calls between her sister and her enthusiastically increased.

"What time would they be leaving – arriving? – Who was bringing what food? – Yes, the children all needed new bathing suits, they'd grown so much."

Spending the summer in Lund Harbour was not just about being there, it was that Mum was at her best; that was the magical miracle of it all. The very place she just had to leave as a new bride was where she was happiest, or so it seemed to me.

Our small family sat in the front pew, and I couldn't help turning around to see who else was there. There was a good turnout. Uncle Brian had arrived the night before. He was a nice man, a kind man. Two ladies from the dress shop where Mum worked smiled at me with pity. A man with red hair sat in the row behind them. I think he had been looking at me but when I looked at him he turned his head quickly. It seemed that people were awkward at funerals. I assumed he had something to do with the dress shop, maybe the accountant. It was strange he was there by himself. A group of parents from our school clustered together. I was surprised to see my best friend Penny and her mother.

"Hi," I waved using only my fingers.

I guess it was out, everyone knew. *What did they know, the truth or the lie?* This hit me like a death sentence.

All those in attendance were invited back to our home for lunch. I spotted the red-haired man slipping out the side door of the church, avoiding shaking hands with Dad and Aunt Joyce. I could see he was crying, blowing his nose, more upset than Uncle Brian. I lost track of him, but it was clear he didn't know the ladies from the dress shop and he was very upset. This puzzled me, and for some reason, made me feel uneasy.

To my great relief, Penny didn't come back to our house for the reception. Funeral protocol dictated that the whys and wherefores for the deceased to be lying in that box was not up for discussion, at least that was the rule at this reception. I also learned that "Thank you," was the correct response to, "I'm so sorry for your loss."

"Sweetheart, come with Gracie and me," my aunt whispered in my ear, breaking the spell of my thoughts.

She took hold of our hands and guided us up the stairs. We followed as if in a trance. On bended knee, saying nothing, asking nothing of me, she slipped off my shoes, stood and fluffed my pillow in preparation for my head. For just a moment, I slipped into being a little girl as my aunt took care of me. I lay my head down and felt the weight of a throw draped over me. I was asleep before she left the room.

It was dark when Grace and I woke. I could smell real food, so different than the smell of cardboard TV dinners. Upon each waking since my mother's death, I had the experience, for an instant or shorter than an instant, of knowing nothing. In that nothingness all was familiar. Mum was alive and life was as usual. And then, like a bomb on impact, I remembered everything. Waking up was torture.

While I waited for my tortured feelings to subside, I listened to my aunt and Dad talking in the kitchen but couldn't make out what they were saying. I watched Grace walk toward the bathroom and saw Mum's silhouette in my sister.

"I think I'm hungry," Grace said, standing over me.

I had pulled the covers over my head, curled up in a ball, thinking of Mum lying dead.

"Okay, I'm coming. Just gotta pee and brush my teeth and get out of these clothes."

They actually disgusted me; I'd never wear them again.

"I'll change too."

"You're in your pjs, I'm gonna put mine on," I said, smiling at my sister, pleased that I gave her the lead.

"Ah, there you are. Do you feel better?" Aunt Joyce asked as we walked into the kitchen.

Geez, do I have to feel better? "Yup, feeling better," I said sarcastically.

"Maggie, there's no need to be rude," Dad said.

I didn't miss the discouraging look the two of them exchanged. I interpreted it to mean that they were going to tell Grace the truth and I was making things difficult with my grouchiness.

"I'm sorry, I'll set the table," I said sincerely.

I gladly headed for the dining room.

"We want to speak with both of you. Come, sit here," Aunt Joyce said, indicating we should sit at our small kitchen table.

She remained standing. My heart pounded. I didn't want to be in the same room. I wanted them to explain it to Grace without me being there. They'd tell her I was scared and that I was sorry I'd lied to her.

My aunt went to the kitchen door and summoned her husband away from the TV with a quick jerk of her head. He quietly picked up the extra kitchen chair from beside the stove and sat at the table. Dad lit a cigarette and dropped his head. My aunt cleared her throat. I stared at Grace. *Poor thing, she is going to find out Mum committed suicide. Oh God, here it comes.*

"Girls, your dad and I — and Uncle Brian," she nodded her head to include him since she demanded he be present. "Well … we've been talking. You've been through a lot."

She looked to the two men for agreement or encouragement or to take over.

My uncle shot to attention and said, "Maggie, you're thirteen now, same age as our Lacy."

I nodded but couldn't figure out what this had to do with how Mum died.

"Grace, your auntie and I would love for you to come and stay with us for a little while." He forced a hopeful smile and clapped his hands together as if applauding himself for bravery. "What do you think about that?"

What on earth is he talking about? I couldn't make sense of it. There was no mention of the lie. I looked at them for clues. *What did he say? Grace — stay with them?*

"How long?" I asked.

"We're not sure yet, darling, maybe until Christmas?"

"Is Maggie coming too?" Grace said, wringing her hands in her lap.

"Well, the house will be pretty full," Dad said, "so Maggie'll stay here. It's just till Christmas. You can go to your cousins' school."

"I have to go to school?"

"Just for a couple of months, honey; it'll go by so fast," Aunt Joyce said, trying to sound upbeat.

The writing was on the wall. There was no way out. The decisions were made. The lie would continue. And Grace was leaving. She looked terrified, and I was terrified for her. Common sense guided me, though, and as much as I wanted to plead with my father, I knew I had to side with him. I pulled my chair closer to Grace and put my arm around her.

"It'll be okay, it really will. Aunt Joyce is like Mum," I said, not believing a word of it.

We both looked at our aunt, she smiled and nodded affirmatively; she was like our mother.

"No, she's not. She's our aunt, she's not our mum," Grace said, bubbling at the mouth with snot running down her face.

Sweet Grace had never been rude or insulting. I'd never seen her this scared.

"You're right, I'm not your mum," she said, placing her slender hand over Grace's. "I'll do my best for you, darling, I'll do my best."

Dad placed tissue and a glass of water in front of Grace.

"Don't make me go, please," she squeaked out between sobs.

"Come with me," I said, taking her hand.

Aunt Joyce looked defeated or maybe exhausted. I lead Grace to the living room sofa, wrapped a throw around her shoulders and sat close to her. No words of reassurance came to me because there weren't any.

"I don't want to go," she squeaked through her sobs. "Why do I have to go? Why can't I stay home … with you. Or why don't you come too?"

There were more whispers coming from the kitchen. My uncle quietly set the dining room table, not daring to look at us huddled on the sofa.

"Come to the table girls," Dad said.

"I'm not hungry," Grace whispered to me.

"I know, I'll be right back."

"She okay, dear?" Aunt Joyce said, putting her hand on my shoulder.

"No — nothing is okay. She needs to be here," I said in a low tone. "She needs to be in her own home — with me." I leaned into my aunt's ear and said, "Why didn't you tell her the truth? I wanted you to tell her. She needs to know the truth and she needs to be home."

My aunt gave me a look of pity that told me I wasn't going to get what I wanted. I put a spoonful of mashed potatoes on our plates, added some gravy and went back into the living room. Grace was sitting up, pale.

A sentence Dad used on me not long ago fell out of my mouth. "I'm not hungry either, but we can eat this much."

We ate in silence. When we had choked down our last mouthful, Grace lay down and curled into a ball.

"Let's think about this for a minute," I said. "You know from now to Christmas isn't that long, really. Just a couple of months. Maybe it'll be like a holiday … sort of. And we can write letters to each other; I'll write to you every day."

I almost convinced myself. I was a star.

"I don't know anyone there. I only see them in the summer on holidays and you're always there with me. I don't want to go."

Her voice was barely audible.

"You know Joy. You two play together more than we do. She's sweet." I paused and stroked her head. "Just like you."

Her tears subsided as sleep took over. I sat with her for a while longer. There was minimal conversation coming from the dining room table. I went upstairs. I wanted to scream. *How could he do this to us, now, we need each other more than ever? They set me up to think they were going to tell Grace the truth, but they've made everything worse.*

Two days later, I hugged my sister goodbye. She sobbed loudly; I swallowed nails. She walked away with my aunt and uncle to board a plane. She looked so small. Aunt Joyce reached for her hand while saying something to her. Grace nodded her head in agreement. What choice did she have?

"She'll be okay," Dad said as we watched them walk out of sight.

But would she? Would I? We drove home in deafening silence.

Chapter 8

Raising Grace

When I was three, I'd wake in the night to the sounds of a baby crying in our parents' room. Grace slept in a crib beside Mum, yet neither she nor Dad woke to her cry for food. I'd go into their room, wait until my eyes adjusted to the dark, retrieve the bottle sitting on Mum's bedside table, reach between the crib railings and gently put the bottle to Grace's cheek. Like a baby bird, her little mouth opened, her head turned with a frantic jerk to find the nipple. She'd look at me in the dark, sitting on the other side of the rails, enthusiastically sucking the bottle. By the time it was dry, she was fast asleep. Sometimes I fell asleep, too, right there on the floor between my parents' bed and the cradle. Neither of my parents questioned this. My little sister was lovely, soft and pudgy. I couldn't get enough of her chubby cheeks. I'd nestle my face into them and she'd push into my face, each of us soaking up the loving affection from one another.

When I was four, I could make scrambled eggs, heat cans of soup, beans, creamed corn, spaghetti and jarred baby food. I could make toast, hot chocolate, hot dogs and spam. I could change most diapers, but some of her overzealous poopy ones were too much. I remember asking Mum to help once. She was napping at the time, one of her all-day naps. She got up, changed the diaper and didn't speak to me for the rest of the day. My father said she needed her sleep and didn't like being interrupted. This was the start of her "quiet times" as my father called them. They could last anywhere from an hour to a month, sometimes more. My father's alcoholism was predictable, understandable, even manageable. My mother was a gargantuan mystery.

Grace was soon moved into my room, and as she got bigger, into my single bed. We slept like two peas in a pod, and she only fell out twice that I remember. My favourite part of the day was getting under the covers with my little sister, the chaos of the day over. We'd spoon, me with my nose just above her head; the smell was intoxicating, it was the medicine that made all bad things go away. I was utterly in love with her and she with me.

As if we'd all been asleep, Mum would enter back into our lives. Although she did manage to take care of the bare-bones basics, showing up long enough to throw in some laundry, heat up a TV dinner and ask us what we were doing as we sat watching TV. Once she had assessed things as fine, she'd retreat once more to her bed. We were, essentially, neglected children.

Forbidden to bathe without an adult present meant we went for days without washing, which also meant Grace's little bottom was purple most of the time; that had to burn. She was smart, though. By observing me, she potty-trained herself by sixteen months. Mum had us both in diapers at night, she'd have nothing to do with wet beds. Grace said my name — "Gee," clear and crisp — before any other words. Mum only tried once to make her say "Mama." She wouldn't say it and that was that. Little Grace was too young to know that not saying "Mama" on command would send Mama to her bed for a week. This was my early childhood, outside of summers in Lund Harbour.

One morning when I was twelve, Mum floated into the kitchen for coffee and saw me sitting at the table eating toast. She looked disappointed to see me there.

"What are you doing home? Why aren't you in school?"

"It's Saturday, Mum."

"Where's Jack?"

"I don't know."

"Great," she said sarcastically while putting the kettle on. "Gimme a bite of that," she said, taking the toast out of my hand. "Mm, good jam. Make me some coffee would you, Mags." She spun on her heel and darted out of the room. The faster she walked, the higher her blue silk robe floated behind her like a cape. I could tell she liked the effect. I could also tell she was bubbling with energy.

The kettle blew and I quickly poured the steaming water over the brown granules in her favourite cup. I didn't want to be there when she returned. And yet, I wanted to be there because maybe — just maybe — she'd be different after she had her coffee. Maybe she'd want to talk or be with me.

"Coffee smells good, Mags, let's see how it tastes," she said, breezing back into the room. "No milk, no sugar, just dark, black coffee," she said, giving me a wink. "Hot hot, but delish. Want some?"

There seemed to be less air in the room as Mum flitted from one spot to another, finally landing on a *Vogue* magazine. She sucked in her belly and stood tall, mimicking the emaciated models.

"Sure," I said, eager to keep her a bit longer.

Three spoonful's of sugar and half a cup of milk later I could barely get that horrible brew down my throat. Mum giggled watching me.

"You hate this stuff, don't you?"

"It's growing on me," I lied.

"I'm bored," Mum said, looking out the window. She turned quickly. "Let's go shopping. I'll buy you something pretty. You're always in the same jeans and sweater, come on, let's get ready. I know just the place to go — come on, get ready!" She said, impatiently flapping her hand for me to move.

"Sure, okay, sounds good," I replied, jumping to my feet.

There was simply no option to tell her that Penny and I had planned to go shopping — no way, no how. I dumped my coffee mixture down the sink, called Penny and headed to my room to "get ready." I have no recollection of our shopping day, none.

Chapter 9

Best Memories

When we were kids, there was no highway from Halifax to Lund Harbour. The country road between the two worlds snaked around corners, evoking motion sickness that could render me semi-conscious, with or without Gravol.

With our spacious Buick crammed to the gunnels, we'd take off with "no time to waste," so Mum would say. I loved that Dad was fully in charge of the day. He and Mum rose early while Grace and I slept. They used this time to pack the car "undisturbed by two excited little girls," Dad would say with a wink.

This year was no exception. I awoke to the smell of percolating coffee that wafted around the corner from the kitchen up the stairs, filling my nostrils with the message, *Wake up, the day's arrived, it's time.* My parents' voices, laced with my mother's laughter, echoed against the walls, filling me with promise. It was better than any Christmas morning.

In a kind of reverent silence, as if our excitement was too grand to be expressed, Grace and I dressed in the clothes that had been selected the night before. My mother's transformation was in full bloom. I couldn't take my eyes off her as she skipped from room to room preparing the house for our absence. Her white, sleeveless blouse tucked snugly into her blue pedal pushers showed off her hourglass figure. Hot pink toenails drew attention to her pretty bare feet. The shiny brown waves of her hair bounced around her face, framing her high, flushed cheekbones, the bow of her full raspberry lips showcased perfect white teeth. Not a spec of make-up needed; she was truly a natural beauty.

Her laughter, now fully emerged from its hiding place, warmed my bones. We'd all laugh along with her — she had no idea the power of it. It was like a song you never wanted to end. I should have told her.

Lund Harbour was my mother's manger. We'd stay in her childhood home that we fondly referred to as the Big House. The Big House sat atop of a hill overlooking the ocean, with a meadow as far as the eye can see out back. Mum was born upstairs in a corner room at the back. From the garden, I loved looking at the wood-framed corner window imagining my grandmother crying out as she pushed her daughter, my mum, into the world.

The car was filled with a simmering excitement that was quite foreign to our day-to-day experience. Lunch would be had at the "greasy spoon," as my father called it, and later we'd indulge in a soft ice cream cone from the Dairy Queen. Other than the odd Sunday drive, our family rarely spent time together, and certainly not in such close quarters. Gas was cheap then, so cramming into a car for family outings was common. No seatbelts meant Grace and I roamed freely around in the back. Which also meant both Mum and Dad barked, "Sit down girls!" every five minutes until we surrendered to behaviour they could tolerate. Children were to be seen and not heard, and in our family not being seen OR heard was better. However, the drive to Lund Harbour was different. Grace and I took full advantage of our parents' relaxed attitude, as we giggled and played with zest. Until, of course, motion sickness took its hold on me. After a roadside vomit, I'd sleep until I heard Mum say, "Oh my, Jack, it's more glorious every year. Look girls, look how magnificent the beach is!"

The vastness and wonder of Sunrise Beach greeted us as we curved our way down the peninsula. The tall sea grasses bowed as if saying, "Welcome." Yes, it was magnificent, but my attention was on Mum's hand reaching for my dad's and witnessing the loving look they exchanged. This interactive snippet of tenderness between my parents was rare. *Why was that?*

"Can we swim at that beach?" Grace asked this every year.

"Only extremely strong adult swimmers swim in that water, honey. Kids can splash in the surf." She'd go on to say, "This beach is for walking and admiring. We'll swim at Lund Beach."

The road came to an abrupt dead end at the bottom of the peninsula. To leave Lund Harbour, one has to turn around and drive the same road out. The Big House was at the end of the peninsula, and then a right turn up a long, grassy driveway. The Buick came to rest on the edge of the open meadow close to the back door entrance for easy unpacking.

The Hester family had arrived a few days before us. This gave them the advantage of settling in, claiming their space, exploring all that was new and different from the year before. Lacy was sunburned, Joy was covered in mosquito bites, and David had caught a fish. This made me feel like I had missed out, or I had to catch up, or that I'd never catch up.

"Oh goodness, Lo, you look like a movie star, as always," Aunt Joyce said, embracing her sister.

"Thank you, *Daaahling.* But honestly that drive seems to get longer every year. Maggie threw up every five miles."

"I did not. I only threw up once!" I said much too loud.

All eyes were on me. The earth could have opened up and swallowed me whole and I'd not have minded. Sensing my embarrassment, Aunt Joyce came to my side.

"Only once? Good for you. I felt nauseous the entire trip; you and I have the same tummy."

She had a way of making everyone wish they had the "same tummy." Just like that, throwing up became envied, in my mind anyway. On the other hand, my mother had a way of making everyone she spoke to feel confused.

"Look at these grown-up people. Who are you all?" she asked.

"I'm John."

"I'm Joy."

Did her nieces and nephews really need to identify themselves?

"Yes, you've all grown up so much and you're just going to grow more this summer. We should measure you all," my aunt said, picking up a box of food and walking into the house. "I'll put the kettle on and we'll have a cuppa while unpacking the boxes, shall we?" She yelled back over her shoulder to Mum, who was carrying in a couple of pillows.

Dad and Uncle Brian shook hands, said a few pleasantries, then got busy emptying the car. Grace and I awkwardly greeted our cousins, assessing our differences and similarities. By the evening of the first day, after a full exploration of the house and bedrooms chosen, the pecking order was established, allowing us to fall into a comfortable rhythm of banter and play that lasted the entire summer.

At first, Mum and my aunt sounded the same, but as the days passed, I easily heard the distinction. The ever so slower and deeper tone came from Laurie, whereas Joyce's voice was higher pitched, as if her collar was too tight around her neck. After a glass of wine, though, they both sounded the same; either Mum's voice rose or my aunt's dropped. They never stopped talking as if their language belonged to only them. Talking and laughing as they chopped, grated, boiled, stewed, stirred, sipped tea, sipped wine, walked, waded, picked berries, washed clothes or toilets. *How much is there to talk about?* In any event, I was sure Grace and I would do the same as adults, only we would be together all the time, not just in summer.

While the "youngsters" did the dishes, the adults played bridge. They sat around a card table that I'm sure was as old as the house, all of them smoking. Well, some smoking more than others. It was all in the technique. Dad dragged on that poison wrapped in paper like his life depended on it, while my aunt and Mum squinted as they brought the offensive thing to their lips. They gently pulled on the plastic filters and immediately released the smoke out their mouths in a gray cloud that hid their faces until they had successfully blown it away. Two puffs, they were done. I could see Mum loved the act of tapping the burnt end of the ciggy until she had successfully snuffed it out. It then laid in an ashtray as a testament to her adulthood.

On Sunday evenings, Dad returned to Halifax for the week to work; he'd be back Friday evening. I secretly worried about him being alone for a whole week. Would he drink himself into oblivion? This particular Sunday evening everyone gathered to say goodbye to him.

"Bye, dear," Mum said as if she said it every day of our lives, wiping her hands on her apron before putting them around his neck. "Drive safely now, and call when you get home." They then kissed — a real kiss, five seconds at least. Their bodies pressed up against each other and Mum lifted her foot just a little, then Dad gave Mum's bum a tap. It was quite a display.

"I will. Should be about two and a half hours. Bye girls, come give Daddy a hug."

It was another advantage for the Hester family to have their father with them for the whole summer, thus a disadvantage for us to not. With Dad not present to keep Uncle Brian company, Mum had to then share her sister's attention with him. If we were at home, this would have put Mum into a real funk, but here, she put on a good face and pushed through.

I hardly noticed my uncle at all, only seeing him at the dinner table. I think he secretly enjoyed being on his own. His wife was having a wonderful time with her sister and he didn't have to be with Dad. He came and went as he pleased. Every morning he'd walk Sunrise Beach. Such a glamorous idea; it was something I intended to do when I visited Lund Harbour as an adult. One summer he taught us all how to play baseball, or a version thereof. A small diamond was cleared at the edge of the meadow overlooking Seashell Island. It was so fun to have both families playing together this way.

The long summer days stretched into long weeks. Time was irrelevant. The rhythm of the sun was our guide, like a heartbeat. We were free as the frigid Atlantic waves that crashed over our young bodies, sending us racing back to the warmth of the sand.

We'd snuggle together under an old sleeping bag turned picnic blanket. Our bodies always touching, the salt and sand exfoliating the dead, dry skin of winter. The last summer there was truly the best. I just had no idea I'd never return.

Chapter 10

Addicted

My car jolted off the tracks of the car wash. A man waved me forward.

"Okay, thanks," I yelled inside the car to myself. I'd pick up some spring bulbs. The nursery had taken on hues of autumn, summer had come and gone quickly. We had spent it moving James, our middle boy, into his own place, with four other young men. At the age of fifteen, James gave Phillip and me a run for our money. We completely missed the signs. It was Brian, our eldest, that pointed out to his clueless parents their son was drinking and hanging out with a "rough crowd." Like his father, Brian was born structured, sensible, disciplined, easy to please and easy to raise. Whereas James was a fireball right from the get-go.

As with all relationships, challenging times will highlight the pre-existing weaknesses in it. Ours was no exception. In essence, Phillip's response to James's drinking was anger and frustration, which only led me to feel angry and frustrated with Phillip.

"What's his problem? He has a great life — he doesn't have to do this. What the hell does he want? He's just doing it to get back at us."

"It doesn't do any good to get angry, Phillip. We have to figure out what to do for him; we need to talk about this quietly."

"Barb's willing to help us, so I don't know why you won't accept her help."

"You know why, Phil: She's a know-it-all. She lords over us how wonderful DJ is, all because of her amazing parenting. And besides, she's married to your brother; families and friends should not counsel each other. I even know that; it's called a dual relationship. Shouldn't she know that too?"

"She's a social worker, she's in the business, but never mind, you do what you want. I have no time — look at the next three months for me. I'm travelling all over the world at all hours of the day and night," he said, sorting his already sorted shirt. "He takes after your Dad — and sister," he added.

"Oh, don't do that," I responded to his back as he left the room.

Suffice it to say, mistakes were made in attempts to harness and protect James. And it all took a toll on our already "tested" marriage.

Mixed in with the chaos, there were times of deep connection with James, giving me false hope that I held onto like a wild animal protecting its young. I'd not lost him completely. Even though I knew all about enabling, I'd believe his promises to never touch booze again. It was like relying on a floating stick to save me from drowning in a tsunami. We'd hug and tearily express our love for one another. Hope bloomed eternal only to wither in another round of binging, or "partying," as James called it.

The girls loved him. He had a sincere, charming way about him that got him through. Teachers liked him. They excused his absences as long as his work was completed successfully and he remained a sweet boy. Mr. Roy, the school counsellor, had a son who was "up to the same business." *So what good was he?* At the last parent-teacher interview, I sat with fifty-year-old Mrs. Wallen, James's science teacher. As I approached her table, she smiled at me with pride.

"James is a lovely boy," she said as if James was her son and she was informing me of something I didn't know.

"Oh yes, he is. How's his attendance?" I asked.

"Well … you know … James is absent now and then. But he's bright — always on time with assignments …." She dropped eye contact.

"He is bright, yes."

There was nothing more to talk about. What could they do? I briskly headed out the door to the parking lot, plunked my defeated self behind the steering wheel and bawled my eyes out. *Jesus, what am I to do? I'm going to lose my son like I lost my sister.* Never in my wildest dreams did I think that one day I'd turn to Dad for guidance, but these were desperate times. I got the same response I'd already heard many times.

"He's gotta want to quit. Can't be forced, won't work. Best you get the support you need to handle it."

"Yes, Dad, but how did you do it?" I wanted specifics.

"Lost my appetite for it; lucky, I guess."

I'd never heard of such a thing but didn't see this happening for James. He was more like my sister then my father. We limped along through the remainder of Grade 10. Right or wrong, I needed Brian to keep an eye on his brother without him knowing and report his findings back to me. I would learn one day that this is called "triangulation" in the counselling world, and it's considered dysfunctional. I saw no other way.

The reports from Brian were much the same. James "partied" on weekends, attended school most days and smoked the odd joint at lunchtime. Even though not perfect by any means, things were not getting worse.

Upon Phillip's insistence, James secured a summer job serving popcorn and drinks at the local movie theatre. We were hoping for a job with daytime hours. He slept until noon all summer, went to work for the 2 p.m. matinee through to 11 p.m. closing, then drank with friends until the wee hours of the morning.

"There's no way in hell my parents would allow me to sleep all day," Phillip said with frustration, his nostrils flaring like an angry dragon.

"I know, I know — but at least we know where he is," I replied with relief.

"We've set the bar pretty damn low if this is what makes us happy."

"I'm not happy Phil — I'm relieved. In this moment, I'm relieved." *Please let me have a little relief.*

Soon into James's Grade 11 year, coach Ted saw talent in his basketball game. It seemed cliché that a school PE teacher/basketball coach would be the one to mentor a struggling young man, but there he was. James had never been a strong athlete, so I had concerns about coach Ted's intentions and thought I'd just have a word. But when a parent is witnessing their derailed child come clean, join a sports team, make new friends and express enthusiasm, it's not so easy to rock that boat. Especially when everything that Phillip and I had tried failed.

"I have basketball practice after school," James yelled as he slathered his toast with peanut butter. I was in the den looking for my reading glasses.

"I'm right here," said Phillip, realizing he was invisible to his own son. "I'm coming to watch — if that's okay with you?" James looked surprised.

"Really? That'd be great!"

"3:30 in the gym?" Phillip asked, putting the paper in front of his face as if he didn't want to scare the boy away.

"Yup, you got it."

"I'm coming too," I said, entering the kitchen with my glasses. James smiled with great pleasure as he stuffed half a piece of toast into his mouth.

"Right on," he mumbled. "Don't embarrass me," he said in his charming way even though his mouth was full of food.

Phillip erected a basketball hoop on the side of our driveway that day — dug a hole deep enough to bury a body, mixed concrete for an hour in a wheel barrel, filled the hole with it, stuck the basketball pole in the concrete and braced it with a wood frame. It took a full week for the concrete to dry.

"Maybe I *did* dig the hole a bit deep," he admitted to the boys, who were chomping at the bit to shoot hoops.

"Ya think?" Brian said teasingly. Well into the winter months, the sound of a bouncing ball could be heard from the backyard as Phillip and his three boys cheered and moaned with each shot, either sunk or missed. I saw every game that year. James was not tall, but he never took his eyes off the ball. Could run in fast spurts. Had a way of crouching and weaving through the players. He knew when to shoot and when to pass. He was so exciting to watch and was touted as the most valuable player on the school team. We had come through the tunnel.

. . .

The nursery was warm and moist. Leafy decorations of fall colours invited customers to prepare for the coming season. Other than white tulip bulbs, I'd skip purchasing anything new and let nature take its course. I never remembered what I'd planted from one year to the next, it was always a surprise, usually pleasant. The tulips would be a nice showing in the spring. White was the colour of celebrations, weddings, births, deaths, graduations, surrender, purity, Godliness, neutrality, truth. *Ah, truth.* I spotted a pot of cut white roses in full bloom, half price. Out of the blue, I wanted to visit Mum's gravesite, which was a first. Armoured with a handful of white roses, I headed for the cemetery.

It was amazing that I remembered where her gravesite was; I drove right to it. I was fourteen years old when we placed her ashes in the ground. Ashes that travelled across Canada. Her resting place was at the top of the hill, in the sunshine. I approached slowly, feeling fourteen again, sad and frightened. Only my dad and I were present at the site. Dad held my hand, a rare gesture of love to me, as we listened to a woman read the Lord's Prayer. We then each dropped a handful of dirt into the one-foot by one-foot grave. That was the end of the service. We drove home in silence.

I recalled this time like it was yesterday. I took a deep breath and placed the white roses by her headstone.

Laurie Marie Holm
1937 to 1974
Loving wife and mother
Rest in peace

Wonder where Dad found those words; maybe from a funeral-home catalogue. I could only recall one time in my life I felt what I think was real love from my mother. I see it less now, but I've spent many hours daydreaming, dissecting each half-second of each movement as if I might see something I missed, giving me more of her.

When I was seven and Grace was four, Mum took us shopping, a seasonal ritual — one of only a few family rituals we had. It was summer and we took a bus then walked quite a distance to Simpsons-Sears, a walk Mum mastered in high-heeled shoes like a ballroom dancer. The purpose of the trip was to buy new nylons for Mum.

Buying nylons was a tedious affair for Grace and me. In those days, the stockings were kept behind the counter. Rows and rows of thin stacked boxes, high up, out of reach. Flat little boxes, each labelled with a colour: medium beige, shear rain, clear taupe, medium dark gray, light charcoal. Hundreds of them. A young, pretty girl, an expert in nylon stockings, stood behind a brightly lit glass counter.

"Not too dark, not too shear, you know, natural, the colour of flesh, but enough to hide veins and so forth," Mum said vaguely.

The sales rep spun on her tiptoes, reached way up, and with great skill, pulled out a box from the middle of a pile without disturbing any other boxes. It was like a magic trick. She opened the box, carefully lifting a layer of white tissue paper to expose the thick top of the stocking that would eventually clasp to a garter belt. The young lady's ringless hand slid into the stocking, nails tucked under so not to snag the nylon. The stocking lay on the back of her hand, both she and Mum paused in anticipation.

"Too dark," Mum said, shaking her head.

With a nod, the girl wrapped the stocking, closed the box and slid it back exactly where it came from. I know this because I had taken note of how many boxes were under the selected box. There was no marker for the girl to find the place where the box had come from, she just knew. She then moved her pointer finger to the row on the right or left, scanning down, selecting, opening, presenting, waiting, replacing, selecting, etc.

Just as Grace and I started displaying we'd had enough, around the fourth or fifth box, the young woman's hand slid under the nylon and my mother announced with complete certainty, "That's the one, it's perfect!"

They met eyes. No contest, it was decided. *Thank God.*

The best part of the shopping trip was a visit to the cafeteria. The lights were dim, creating the illusion of nighttime. We would sit atop the high, red vinyl stools at the bar. Mum sat with her legs crossed, dangling her high-heeled shoe off her toes, looking like she should order a drink. I was startled and somewhat embarrassed seeing Mum posed in such a manner. I had seen women in movies sitting just this way, holding a cigarette and always saying something clever to a man.

"Ice cream or French fries, girls?" Mum said, offering no other choices.

Grace squirmed with indecision, but I knew exactly what I wanted because I had a system.

"Well," I spoke with conviction, "it's warm outside so I'm having ice cream because it will cool down my insides. In the winter, I'll have French fries because it's cold outside and I'll need to warm up my insides."

I met Mum's gaze and she smiled at me with enamoured beauty. She loved me. I felt it in my heart and deep in my belly. My skin tingled with life. In that sentence, I had said something that connected her to me. It happened only this once. After that time, no matter what I said or did to connect us was never the right set of words. In fact, what I said often had the exact opposite effect. But I never gave up trying. Once you taste a mother's love, you're addicted and the rest of your life is spent looking for morsels.

Stretching out on my back, I sighed, pushing the memory away. I thought of her toenails, a pretty pink. The sky stretched above like a big blue prairie. The speck of a plane could be seen but not heard. Always, at the sight of a plane, was Phillip. I closed my eyes.

Oct 4, 1974

Dear Grace,

How are you? Are you use to being at Aunt Joyce's yet? Do you have your own bed? Do you share a room? I hope you're having fun with our cousins. Do you play with Joy?

Dad and I are okay. Dad goes to work and I go to school. Then I come home right after. I don't feel like playing with anyone. I'm still friends with Penny, but not as much as before. She sort of hangs around other kids that I don't know, but sometimes she'll invite me to her house. Her Mum's really nice to me, it makes me sad though. I watch Penny and her Mum talking to each other.

I can hardly wait till Christmas till you're home. I really miss you and I'm sure you miss me too. I bought a transistor radio with money I got babysitting. I babysit every Thursday night, 2 little girls. The Mum's really pretty, her name is Isabella, isn't that a beautiful name, I just love it. If I have a girl I'm going to name her Isabella. She told me it's a Spanish name. She was born in Spain.

What's school like? Do you like it? It doesn't matter if you don't because you're only there till Christmas anyway. Are you going out on Halloween? What will you be? I don't know if I'll go out yet. What kind of food do you eat? Does Aunt Joyce cook dinner? I picture you like Father Knows Best, you know, like the Mum and Dad and kids all happy and stuff. I wish I was there too. That would be too many kids for them, and I guess Dad would be all alone then.

Seems like I have more to write but I'll save some for my next letter. I'll mail this letter tomorrow. Please write me back soon. Dad says we can talk on the phone on your birthday. I can hardly wait.

Love Maggie xo

Chapter 11

Learning to Navigate

Paranoia had me proofreading my letters to Grace at least twice, examining each word, phrase and sentence for the slightest hint that would reveal the secret. Had she known the truth about Mum's death, we could have shared our thoughts and feelings with one another in our letters. I had no one. Dad sure wasn't going to talk about it, and I didn't want to talk to him anyway.

"Maggie," I turned towards the voice.

It was my first day back at school after Mum died and Grace had been taken away. It was Mrs. Radcliff, the school secretary, calling me into the office. *What was happening? Who knew? What did she want?*

"Can you pop in here for a minute, dear?" she asked, holding the office door open for me.

Do I have a choice? Everyone in the hallway was looking at me and whispering to each other.

"I'm so sorry to hear about your mother, dear," Mrs. Radcliff said with just the right amount of kindness; made me want to cry. Reaching into the pocket of her big blue sweater that she wore every day of the year, she said, "I have this to give you." She handed me a folded piece of paper. "Read it here, dear. You can come behind the desk if you like."

"No, I'm okay."

No, I'm not. The paper flapped in my shaking hands.

"Oh, come in here."

Such a loving voice. I followed and sat where she indicated, out of sight, behind the desk. The note said that the school counsellor wanted to touch in with me today. *Maybe the counsellor's like Mrs. Radcliff.* I looked up at her and nodded.

"Wonderful, come see me after lunch break. You're excused from first period to see Mrs. King, she's the school counsellor, she's lovely." I trusted everything Mrs. Radcliff said.

The morning was tricky. Some classmates knew my mother had died, some didn't. Word spread fast. Most didn't know what to say, even teachers. Lots of awkward silence around me. I skipped lunch and headed straight to the school office. Mrs. Radcliff had the phone tucked between her ear and shoulder and was flipping through papers.

"Where is that darn thing?" I heard her say.

She was slim, around fifty. Every year her hair got shorter, and it was too short right now. Family photos in matching frames sat in front of her, the smiling faces of her twin boys in graduation caps and gowns. A more recent one last Christmas in front of the tree in her home. *She has her own family. I'm a student, that's all.*

"Oh, you're here," she said, spotting me at the desk. She smiled, stood and said, "You're early — did you eat lunch?"

"I'm not hungry — I'm okay."

"Come through here, dear."

I followed. With a bent finger, she tapped lightly on a door labelled COUNSELLOR in black. While we waited, she smiled at me and took a deep breath as if encouraging me to do the same; I did.

The door opened and I saw that the counsellor stood about four feet tall at most. She seemed used to looking up, wasn't bothered. I turned to say goodbye to Mrs. Radcliff but she was hustling down the hall onto the next thing.

"Hello, Margret. My name is Mrs. King. Would you like to take your jacket off?"

Should I correct her? "No, thanks." *That's not true. I'm hot and sweaty; it has to be a hundred degrees in here — no windows?*

"Well, I just wanted to touch in with you. Why don't you take a seat?" she said, pointing to the chair I was to sit in. It was directly across from her, face to face. "Are you comfortable — can I get you some water?"

No, I'm the opposite of comfortable. What does she want to know? She spoke like she was singing off-key, almost like yodelling. Her voice went up and down, up and down; it was irritating.

"No, I'm fine, thank you," I said politely.

As I stuck my bottom out to sit, I nudged the chair back a few more inches and placed my books on my lap like protective armour. Mrs. King sat down, plunking her hands in her lap. She wore tight purple pants that forced her belly to protrude and the zipper fold to flap up, exposing the metal thread. Her flowered blouse was equally tight. Each button under great strain to keep soft flesh from escaping, which it did anyway. I couldn't stop staring at the tension on those things. I expected them to pop any minute. I caught her mid-sentence.

"— you know, see how you're doing. I know you must be going through a hard time right now."

"It's okay," I lied again.

"Can you tell me what's okay, I mean, tell me how a usual day goes for you?"

"I get up, Dad makes me breakfast …" — lying — "… then I come to school, then go home and do my homework. Then Dad comes home and makes dinner." *That sounded pretty good.* "We watch some TV together, then I go to bed."

Mrs. King's tiny feet didn't reach the floor. They dangled like Christmas ornaments in little red pumps. Her purple pant legs had ridden up, showing off smooth, white, fleshy ankles that kept expanding into fleshy calves.

"Oh, I see, okay. Are you sleeping okay?"

Look at her face. "Yes, I sleep fine, thanks." *Geez, sleeping is all I do.*

"Do you and your Dad talk about what's happened at all?"

Why am I here? Who sent me? I don't want to talk to you. I'm not telling you my name.

"Sometimes."

"Do you make plans for the future? I understand your sister is now in Toronto?"

Future plans? Hilarious. "Yes."

"You must miss her."

"Yes," I said, trying to squirm out of my coat.

"Are you sure you wouldn't like to take your coat off?"

"No, I'm fine thanks," I said, looking for a window that wasn't there.

The room smelled like gasoline and vinegar. I nudged my chair back another inch. *Don't think she noticed — still talking.*

"— a girl of your age is going through many changes. This is a time when she would lean on her mother for advice and guidance to help her through. I want you to know that I'm here for you to talk any time you want."

I'd not have known she wore a wig until it slipped slightly to the left. A short, wavy, brown wig now covered her left ear. *What does her real hair look like?* I imagined her bald. Her eyes were beautiful; big and brown, like Mum's. Her skin was light, full, soft, like Grace's baby cheeks that I couldn't stop kissing.

"You just have to tell the school secretary that you'd like to speak with me and she'll make an appointment for us to meet, like this," she said sticking her hands out like flippers coming from the sides of her body. "Would you like that?"

"Sure, okay — thanks," I said to the plastic palm tree in the corner.

"Is there anything you'd like to ask me today? Do you have any concerns about school or friends, or anything?"

"No, I'm good — thanks." *Just need to get out of this stinky oven.* "Oh, just one thing," I said, standing.

"What is that?" she said excitely as she shuffled forward in her chair so her feet touched the floor.

"Will anyone know that I came in here, with you? You know, teachers or other kids — anyone?"

"No, Margret. Everything we talked about is completely confidential," she said, pushing herself up with her hands.

I tried not to tower over her but it was impossible. She was short to begin with and I towered over everyone.

"Ya but, will anyone KNOW that I came here?"

"Well, some people. Our principal, Mr. Brady, and the school secretary, Mrs. Radcliffe, that's all. They need to know, of course, but again, they have to abide by confidentiality rules. They won't be saying anything to anyone. Do you feel better about that now?"

No, I feel like shit. "Yes, I guess so. I just wish no one knew."

"I understand. You just want things to be normal. That's because you're young. You'll understand one day that both Mrs. Radcliffe and Mr. Brady only care about you, they have no interest in gossip. I understand how you're feeling, but I don't want that to stop you from coming to see me again. Only Mrs. Radcliffe will know so she can make the appointment, okay?"

I felt a headache coming on. The smell, the heat, the yodelling mixed with my sudden hunger.

"Sure." *Just please stop talking and let me go. How am I going to get out of here with no one seeing me?*

"Okay, Margret."

I was glad she didn't know my name. She knew I'd not be returning. But it was too late. In my mind, everyone knew I had seen the counsellor because I was crazy, or at the very least, weird. Damaged goods, now a motherless child.

My so-called friends became increasingly uncomfortable around me. After all, how do you talk to a girl who has no mother? Most conversations were all about how unfair their mothers were, so my presence only made them feel mean and ungrateful. The isolation was fine with me. Not only was I somewhat of a freak for not having a mother, but I also had a lie to guard. The lie had bored its way into my brain cells, causing my lips to remain in fearful lockdown lest I say the wrong thing.

With the exception of my Thursday night babysitting, TV was my best friend. I spent the weekends sleeping and the weekdays checking the mailbox. That was my life. Finally, after what seemed like an eternity, a letter arrived from Grace.

Oct 28, 1974

Dear Maggie,

So much has happened. The best thing is your letter. I sleep with it under my pillow. I have my own bed in Lacy's bedroom. Lacy is 14 but she's not like you at all she's like 16. She wears make up and smokes and swears. At first she was really nice to me telling me stuff about her friends but then she changed. I don't know anyone in school just Joy. I miss my old school. They play loud country music all the time and they have all the lights on all the time. I miss home so much and I miss you. Aunt Joyce lets me stay home from school if I want to. She says I have homesickness because I cry alot and I just want to go home. I don't tell her because I don't want to be rude or hurt her feelings. But I just want to come home.

I got my hair cut for a treat. I have bangs now. I can still put it in a pony tail but its a short one. Flying was scary at first, the plane speeds to take off then just starts flying. It goes above the clouds. It was like being in heaven. I watched out the window the whole time looking for Mum but I don't think I saw her, but maybe I did. It was kind of like a bunch of sparkles on the wing of the plane like an angel. It just stayed there for a really long time. I think it was Mum. I didnt tell anyone, just you. She was like an angel. I kept looking out the window in case she came back. Anyway don't tell anyone. Tell me what you think, do you think it was Mum? I think it was.

Its weird to be here with Aunt Joyce but not Mum or you. Everything is so different now. I think of you and Dad and get so sad I cry alot.

Aunt Joyce is sewing Joy and John and me Halloween costumes. John is going to be superman and Joy is Barbie and I'm Tinkerbell. Lacy said she's going to a party and out with her friends, she said she's not taking Joy and me trick or treating. Aunt Joyce and her got in a big fight about that. Its too bad about your friends at school, they sound mean. You can get other nicer friends. Are you going out on Halloween? What will you be?

Aunt Joyce bought me this writing paper that I am using to write this letter with my own envelops and stamps so I'm going to mail this to you today. There is a mail box right on the corner. They have a cat and I'm alergect so I'm not allowed to touch it. My eyes get all red and itchy and my nose runs like I have a cold. His name is Smokey I like him so its to bad I'm alergect.

Dave is really nice to me. Hes learning how to drive and he told me that when he gets his license he'll take me for a ride. Its really neat that you babysit and make money and you bought a transistor.

Well I hope you have fun on Halloween. I wish you were here so we could go together. I cant believe that Mum is dead. I just pretend she is at home with you and Dad and I am on a holiday to visit our cousins. Its weird but I get sad if I don't think that. Write me back soon. I miss you so much.

Love Grace xo

Did I think it was Mum sitting on the wing of the plane? No, I did not think it was Mum. How could she be an angel? She's in limbo. She killed herself. She left her children, forever. Angels care about children and look out for them. Why would Mum sit like an angel on the wing of the plane so Grace could see her?

I sighed. I felt tired. I imagined my little sister staring out the window in heaven waiting for Mum to appear. I could see the back of her head, her shoulders tight, eyes wide open, holding her breath in anticipation for a glimpse. Could it have been Mum? I brought the letter to my lips, the closest I'd been to Grace in over a month and kissed it as if I was kissing her. *She wrote all these words to me.* I crawled on top of my bed, curled into a ball holding her words to my chest and cried myself to sleep.

"Maggie, are you home?" Dad called up the stairs.

Where else would I be? "Yes, I'm here, just sleeping." I felt weighted, like a drowning dog.

"I'll heat dinner."

We'd be dead without TV dinners. To this day, I cannot tolerate the smell of them — turkey, stuffing, gravy and cranberry sauce — yuck!

My reflection in the bathroom mirror exposed the truth. Puffy flesh around my eyes kept me from seeing what I couldn't endure. Dry, cracked lips from a thirsty heart. Sunken cheeks lost in a relentless world of cryptic lessons. I wanted to crawl under the covers and sleep until the nightmare was over, just like Mum did.

"I'll be right down."

I wouldn't tell Dad about Grace's letter, just as he wouldn't share his conversations with my aunt except to say, "Grace was doing just fine; we made the right choice."

"WE did not make the choice."

"Maggie, leave it."

The thought of living in a brightly lit house with country music twanging in the background made me *almost* grateful I was left behind. I was accustomed to, and preferred, a dark, quiet house save for the noises that beckoned out of a TV and lured me into a make-believe world. But my sister should be here with me, living in her own home.

Chapter 12

Letters and Dreams

Even as a small child, Lacy was a powerhouse, defiant beyond her young years. I was already a people pleaser with no developed opinions of my own. Lacy, on the other hand, seemed to have something to say about everything. Adults laughed at things she said, which only incensed her more. It was all above my head. But I admired her expressive ways, and to demand something of the adults in her life. This would never have occurred to me simply because Mum and Dad used up all opportunities for the likes of such expression, whether silent or loud, there was conflict.

Each time I reread Grace's letter, which had to be at least ten, explosions of thoughts and feelings erupted. Jealously caught in my throat. *If I was there, I'd be sharing a room with Lacy, and maybe I'd be rebellious too; and Dave would invite me for a drive;*

I'm closer in age. And so began the arduous task of comparing my life to my sister's. The Great Divide.

. . .

Had I known how peaceful a resting place my mother occupied, I'd have visited more often. *Or not; most likely not.* There were no trees on the hill to block the sun, and I enjoyed the warmth. I shifted up onto my elbow and read the stone again, lightly touching the letters of *Loving wife and mother.* Poor Dad, he knew so little about the woman he'd married. My father and I never spoke about the stone, the words, the plot, nothing. We dealt with her death in private, in our own heads. We fell into a new routine that suited both an adolescent girl and a man whose mother and wife had left them alone. Dad's second wife, now gone; schnapps his only remaining love. Unbeknownst to me, I learned how to isolate my heart from an untrustworthy world.

Memories of childhood were a series of fleeting thoughts that flashed by at lightning speed. Grace's coral bathing suit, knees together, toes curled into the rippled sand, arms tucked into her tummy, wisps of hair blowing across her face as she scanned for sand dollars. The most pleasing memories were always those of Lund Harbour and the mixture of sea salt, dust and wood that permeated the Big House. Comforting sounds of squeaky floorboards under my feet as I walked up the grand staircase and down the long, narrow hallway. Stories of my mother and her sister as children emanated from those floorboards.

The house was alive with two little girls excited about a special dessert or fresh bread. It was like a movie in my mind. I yearned to be my mother as a child in those memories.

Although the Big House needs serious repair, it basically remains the same. A large bathroom sits at one end of the hallway with the original claw-foot tub. At the other end of the hallway, a door leads outside onto a small balcony, for design only, the architecture of the day. There were bedrooms of all shapes and sizes, each with their own dormer window off either side of the long hallway. It was ecstasy for Grace and me to pick a bedroom with an old double bed that swallowed us up in luxurious flannel comfort. The deep bass of fog horns rhythmically lulled us to sleep, carrying us out to sea.

There was nothing better than waking to the sound of laughter, especially Mum's. It welcomed us into the large, old kitchen for a hearty breakfast "To start the day right!" my aunt would say.

The summer I had just turned eleven, my godmother and great-aunt, Marget, who I'm named after, arrived early one morning.

"Ah, there's my sleepy godchild, my namesake. Goodness you've grown," she said, holding open her arms.

Even though I saw her only once a year for a week, she felt like home to me. I nestled into her; she was like a soft pillow. I was only eleven, but we almost stood eye to eye. As if always on alert, her eyes were almost completely black, just a hint of dark brown circled her large, open pupils. She held my face in her hands and placed a knowing kiss on my forehead.

"It's good to see you," she said simply, no gushing.

One by one, others filled the kitchen. She squeezed my hand and winked; I was her favourite and I imagined I would live with her someday when I was older and going to college. Aunt Marget was smart; she would tutor me and make sure I had everything I needed to be successful. And then Grace would join us and we'd live together. This is why her passing that winter devastated me so. A particularly cold Atlantic storm placed pneumonia in her lungs. Even though she lived and died a few hours from Halifax, we did not attend her funeral. My childish dream of living with Aunt Marget had nowhere to go. It sat stagnant in my head, mocking me. I had only shared this dream with her silently in my mind, and I imagined she delighted in the possibility. But the dream died with her.

That Christmas before the winter took her, she sent me a card with a small heart on the end of a chain. I wore it for years, until the chain broke. The heart, her heart, was laid to rest in my jewellery box.

Nov 16, 1974

Dear Grace,

It was so great to get your letter. It's weird picturing you there, eating dinner and everything with our cousins. I imagine this really bright house with loud music. It's too bad about Lacy not being nice to you, did you tell Aunt Joyce? Maybe you could share a room with Joy.

It was a long time ago but did you go out on Halloween? I ended up going out with Penny, just the 2 of us. She was in a bad mood though, I don't think she wanted to go out with me, I think her Mum made her and now she hardly talks to me. I don't care anyway, I don't like her anymore. All the girls at my school are stupid. Don't tell Aunt Joyce, but I skip a lot of school. I get home before Dad so I get to the mail first and just throw away the school notice. DON'T TELL!

Did Dave get his drivers license? What TV shows do you watch? Are you ever alone or is there always someone there? I'm alone most of the time. I keep looking for you or expect you to come around the corner. Nothing's the same here. I watch TV all the time and I eat when ever I want, mostly cereal or toast. Dad stays late at work a lot.

It snowed yesterday. I love how the snow makes everything look so clean. Remember you and I would go out and make a snow man as soon as it started snowing?

Well your birthday is coming soon. Dad said I can call you. What will you do for your birthday?

I'm saving money from babysitting. I'm saving up for a car. Dad said if I start saving now by the time I turned 16 I'll have enough. It seems a long time from now but cars are expensive so I have to save a lot. I really like the family I babysit for. I call the Dad Mr. Campbell but the Mum says she doesn't like being called Mrs. Campbell, and I must call her Isabella. She's so nice. The little girls are so cute, Jennifer is 6 and Julia is 4 and ½. Julia copies everything that Jennifer does, it's so cute. They have a really nice home and fun toys and stuff. Isabella cooks me dinner too, so I eat with them and then they go out to the camera club. They take beautiful pictures of Jennifer and Julia, they're all framed and hanging all over the house. I get them ready for bed, read them a story or play snakes and ladders then tuck them in. They always have stuff to tell me when they get in bed. I feel like their much older sister. Isabella told me that they just love me and can hardly wait for Thursdays when I come.

Ok, that's about it for now. I'll talk to you before I write you again... I feel like crying thinking about talking to you, I hope I don't cry on the phone.

I miss you.

Love Maggie xo

Dad dialed the number.

"Hi Joyce," Dad uncharacteristically chuckled with delight. "Seems we have some pretty excited girls here. I'm handing the phone to Maggie."

He gave me a nervous wink, maybe in anticipation of what was to come. He'd have to do a lot more than make a phone call before I'd succumb to his charms.

"Grace?"

The dam broke, tears flowed, and as if contagious, Grace started crying too.

"Maggie — I want to come home," she loudly sobbed.

Dad shot me a look that said, *You're not making it any easier*, and in my usual "save the day" fashion, I sucked in my sorrow, swallowed hard and chirped, "Hey, Grace, it's okay. You'll be home soon. Hey, happy birthday! You're twelve now — one more year till you're a teenager. What did you get for your birthday?"

Phlegm filled my mouth as if my sadness had nowhere to go. Grace was now sobbing uncontrollably, so Joyce took the phone.

"Hi Maggie dear, just give her a little minute. How are you?"

There it was again, Mum's voice.

"Okay, how are you?" I said by rote.

"Oh, here's Gracie dear."

"I'm okay now," she said stoically.

I wanted to yell, "MUM KILLED HERSELF, SHE DIDN'T DIE OF A HEART ATTACK, AND YOU NEED TO COME HOME NOW!" Instead, I said, "Are you having a good birthday? What did you get?"

"I got a new pair of jeans and new shoes. We just had dinner … Aunt Joyce made my favourite, shepherd's pie." She lowered her voice as if she was filling me in on a juicy bit of gossip. "We're gonna have cake now."

Dad lit a cigarette, making me conscious of how much this was costing him and that he had not yet spoken to his daughter.

"I guess I better let Dad say hi to you. I'm glad you're having a good birthday. It'll be Christmas soon and you'll be home. So just keep thinking about that — and write me letters and I'll write you. I'll buy you a birthday present and a Christmas present at the same time and you can open them when you're home."

Silence

"Okay, bye," I said through a tight throat.

"Bye …" she said through an explosive sob.

I handed the phone to Dad. With the help of some almighty power I got to my room and immediately escaped into the safety of sleep after crying.

"Loving wife and mother," I read again out loud. Could I squeeze Mum into that role? Maybe sometimes. There were loving moments, I guess. Times that suited her when she felt in the mood to express a loving gesture, but other than our magical moment in Sears, I don't really recall them, I just imagine they exist. Did Dad feel loved? I think not, but she most likely didn't either.

Chapter 13

A Good Day

The sun's warmth comforted me as I sat at the top of the hill beside Mum's gravesite. I felt reluctant to leave. *When will I return?* I pulled the roses to my face and inhaled the scent one last time before placing them gently over her stone.

Had I forgiven her? How could a secret be kept for so many years? Would it be easier to take it to my grave? Not anymore, I was exhausted. Every cell in my body screamed for peace. I moved the roses off the stone, as if to improve Mum's ability to hear me, and leaned in close. Never having spoken to Mum in a loving, intimate way, I paused to collect myself and clear my throat.

"Mum, I'm telling Grace the truth," I whispered. "Did you come to help me this morning? Are you here? I need your help. I know you regret what you did. I know you loved me — I want to be free of this — I want to forgive you — I do forgive you — I forgive you, Mum."

I stretched my arms over her stone and cried with undeniable honesty, like I was fourteen again and needing to understand and forgive.

Forgiveness is a powerful thing. It's like sobriety, can't be forced or faked. My tears weren't heavy with grief but light with what felt like love. I rearranged the roses again, carefully this way and that on and around my mother's resting place. I kissed my fingers and placed them on her name.

"I love you," I whispered.

Light as a feather, weightless even, I seemingly floated to my car. I was acutely aware of the absence of something. *My mind — have I lost it? What is it — what's missing? Resentment?* I searched for it, I even tried to muster some up. Nothing. Even the memory of it was nowhere to be found. I pictured Mum lying on her bed, still, dead, but it was fuzzy, as if butter had been smeared on the lens of my imagination. Her green skirt and yellow sweater faded and blurred as she grew smaller and smaller until there was nothing to see. No emptiness in my belly and no tightening in my heart. I glimpsed at myself in the rear-view mirror to wipe tear stains from my face. *Who are you, looking ten years younger — brighter, happy.* I drove home in an altered state, a peaceful state. How does a person know if it's peace they're feeling? Is it a thing? Or is it the absence of something, like resentment?

It was that strange time of year when it's cooler inside the house than outside. I stood on the deck that overlooked a rather pleasant backyard, albeit with a neglected garden. I'd get to it in good time. My newfound peace permeated outwards, so everything could wait, there was no rush.

The oak tree, as we called it before the swing was erected, had not yet started turning colour. Slippery green slime now covered the wooden seat. The boys were young, heck Phillip and I were young, when we erected the swing. We had talked about it for weeks.

"Well, the branch is perfect, no doubt about that," Phillip said for the umpteenth time.

It stuck straight out from the trunk at just the right height and just the right thickness.

"But we need a certain kind of rope, and wood for the seat. Wouldn't want any accidents, must be done right."

The boys and I spoke for the tree branch.

"Put a swing on me right here — Hey! Where's my swing? I've been waiting a long time for a swing!"

Phillip's rebuttals included poor weather, his work schedule, the store didn't have the right rope. However, the boys were relentless. At long last, on a warm day in June, Phillip got to it. He had educated himself on how to build a swing and how to attach it to a tree branch, and he laid out all the equipment on the grass. The boys were out of their minds with excitement. It was a rare thing to see all three of them play together; it relieved me somehow, like I knew they would eventually come together, as adults, to look out for each other after Phillip and I were gone. It was evident that they, too, enjoyed this time. At one point, James paused to observe his two brothers interact in a way that can only occur when there are no mysteries about who the other is. Like a blissful sunrise, he smiled and exuberantly jumped in to rejoin the fun.

In between gazing at this wonderful display of sibling bonding, my job that day was to keep the food and beverages coming. By late afternoon, it was all about who had the longer turn, how high could it go, was the branch going to break, give me a push … again.

As the honeymoon of the day was nearing its end, I could feel a pull on my heart. *When will I experience such close family time that isn't dictated by a celebration or family holiday again?* This had been a spontaneous day where free will ruled our decision to be together, just us, in our own backyard.

Just as the build up to Christmas is more exciting than opening the gifts, after the third and fourth turn, the thrill of the swing began to decline ever so slightly. Brian found other ways to keep the play going, shinning up the ropes and throwing the swing around the branch to make the swing higher, standing on the seat to swing and so on. The competition between James and him was evident. Brian was built like Phillip with excellent athletic abilities, a natural at all sports. Not only was James younger, but he was also not a natural athlete. Brian was completely unaware of James's need to prove himself to his older brother. James was hard enough on himself and envied his brother's seemingly easy approach to life. That's what was so remarkable about this day; they were all equal in their anticipation and excitement. I could see they wanted to keep the momentum going as if they, too, knew it had been a miraculous day.

To everyone's delight, I spread our well-travelled picnic blanket beside the tree that we now referred to as the swing tree for a picnic dinner.

"Okay everyone, I made a spread of food, need help bringing it out."

The boys, always ready to eat, raced each other into the kitchen.

"Right on, Mum's potato salad!" Brian announced.

Only took a large bag of potatoes and almost a full jar of mayonnaise. There was a platter piled with chicken drumsticks — twenty to be exact — a very large bowl of green salad from two heads of lettuce, four tomatoes, six mushrooms and quarter of a jar of Thousand Island dressing. We followed that with half a pan of chocolate brownies washed down with a quart of milk. The spread was impressive, one for *Better Homes & Gardens*, so Jeffery said.

After dinner it was my turn to swing, and Phillip pushed me. It *was* truly thrilling, even for the boys. The seat of the swing was long, room for two. The rope thick and sturdy. There was the slightest give in the branch as the swing descended, giving the impression you just might hit the ground. I squealed, feeling ever so young and pretty. The boys jumped and clapped, taking pleasure in my enjoyment.

It was a good day and is a wondrous memory. In honour of that day, I filled a bucket with hot water, added a combination of TSP, dish soap and a splash of bleach, and got busy scrubbing that seat. I wished Phillip and boys were here to see the end result; it looked spanking new, with a titch of weathering.

Chapter 14

Don't Get Your Hopes Up

Dec 18, 1974

Dear Grace,

Dad just told me that you're not coming home at Christmas. He said that you're doing well at Aunt Joyce's and that moving you again would not be good for you. How do they know what's good for you? Being away from your own home is not good for you. You told me you were homesick. That's because you should be here, not there.

What am I going to do for Christmas? It'll just be Dad and me here, and I'm not buying him a present and I don't want one from him. I don't even have time to send you a present. I thought you'd be here to open it.

Our box of decorations is sitting in the middle of the living room floor. I guess Dad thinks I'm going to decorate. All the other houses have lights except ours. We don't even have a tree. Sometimes I wish I lived somewhere else. I miss Mum a lot. She loved Christmas and always made everything so special.

It must be different for you, at least you have other people and kids around. I'm sure there's decorations. I don't blame you if you don't want to come home.

Don't tell Aunt Joyce but I think I'm failing some classes. The principal told me I'm going to have to go to summer school for math and science if things continue the way they're going. I don't care, there's nothing else to do. I asked Dad if you were coming home in summer and he said he didn't know.

Penny is so mean to me now, I don't know how she was ever my friend. I don't care, I don't like any of those girls. Do you have friends at school now?

Are you still homesick? I wish it wasn't Christmas.

Write to me soon…

Love Maggie xo

"Look, it's not that simple. You can take care of yourself. She's still a little girl. I know you think you can take care of her, but you can't be there 100% of the time and neither can I," he said, averting his eyes as if not to poke the bear.

"I've looked after her all my life. I know her better than anyone. But I can tell your mind is made up and that's that!"

It was imperative that I not cry; I would not give my father the satisfaction. My lips pursed and I swallowed the metal taste of bitterness. This conversation was over. Certainly I was not bringing it up again, I would not beg. And I would not give my dad the impression that I was suffering because of anything he did.

Eventually he did adorn the front door with a string of lights haphazardly draped over the frame. It was pathetic. On Christmas Eve, we watched *A Christmas Carol*, the classic with Alastair Sim, and ate deluxe Christmas turkey TV dinners.

"How bout you open your gift tonight?" Dad suggested when the movie paused for a commercial.

"I don't have anything for you." I felt horrible.

"Don't give that a thought, I don't need anything."

He retrieved the gift from the kitchen and I opened it.

"A watch," I said, thinking I have a watch but didn't want to be rude.

"It's battery operated, no need to wind it."

"Oh cool," I said. "I like it, thanks."

I thought about giving him a kiss, but the movie started so I didn't have to decide. I put the watch on right away and showed it to him with pride. After the movie ended, Dad started cleaning up and I turned off the string of lights.

"I'll make French toast for breakfast," he said.

He was doing his best.

"OK, thanks again for the watch."

I headed up the stairs, and before I closed my bedroom door, I heard the sound of liquid being poured into a glass. It all felt surreal.

There was one ray of sunshine. Isabella invited Dad and me for Christmas dinner. A non-alcohol Christmas dinner, a novelty for us both. With my stash of babysitting money, I painstakingly selected and wrapped the perfect gifts for Jennifer and Julia. Dad rose to the occasion, buying a poinsettia for our hosts. Their house was like a real home, full of Christmas smells, shiny ornaments, reds and greens, Andy Williams' Christmas hits swooning from the record player and two little girls who were over the moon to have us there. Isabella told me the girls hounded her all day about my arrival time. Little did she know that I would have come at the crack of dawn and stayed forever.

"Jack, I'm so sorry for your loss," Isabella said, shaking Dad's hand.

I came to attention. How much or what did she know about that? We'd only mentioned it briefly.

"Thank you, yes. It's hard on Maggie, you know?" he said, clearing his throat and glancing at me.

"Of course, yes. You know our girls just love her. She's a lovely girl, Jack. Dick and I can't believe our luck."

Dick? How could an Isabella be married to a Dick?

"Well, she enjoys babysitting here, that's for sure," he said with far too much enthusiasm in his voice.

He was sweating, which was a cue that the subject of his wife's death was over. Grace was never mentioned; she seemed to have vanished along with our mother.

As if in a TV commercial, we sat around the Christmas tree and opened gifts. It was heaven, real heaven. I wanted to stay right there, in that family. I wanted that family to be mine. Part of me wished I'd never met the Campbells. It was like being offered a morsel of love: *Here, have a taste of what you'll never have.*

"Would you like to help me in the kitchen?" Isabella asked, placing her hand on my knee.

"Yes, sure," I said, dying to be part of it all.

"Thank you for the beautiful teddy bears for the girls. That was very sweet of you, but it wasn't necessary."

What does she mean? "Sure, I still have my teddy that my Aunt Joyce gave me when I was three and Grace had just been born," I said, stirring gravy that didn't need stirring.

"I'm sorry Grace isn't here with us. I'm sure the girls would love her too — if she's anything like you. Do you miss her?"

"Uh-huh ...." My throat tightened and I took a deep breath, "I love my hat and gloves set. You remembered my favorite colour, raspberry!"

"Jennifer remembered — I thought it was purple. Happy to hear we got it right!"

We gathered around the table just like *Father Knows Best* and not unlike our Christmases when Mum was alive. We started by opening Christmas crackers, putting on our paper hats, reading jokes written on little pieces of paper, then holding hands to say grace. From beginning to end, the lively conversation never stopped. Dad chuckled at the two little ones, and I wondered if he ever laughed at Grace and me.

After helping with the dishes, I stuck with the girls but couldn't help observing my father as if collecting data for analysis. He was well read in his own right, and to my surprise, he appeared relaxed and conversed easily with Dick and Isabella.

The silence upon entering our house was deafening. Little girls' excited giggling echoed in the empty space, and Dad was well aware of the contrast too.

"Well, they're a nice family," Dad said without looking at me. "Kind of them to invite us, very enjoyable evening."

"Yup," I said, struggling to stay angry. I couldn't. "You see why I like babysitting the girls? They're so cute," I said, remembering he smiled at their antics.

"They remind me of you and Grace."

"They're pretty lively, always talking and laughing," I said on purpose because my sister and I played quietly; we weren't permitted to run and laugh in the house.

I put the Christmas dinner leftovers from the Campbells in the fridge, yawned and said, "I'm tired, Dad, going to bed. Goodnight."

"Goodnight, Merry Christmas," he said, heading to the den.

Christmas was over, thank God.

. . .

Jeffery sent a text saying he'd not be home for dinner. The house seemed eerily quiet. There's not a doubt in my mind that I overcompensate for not having a mother of my own, but Phillip accuses me of not letting the boys figure anything out for themselves. Even though I'm completely aware I pamper and cater, I disagree that I don't let them suffer their own trials and tribulations.

Their aunt Grace has been kept at a distance lest the wrong thing be said. I never intended for my boys to know the truth about Mum, but at the age of eight, James overheard Phillip and me talking about her suicide. James's precocious nature dictated that he inquire further, with tenacity. I couldn't burden him with having to keep the secret from his brothers, so I told them all.

"When are you going to tell Aunt Grace the truth?" Brian asked, taking the news in stride.

I hung my head and said, "I have no idea."

Jeffery, six at the time, lovingly put his arms around me and said, "That's okay, Mummy."

But James took it on as if I had committed suicide myself. Was it his nature or age that caused him to seemingly be traumatized by this information? The expression on his face actually scared me.

"Boys, you don't need to worry about me; I would never do that to you. I intend to be around for a very long time. You'll all be sick of me by the time I die of very old age."

James's jaw clenched and his eyes watered, but there were no tears. Unfortunately, I neglected to confer with Phillip about my decision to tell the boys. There were, I suppose, other ways I could have explained the conversation James overheard, and Phillip accused me of unnecessarily burdening the children. At the time I felt sure that I'd done the right thing in the right way. But when James struggled with alcohol abuse, I felt responsible. In Al-Anon, I learned one of the reasons we enable is because we think we're responsible for our loved one's substance use. This was certainly the case for me.

I thought about my own mother's parenting. She was a terrible mother, but I didn't care. Her parenting had nothing to do with me. Maybe as a child, yes, I needed her, but I'm not a child anymore and she was sick. *Deal with it, Maggie. Let the woman rest.*

. . .

When I opened Grace's letter, a picture of Mum and Aunt Joyce standing on Sugar Hill, waves splashing at its base, dropped out. I knew that rock, I'd climbed it myself. It was at the far end of Sunrise Beach. They looked to be about eleven or twelve, both smiling with their arms draped on each other's shoulders. Mum had a straight bob haircut, and Aunt Joyce's head was adorned with untamed curls blowing this way and that. Lacy looked just like her. It unsettled me to see Mum so young, full of potential for all things, before I came along and forced her to shrink.

Jan 1, 1975

Dear Maggie,

Happy New Year. I got your letter before Christmas but I knew if I wrote back it wouldn't arrive in time for Christmas. So I'm writing now. I was really sad when I found out I wasn't going home, not even for Christmas. I won't be coming home until summer. My homesickness got worse so I didn't go to school for the last few days.

Christmas was okay. I got lots of stuff,
a new jacket,
a 500-piece puzzle,
new pajamas
a small dictionary so I can look up
words I don't know how to spell for my
letters to you,
a new tooth brush
and some other stuff.

The kids don't buy gifts they give each other something that they don't want or use any more, but it has to be nice, not broken or stained. Lacy gave me her nail polish kit with 3 different colours. There's scissors, a nail file and another thing that I don't know what its for. I gave Joy my old jacket, which use to be your jacket. Aunt Joyce said it was still in really good condition, it just didn't fit me anymore.

We had to go to church, just like at home. Aunt Joyce says she goes once a year and this was it. It was okay, I liked singing Christmas carols except I missed being with you.

There were lots of people for dinner. The next-door neighbors came over. They have a baby. I'm glad you got to go for Christmas dinner at Isabella's house.

I'm still in the same room as Lacy. She ignores me most of the time. I'm not allowed in if she has a friend over. I don't care though. Aunt Joyce lets me stay home if I don't feel like going to school. We look through photo albums full of pictures of her and Mum. She tells me the story of every picture. Like how old she was and how old Mum was and where it was taken and what they were doing. They use to pick wild strawberries in the field and then baked pies together. They would have tea parties and all their relatives and friends would come for tea and pie. There are lots of pictures of our Grandparents. There's a picture of Mum and Aunt Joyce about three and four years old in a rowboat with our Grandfather. She said that's the first picture of them as children. There's a picture on the wall of us all in Lund Harbour standing in front of the Big House. I can't stop staring at Mum in that picture. I can't believe she's not alive anymore?

I was allowed to pick any picture I wanted to send to you, except the one of them in the boat, so I picked this one. I hope you like it.

Dave got his drivers license but Uncle Brian said he can't take me for a drive until the spring when there's no snow on the roads. I don't think that's fair because there's no snow on the roads now but we still have to wait for spring.

I have something to tell you. I'm scared your going to think I'm crazy. I haven't told anyone, not even Aunt Joyce. Okay, here it goes. At night, when all the lights are out and I'm in bed I think I see Mum in the corner of the room. It's like a light, not bright, it's kind of round and it moves a little bit. I've looked outside for a light that would reflect into the room but there isn't one. There's nothing that would make that shape on the wall. It's there every night. Do you think it's Mum, like an angel? I think it is. It's not sparkly like I saw on the airplane wing, but I just think it's her. I can tell.

Well I hope you like the picture. Maybe if you go to school every day you won't have to go to summer school. When I get homesick I just think about something different, like my new jacket, or work on my puzzle. It's on a card table in the corner of the kitchen so that the whole family can work on it every time they walk by. I can tell Lacy really wants to work on it but she's defiant, that's what I heard Aunt Joyce tell Uncle Brian.

Okay, that's all for now, write me back right away.

Love Grace xo

It took time for the familiar swirling in my head to settle. I sat, staring off into space and feeling numb, picture in one hand, letter in the other. I examined the picture carefully, holding it close to my face. Grace was right. How could this young girl be gone? *Why her and not her sister? What was so different about them?* Did she know then, standing on that rock, that one day quite soon she'd be dead?

I read the letter again and again. Visions of a family singing Christmas carols haunted me. Then more visions began to cascade, free falling on top of each other: children wearing red flannel pajamas and opening presents from each other; an angel in Grace's bedroom; Mum lying on her bed, green skirt, yellow sweater; Dave driving, smiling; Grace wearing Lacy's nail polish; turquoise carpet; Grace and Aunt Joyce sitting close to each other looking at pictures; Grace crying as she walked away from me. It was my own personal photo album in my head with no sequential order. Like a car with no brakes careening downhill.

I needed distraction from my thoughts, so turned on the familiar face of Opie in the sunny town of Mayberry. He'd been keeping me company after school these days. Opie, a happy child whose mother was dead. He seemed not at all affected by this. I longed to get to that place, where I simply didn't think about her, like she never existed. *Was that even possible?*

When Dad arrived home, he said, "Turn on the lights when it gets dark; looks like no one's home." He flipped on lights as he walked to the kitchen. "I'll call you when dinner's ready, I got roast beef tonight."

I knew exactly what dinner was going to taste like — salty cardboard. I picked up the letter and picture, didn't want Dad to see them, didn't want to talk. This one really got me. Our lives that were once the same not so long ago were now so very different. I missed my sister more than my mother. We should be watching Opie together. She'd tell me about a teacher, a kid at school, something that happened, she'd ask me what to do, I'd tell her. We'd eat roast beef dinner together and it wouldn't taste like salty cardboard.

Chapter 15

Finding a Niche

Dad's tire business wasn't doing as well as his drinking, which was alive and thriving. To save the shop, he took on a partner but, sadly, the new guy also enjoyed liquid spirits. After the shop closed for the day, the two of them sat to "discuss business." Dad drove home drunk on a regular basis. We continued to live on TV dinners, but more often than not, I ate cereal three times a day.

"How are you?" Isabella asked one Thursday night.

The question held a punch, like she didn't want to hear "fine" or "good." She wanted to know how I really was.

"I'm okay, thanks," I lied.

"I just noticed that you've lost some weight and I'm concerned that maybe you're not eating enough," she said, getting right to the point.

"Um, yeah, sometimes I'm not hungry." I was caught. *How much do I explain? Where to begin?*

"Well, you know the girls always ask me if you can come over to play, so how would you like to be my 'mother's helper' after school? It would mean that you come here right after school and play with the girls for a while, help Jennifer with her spelling words and do your homework at the same time. You can stay for dinner, and while I do the dishes, you can bathe the girls and get them in their pajamas. I will pay you, of course. And on Thursday nights you can babysit as usual. How does that sound?"

I didn't know whether to laugh or cry. "Yes, that's great, I'd love to. Should I start tomorrow?" I said without hesitation.

"Well, talk to your dad about it first and you can let me know on the weekend. If it's okay with him, you can start Monday."

I didn't ask Dad, I *told* Dad. Of course, he loved the idea. It was almost as good as sending me away to live with another family, less for him to have to deal with. And yet, every so often while surrounded by this loving family and eating a delicious home-cooked meal, I thought of him, alone, eating his TV dinner, and my heart broke. By the time I arrived home, he was well nestled into the land of no pain. There'd never be a conversation about my life or his.

Isabella managed to mother me just enough. She took delight in paying me, which in turn made me feel good about myself, and I wanted to please her. Pictures of me started showing up in their house. Me with Jennifer and Julia on my lap; me helping each one blow out their birthday candles; me standing beside Isabella oblivious to the fact that she was looking at me as a loving mother might look at her own child. This picture sat on my dresser alongside the one of Mum and Aunt Joyce on Sugar Hill.

One Thursday evening when they arrived home from the camera club, Isabella said in a very excited voice, "Mary from the camera club has a daughter who volunteers as a candy-striper at the General Hospital on Saturdays. I was telling her about you and how great you are with kids. She said it takes a special person to be good with kids and that you might enjoy doing that too."

I stood with my mouth open, and Dick started laughing at both his wife and me.

Isabella laughed and said, "Am I speaking Spanish or English?"

More laughter.

"English, but it sounds like Spanish," Dick said. Then he turned to me and said, "Did you get all that?"

"I think so," I said and laughed since they both were. "I'll check into that." *She talks about me to other people.*

Pretending to be a member of Isabella's family — a cousin or auntie, Auntie Mayme — was the closest thing I had to a safety net. It wasn't as secure as what Grace had, but I felt anchored for the first time since Mum died. Secretly, I wished she'd ask about Mum; I wanted to tell her the secret. I wanted to ask her how to tell Grace in a letter. But as each day went by and I said nothing, it became harder to talk about.

Feb 9, 1975

Dear Grace,

Right now I'm sitting with Jennifer and Julia while they colour, so thought I'd write you a letter. Julia calls me Mayme because she can't pronounce G. I just love her little voice calling me Mayme. I haven't had time to write before now because I'm working for Isabella every day after school as a mother's helper. I stay for dinner every night and get the girls ready for bed. I love doing it. It's fun AND I get paid!

You'll be happy to hear I'm not skipping school anymore and my grades have come up. I do my homework when the girls practice their spelling and drawing. I really like the picture of Mum and Aunt Joyce you sent me. You look like Mum.

Isabella said that she's going to take me shopping in the spring for new clothes. I'm so excited for that. She always looks beautiful. She has really short dark brown hair, it's so cute on her. Her eyes are blue which she says is unusual. Usually people that have dark hair and skin are brown eyed.

She said she inherited her father's blue eyes and her mother's dark hair. I know she'll pick out nice clothes for me. She also suggested I volunteer as a Candy Striper at the general hospital. She thinks I'll be good at it. I might do that on Saturdays.

How are you feeling these days? Is your homesickness better? Have you finished your puzzle yet? What's your new jacket like, what colour? I always listen to the weather report for Toronto and I think you're getting a big snowstorm right now.

We're having sausages for dinner, they smell so good. Isabella is cooking right now. She's a good cook. I like Mr. Campbell too. He seems to like me being here. He's really nice to Jennifer and Julia. He always spends time with them when he gets home from work. Like he sits down with them and asks them about their day. He listens to them and makes them laugh. He includes me in their talking as well so I don't feel left out. He doesn't drink. Well he drinks milk and water HA HA.

I have to go now and tend to the girls. How are you doing in school? Have you made some new friends yet?

Write me back soon. Say hi to Aunt Joyce.

Love Maggie. xo

"I'm looking to volunteer as a candy-striper."

"Okay, great," said an older woman with a sweet round face like a rosy-cheeked pumpkin, smiling up at me from the other side of the counter under the Information sign.

"Here is the form you fill out. Just leave it with me when you're done. Also, you'll need to visit your doctor to have a TB test. Okay?"

Her face was so angelically sweet I knew exactly what she looked like as a baby.

"Okay, thanks."

I filled out the form and handed it back to her.

"Okay, Margret, that's fine. I'll pass this along to Merriam. Once she receives your TB results, she'll give you a call."

"Okay. Oh, could I have that paper back, please? I just need to change something."

"Sure, what is it you want to change?" she asked with curiosity.

I put a line through Marget and wrote Maggie. The reality of my name was that no one was ever going to get it right, so I had to stop testing this theory. It just frustrated me, and I didn't like the thought of being frustrated at this cherub in front of me.

"My name," I said, handing her back the paper. "I prefer to be called Maggie."

She examined it and looked at me. "Oh, I see. Good then — good idea ... Good idea, Maggie," she said, emphasizing my name.

The TB test results took a couple of weeks to land on Merriam's desk, but I finally got the phone call, followed by an interview. I would start that Saturday, four hours from 9 a.m. to 1 p.m.

"What?" Isabella said with delight. "You just went and did this? I'm so impressed, Maggie!"

She wrapped her arms around me, which was so overwhelming that my knees buckled. I had not been hugged in a very long time. I couldn't remember — maybe when Aunt Joyce came for Grace?

"I am so proud of you," she said.

With her and the girls in my corner, I was on track, but Dad continued to spiral down. I'd often find him passed out in the den when I got home from the Campbells, always in his chair. But this particular night, he was on the floor. *IS HE DEAD!* I ran to him yelling, "Dad!" I shook his shoulder. He moaned and coughed, confused about where he was. My heart was pounding, I gasped for air. The empty bottle lay beside him.

"Get up, Dad, for God's sake!" *Why didn't you let me go with Grace? You don't care about me.*

Once he pulled himself to sitting, I left, went to bed and cried myself to sleep. I could not get off this roller coaster.

Carrie, a fellow candy-striper, became my Saturday friend. She satisfied my desires to talk music, TV shows, fashion, hairstyles and acne. It was as if I had unknowingly buried that part of myself and was unaware it was missing until Carrie unlocked it. We got along well, but there'd be no relationship outside the hospital setting — too risky. But for those four hours, I became someone else. It wasn't as if I was a total fake. On the contrary, I loved acting my age, but it was just that, I was acting. Saturday afternoon, I'd return to my former self, ageless with an alcoholic father and a deep secret.

Our job was to visit each floor pushing a trolley of various magazines to offer patients. We were instructed to only approach patients who were awake and alert. Each room we entered had its own unique smell, none of which was pleasant. Variations of urine, blood, bleach and death.

Four people crammed to a room. The elderly and confused were often tied to their beds, their wrists red and bruised from fearfully pulling on restraints trying to set themselves free. No one looked well in those faded hospital gowns. Tubes of all colours that drained liquids from body parts hung off the bed rails. IVs dangled off poles, with needles the size of straws plunged into bruised arms, hands and wrists. Cups of water, once ice chips, sat beside drooping flowers left by a loved one who would have popped in for only a minute, so not to disturb. Couldn't fool me; visitors couldn't wait to get out of there. They looked so out of place — dressed up, hair coiffed, tube free. They resisted looking at anything other than the person they came to visit, lest they saw blood or vomit or worse. Much of what Carrie and I saw left us wide-eyed and slightly shaken.

One Saturday morning a month or so into the job, we had developed a level of comfort so I suggested we venture off into places unknown.

"I want to see the newborn babies," I said, looking at her eagerly.

"I don't think we're allowed to go there," she said sheepishly, but I knew I could talk her into it.

"We'll just say we got lost," I said with a smile and a nod.

"Okay, let's check it out, I guess."

Armoured with our trolley that carried a delightful array of current magazines, we hit elevator buttons not meant for candy-stripers.

"Hey, girls, wait a sec," a young nurse on the third floor called out to us.

We stopped, expecting to get in trouble.

"What have you got here? Let's see," she said, picking up the latest *Glamour* magazine. "Honestly," she said, looking at us, "I'm never going to look like any of these girls; I don't know why I torture myself." Then she looked directly at me and said, "You — you could be a model; how tall are you?"

"Oh, I'm not sure, but yeah, I'm tall … like my Dad."

"Do you want to see the newborn babies?" she asked, putting the magazine back on the trolley.

"Could we?" Carrie said.

"Sure, come on; leave your trolley here."

We followed this ever so spunky nurse through the double doors and into the nursery area.

"You have to stay in the observation area, but look," she said, holding out her arms towards the infants as if they were all hers. "Here are the newborn babies."

Little pink and blue bundles lay swaddled in their plastic beds. There were three rows of five or six beds.

"See that little girl right there?" she said, pointing with pride. "She's twenty minutes old."

Carrie and I looked at each other with delight.

"Wow, twenty minutes old!" I said, thinking of Grace.

"Okay girls don't stay too long and don't forget your cart's out there," she said, turning with a skip.

I watched her scrub her hands and put on a heavy blue cotton gown over her uniform. She then pulled a tight-fitting blue cotton hat over her fly-away hair. She entered the nursery, picked up the newest little pink bundle and brought her to the window. Her little face was rusty, blotchy, scrunchy — nothing like Grace's perfect, angelic newborn face.

"Geez, she's red," Carrie said.

"I was just thinking that. I wonder if there's something wrong with her?"

If there was, the nurse didn't seem concerned. She took hold of the infant's tiny hand and waved a pretend "bye bye" to us. Carrie and I waved a doubtful bye back, as if that kid was doomed and nobody knew it but us. We hightailed it out of there.

Feeling undeterred, we hopped on the elevator and hit pediatrics. We were again greeted with enthusiastic nurses swarming the trolley as if they hadn't seen a magazine for years. My eyes couldn't take in the sights fast enough. Sick kids everywhere. Even the kid in the small playroom at the end of the hall looked lethargic and pale. The child's mother sat on a big blue rubber cube with a strained smile on her face as if she was hiding something. I could read people from an early age, and she wasn't hiding anything from me in her sad eyes. I picked up a small selection of magazines and walked towards the playroom.

"Hi, would you like something to read?" I asked, fanning the selection like a deck of cards in front of the woman.

She looked up at me as if she'd been asleep.

"Oh, gosh, I didn't see you there. Thank you, yes."

She selected the *Woman's Home Journal* and plopped it in her lap, didn't open it. I figured if her child was in the hospital there'd not be much in the *Home Journal* of interest. I glanced at her little girl.

"Hi," I said softly, squatting down and picking up a toy. "My name is Maggie, what's yours?"

"Ellie."

She did not look at me. She had a big, round, bald head save for a few random hairs sticking out here and there.

"Is that your mum?"

She went to her mum and leaned into her leg.

"Ellie, can you say hi to Maggie?" her mum said as she caressed her daughter's head as if feeling the smoothness of a bowling ball. Ellie looked at me but did not say hi. "She's a little bit shy these days. My name is Ruth."

"Hi, Ruth." I smiled.

"Well, Ellie, I have to go back to work, but I'm finished in ten minutes so I think I'd like to come back and find out what toy you like the best in this room. Will you still be here?"

Ellie looked at her mum with the tiniest bit of excitement.

"You *bet* we'll be here," Ruth said, nodding to Ellie.

Ellie looked at me as if it was all set and we'd all be here to play a game very soon.

"Okay, see you in about fifteen minutes."

Ruth smiled — with her mouth and her eyes.

I joined Carrie at the cart. "Let's go," I said, pushing the cart to the elevator. "You want to come back up after we change to play with Ellie?"

"No, not my thing," Carrie said. "Especially sick ones."

"You don't like kids? How can you not like kids? They're hilarious and innocent and sweet."

The elevator opened and I rushed to our station, changed quickly and zipped back upstairs. As I approached the playroom, I saw Ellie and two other excited children waiting to play with Maggie "the pretty nurse." Before I knew it, we were all giggling

— like belly laugh giggling. We had a great time, and Ruth ended up writing a letter to the hospital volunteer coordinator. Later that week I was promoted and became the first specialized candy-striper for pediatrics.

Luckily, I saw Ellie go home after her third two-week round of chemotherapy. On her discharge day, we all cried with both joy and sadness. The thank-you note from Ruth said I was a bridge between Ellie and her finding joy between sickness and wellness, between forgetting and remembering, between sadness and happiness. Ruth wrote, *"Without you, we would not have found that bridge."* It occurred to me that, in the end, the *Ladies Home Journal* did have the answer. The letter went on to say that Ellie stayed well for three months but died at home, surrounded by family. She was holding her favourite toy.

. . .

The salty Lund Harbour winds, frigid Atlantic, open meadows and the coziness of the Big House transformed all that visited. Being one with nature, left to run, explore, gaze at the sky and rely on each other grew our bones bigger, shaped our faces to show confidence and expanded our minds so we saw our place in the world.

After another long day of play, Grace was tired and wanted to go home, but I, being the older sister, ignored her request. At ten years old, I was in control and she did whatever I wanted. I was intent on finding a garter snake so had ventured off the path into the thicker grass. Suddenly, Grace shrieked. I thought she saw a snake, but she'd actually been stung. The piercing sound caused Mum to bolt from her resting place, book flying. I panicked. In minutes, Grace's throat began closing up, her skin puffed up in hives the size of ping pong balls. Mum scooped her up, threw both of us in the car and took off like a bat out of hell.

What have I done?

The nearest hospital was twenty miles away. We flew through the hospital doors, Grace was whisked away on a gurney, Mum ran attentively alongside it. She turned to me and shook a frantic finger.

"Stay. Right. There."

They vanished around the corner.

Grace is going to die and it is my fault!

I was old enough to know I had been mean not taking her home. God was punishing me for being a mean person.

It was a long wait, but I was finally allowed to see her. Her face was puffed up like a balloon, and the colour of lobster. I burst into tears.

"I'm sorry," I sobbed.

Mum looked confused, like — why was I apologizing? What did I have to do with this?

"It's okay; it's not your fault," she said.

Grace sounded much younger, like a little girl. My little sister that I almost killed.

"Does it hurt?" I asked, looking at the needle in her arm while sniffing up my runny nose.

"No, it doesn't hurt at all — but my face feels ... full," she said through swollen lips.

We giggled as she said, "Face feels full," over and over trying to say it without slurring. Soon, even Mum was laughing. This scary event drew us closer and meant we discovered Grace's life would be threatened if stung again. My mission was to make sure that didn't happen. I was vigilant and solicited my cousins to watch out for killer bees. The rest of that summer was all about keeping Grace alive. She loved the attention.

Chapter 16

The Divide Widens

Feb 28, 1975

Dear Maggie,

I got your letter. Aunt Joyce said to say hi. Something terrible happened that I have to tell you about. It was Lacy's birthday last weekend. She wanted to go to a movie with her girlfriends. Aunt Joyce made Lacy invite me. I didn't even want to go. Lacy wanted to go see a scary movie but Aunt Joyce said that she wasn't allowed to. When Lacy and me were alone in the bedroom she told me that we were going to see a scary movie and I better shut up about it or I'd be in big trouble. Uncle Brian drove us to the movie but when we got out of the car Lacy said we weren't going into that theater to see a dumb movie.

We met her friends on the street and they smoked a joint and they made me take a puff. I choked and almost threw up. Then they put make up on me. They pretended like they were being nice to me saying that I'd be pretty. The pot made me dizzy. We went to another theater where the scary movie was and I got so scared I had to leave. I went to the washroom and I saw that I had black make up all over my eyes. I started crying in the washroom and a woman asked if she could help me. I was so scared Lacy would kill me I just said no I'm ok. I waited the whole time in the washroom. When Lacy came out of the movie she couldn't find me and she thought I left so they all left without me. So when they got home they made up this story that I just walked away from them and they didn't know where I went or what happened to me. They said they thought I had walked home on my own. A person that worked at the theater called Aunt Joyce, and Uncle Brian came and got me. Anyway Lacy got in huge trouble, she's grounded for a month. But the good thing that happened is that I got moved into Joy's room and Aunt Joyce doesn't make Lacy and me be together anymore. Lacy doesn't even talk to me anymore and that's fine with me. David and Lacy fight a lot because Lacy tries to hang out with his friends even though she's way to young. I hear Aunt Joyce and Uncle Brian sometimes fight about Lacy.

So that's what happened. School is better now. I still feel homesick sometimes. I have 2 friends at school, Alison and Shirley. They both live down the street so we walk to school every day. Alison lives with her Mum, her parents are divorced and her Mum works so we hang out at her house after school. Shirley has a younger brother and her Mum is really nice, they have a dog that I was scared of at first but not anymore. They have a trampoline in their back yard! It's covered with snow right now but Shirley said in the summer they put the sprinkler under it and jump. I can hardly wait. I've never been on a trampoline!

It's great that you have your babysitting job with the little girls. They all sound really nice. What does Dad do all the time, he must miss Mum. The only sad thing about not being in

Lacy's room is I don't see Mum in the corner anymore. I miss seeing her every night. I look for her in Joy's room, but so far she's not there and I wonder if she's mad at me because I moved from Lacy's room, away from her. Do you think that? I still cry when I think of Mum and home. I can't believe I'll never see Mum again EVER. Do you still cry?

Aunt Joyce just called us for dinner. I'm use to all the lights on and music playing all the time now. It's my turn to wash the dishes tonight. Lacy and I use to do the dishes together but not anymore, I wash and Joy dries now, just like you washed and I dried.

Write me back soon and tell me all your news.

Love Grace xo

p.s. Aunt Joyce and Uncle Brian call me Gracie, I like it.

I didn't know what to make of Lacy and her friends. Grace hadn't done anything to them, why were they tormenting her? Didn't sound like the same Lacy I played with in Lund Harbour.

Poor Grace. Even with Mum dead she worried about making her mad. *Wonder if you'd want to see*

Mum every night if you knew how she really died? A veil of cynicism strangled my thoughts. Mum's dying would be forever romanticized in my sister's mind and she had the satisfaction of fictional storytelling, believing it to be true. I rolled the story off my tongue to taste the freedom of it.

"My mother died of a heart attack when I was just thirteen years old."

Everyone can tell a lie from the truth, so remaining silent was my only recourse. The closest I could get to freedom was pretending my mother never existed, like Opie. My offering to those salivating for the story was a simple, "My mother died when I was very young, I'm fine now." It was helpful to learn at an early age that if one presents as "fine" with a situation, then it puts everyone at ease and the conversation ends.

It seemed that Grace and I were neck and neck on life's satisfaction scale. Our past life together took shape in our imaginations. Occasions and events were remembered in our own memories like an ice sculpture slowly melting, drip by drip, changing the shape and form into something unrecognizable and different than the original creation.

The routine of winter grounded me, offering me the illusion of stability. I came to learn that my mother suffered from undiagnosed bipolar disorder. It explained everything about her; well, almost everything. Whether manic or depressed, I was never relaxed around her. In her depressed state, she slept twenty hours a day, wore the same sweatpants and shirt for days, and rarely bathed. Even though the silence in the house offered relief from chaos, it harboured angst. Her depression was the pregnant pause between rounds of mania.

Mum arose from her atrophy as if the world had also slept. A month or two in bed ended just like that. I'd come home from school to find her in the kitchen, singing, baking cookies. The cookies smelled good but not good enough to drown the stench of dread.

Her manic states were worse to live through than the depressed. She'd often disappear for days. One time she arrived home with a new car after a week's absence. I have no idea how that got resolved. My job was to take care of Grace. Dad reminded me of this while he put out fires Mum's exuberant behaviour lit.

Her transformation was remarkable. When wallowing in depression, she looked pale, old and tired. Really, though, she was a beauty. Dark, rich, lustrous hair, dark brown eyes, thick, perfectly shaped eyebrows, high cheekbones and full lips; a strange mixture coming from English heritage. My mother knew and loved that she turned heads. The way she dressed and sauntered about was too much — too much for me. I'd tell her to keep her voice down, she was too loud, everyone was looking. This thrilled her to no end, and she'd throw her head back, tossing her locks, and laugh her sensual, intoxicating laugh that every man, woman and child surrendered to. There was no containing her, she just wouldn't have it. That was my mother.

Responding to Grace's letter was difficult. She lived in a fantasy world, thinking her poor mother died of a heart attack, and appeared as sparkles and light. She was making new friends, and surrounded by a big loving family. If I could not write an honest letter to Grace and say, *How could she do this to us? Didn't she love us at all?*, then I would not write.

May 11, 1975

Dear Maggie,

I'm sorry I haven't written you in so long. I've been busy with school and stuff. But that's no excuse. I haven't heard from you either, I guess we're both busy, which Aunt Joyce says is good.

But I don't know if Dad has talked to you or not but they're wondering if it's better that I stay living here for another school year. Did you know that? I hope I'm not making you mad by writing this, I hope Dad told you.

What do you think about the idea? I still get homesick and sometimes I just want to come home so bad. But then other times I don't want to leave my friends and Aunt Joyce is so nice. She says she loves me like I'm her own daughter. It's weird but I never remember Mum saying she loved me. Maybe she did and I just don't remember. I'm sort of forgetting Mum a little bit but Aunt Joyce says that's normal and then she shows me pictures of her and tells me stories about her and Mum. There's lots of stories that I'll tell you when I come home.

If I don't come home in the summer it seems like such a long time before I'll see you. Please don't be sad, if you want me to come home for sure I will. I think it's up to me. I just don't know what to do.

Lacy doesn't bother me anymore. She got suspended from school for drinking on school property. She smokes cigarettes and pot. I think she has sex with boys to. I think she's on the pill. I heard Aunt Joyce say to Uncle Brian, that's all she needs is for Lacy to get pregnant. David finally took me for a drive. He's so cute, I secretly pretended he was my boyfriend and we were on a date. Just kidding.

Hope you like the picture. It was taken at Christmas, but I guess you can see that. Do you see how cute David *is? He's standing beside Uncle Brian behind me.*

What do you want for your birthday? Aunt Joyce said I can send you a present if it's not to big. But she said we have to do it soon so it gets to you on time. So what do you want? You're turning 14, I can't believe it, I can't believe I won't be there. When I think about this I feel homesick. What do you think I should do?

Write me back soon and tell me what you want for your birthday.

Love Gracie xo

Another picture to examine. I didn't recognize any of the clothes Grace had on; I barely recognized her. Of course, the decision had already been made long before I got the news. I was just the last to know. Nothing was up to my sister or me. I sadly accepted it with resignation. In comparison to what she had, what could I entice her with? I had nothing that resembled a cute David. This, though, could not hold a candle to what was to come.

Chapter 17

Breaking News

Isabella insisted I invite Carrie to a dinner celebration in honour of my fourteenth birthday. Carrie didn't quite know what to make of the invitation. Our relationship started Saturday at 9 a.m. and ended at 1 p.m., all winter. She also seemed happy with this arrangement, so why was I confusing things? But she graciously accepted. I wore my new bell-bottom jumpsuit and sandals, a gift from Isabella from our shopping excursion, a day I'll hold in my heart forever. Carrie was a nice girl and didn't ask where my dad or other friends were. She fit right in, and I suspect that if she, too, went into nursing, she'd be a good one.

Dad had been invited but forgot. I didn't care; I'd forget his too. A camera and three rolls of film had arrived in the mail from Grace three days before my birthday with instructions to take pictures of myself and send them to her. Pretty good gift. Many pictures were taken that evening: me with Jennifer and Julia, us around the table, me blowing out candles with the girls, Carrie and I together like best friends, and, of course, Isabella and me, my arm looped into hers, my head tilted towards her. I loved every minute of it but it didn't stick. It couldn't. It was a make-believe birthday with a make-believe friend and a make-believe family. My real family forgot.

So now both Grace and I had survived birthdays without Mum. In reality, we had celebrated birthdays without her before, but she was alive and we wished for things to be different the next year. Guess we got our wish.

Soon after my birthday, Carrie stopped volunteering; she just didn't show up. I never called her. Ashley took Carrie's place, but I kept my distance. We were like night and day, and I suspected she would not become a nurse; she'd be a mean one.

Isabella suggested I get a summer job, maybe at the Corner Cafeteria near my house. I could clear tables. She said she didn't need my help during the summer and the camera club didn't meet, so they were planning a trip and would be away. My babysitting jobs would be few and far between.

Even though being with Isabella and the girls was my favourite thing ever, the idea of a real job was an exciting prospect. I would talk to Dad about this one. He was under the kitchen sink fixing a dripping pipe when I walked in.

"Dad, I want to get a job this summer," I said to his feet. "I want to apply at the Corner Cafeteria to clear tables or wash dishes or something like that. What do you think about that idea? I'm fourteen now, so I can work." Then I added sarcastically, "And Grace isn't coming home, so I'll have nothing to do."

His arms dropped and he rested the wrench on his chest with a bothered sigh.

"I don't know if that's a good idea. Why don't you wait a bit? We can talk about it another time. You can see I'm busy right now."

He resumed working. He had absolutely no time for me at all. A vision flashed through my head of kicking his leg, but I kicked his heart instead.

"You're a fucking asshole. You forgot my birthday, you don't give a shit if I go to school, you don't give a shit at all about me. And you gave Grace away. I'm going to work this summer and you can't stop me. I do what I want anyway and you don't even know what I do because you don't care what I do. I could die and you wouldn't even know because you're drunk all the time. I HATE YOU!"

I went to my room and slammed the door so hard it bounced back and hit me in the butt like a spanking. He would not here me cry, ever. I started to write Grace but was too angry and too sad. An hour later, he knocked sheepishly on my door.

"I have some supper for you."

"I'm not hungry."

"I have something to tell you."

"Well, tell me then."

"Open the door. I don't want to talk through the door."

He was sober. I opened the door.

"Canned beans — now cold."

I turned around and shoved the writing paper under my pillow. He put the plate on my dresser and sat on the bed; I hated that he sat on my bed. He hung his head, wrung his hands and sighed. *Oh sweet Jesus, what now?* I moved to the open door, either for a quick escape or indicating for him to leave, or both.

"You know my shop hasn't been doing well for quite some time now. The big stores are putting me out of business. I can't offer the customers the deals that they can."

"Yeah, so?" I said, standing, arms crossed.

"I've been offered a municipal job as a bus mechanic. It's a solid job, good pay, a pension, good hours and I won't have to worry about the business end of it. I can just go to work and come home and not worry."

I sensed a "BUT."

"But it means we have to move."

His head remained low, but his eyes raised for just a second to check my reaction. Or maybe to see if I had a knife in my hand.

"Move where?" *Toronto?*

"British Columbia."

"No Dad, I'm not going. I'm staying here. I look after myself anyway. I can live with Isabella if I have to." My words came out short and quick, like electric shocks.

Dad shook his lowered head and said, "No Maggie, you can't stay here by yourself. You have to come with me. You're still a minor and I'm your guardian by law. I can't leave you here."

I'm not a daughter, I'm a minor. Didn't have a parent, have a guardian.

"You do things your way, I'll do things my way. I'm going to ask Isabella if I can live with them as their nanny or something."

Even as I said this I knew it wouldn't happen. I couldn't breathe.

"Okay now, you have to know something. The Campbells are going travelling through Europe this summer. They'll be gone for the months of July and August, the whole summer. She was going to tell you, but I suggested that I tell you about the move first."

When had they talked to each other about me?

Dad stood up and walked towards me at the door, but I didn't budge. He had to turn sideways to walk past me. He stopped with his back to me at the top of the stairs.

"I'm sorry, Mags. I know things have been hard for you with your mother gone."

I didn't even know what that meant. I placed the plate of beans outside my door in the hallway and crawled under my blankets, wide-eyed, staring at another empty tomorrow, an unpredictable future.

Reluctantly I continued my job as Isabella's helper, but everything felt different. It was all coming to an end. She attempted to talk to me about the move and how sad she and Dick were. She said she knew how difficult this was for me and that she didn't know about it when she suggested I get a job for the summer.

"It'll be okay, I'm fine," I said.

Inside, I was terrified. I was moving very far away and I'd never see her or her girls again. A stark reminder that I was not her daughter — no more pretense. I was asked not to tell the girls I was moving and that I would not see them when they returned home from Europe. Keeping secrets wasn't a problem for me and I maintained my playful nature with them. After all, it wasn't their fault.

School closed and our moving plans were in motion. The Campbells left the Saturday before, and I made a point of not being around. Dad was there to apologize for my absence.

"You should have been home to say goodbye. The girls didn't want to leave without saying goodbye. Isabella said she understood."

Then why don't you understand?

"You should have been at my birthday," I said quickly with no thought.

He sighed, handed me a large envelope and said, "This is from them."

Feeling like the most horrible person on the planet, I took the package to my room. I smiled through tears at the drawings the girls made of the three of us. All stick figures with smiles from ear to ear bigger than our heads. A small locket lay tucked inside a letter from Isabella.

Dearest Maggie,

I know you are very sad about moving away even if you didn't say so. I'm also sad. I know firsthand the difficulties of leaving one's homeland.

You have been excellent help for me this past year. Please use this letter as a reference for future employment. You are reliable, hardworking, patient, kind and trustworthy.

It is a rare thing to find someone that's not family to love your children as much as you have loved Jennifer and Julia.

I hope our paths cross again, and I hope your new life will be rich with experience, friends, and most of all, love.

Love,

Isabella, Dick, Jennifer and Julia.

The smiling faces of Jennifer and Julia looked out from the inside of the locket. I cried hard. *Sorry for your loss.* As Isabella recommended, I kept the letter, for a reference.

Chapter 18

The Letter

June 16, 1975

Dear Grace,

Thank you so much for the camera and film. I've taken some pictures so I have 19 more left on the roll. My birthday was pretty good. My friend Carrie that I Candy Stripe with came and Isabella made us a delicious dinner. Unfortunately Dad didn't make it, HE FORGOT! Did you ask if you could come home? I don't think they'll let you. I know that sounds mean, but they make plans behind our backs. Like you moving to Toronto, that was all planned way before they told us. They think it's for our own good. Dad just ignores me, and he missed my birthday.

I forgot to tell you that I think I started my period. It was kind of weird, not like blood so I'm not sure but I think it's coming soon. Lots of girls in school have their periods already. If I wanted to talk to someone about it I could talk to Isabella but I know all about it so it's fine. I gave Isabella a mother's day card, well it was from Jennifer and Julia, but I signed it too.

I wish you were coming home. I was looking forward to you being here this summer. I even thought maybe we could go to Lund Harbour. Dad could drive us and we could just stay with our cousins in the Big House.

But now I think I'm going to work. At the Corner Cafeteria. It was Isabella's idea because she doesn't need a mother's helper in the summer, and honestly I don't think you'll be coming home. I wanted you to meet Jennifer and Julia, they're so cute, they giggle all the time, they make me giggle just hearing them giggle. I don't even know what we're giggling about!

Have you been driving with Dave lately? How are things going with Lacy? Will she work this summer? Is Uncle

*Brian around much? Does he drink? I'm
going to talk to Dad about applying for
the job tomorrow. I'm so excited.*

*Write soon, hope I didn't make you
sad, but like I say, either way I don't think
we get to decide what happens to us.*

Ok bye for now.

Love Maggie xo

Dad placed three empty cardboard boxes of
various sizes in my room.

"Time to start packing, so you're going to have
to throw things out. Your stuff has to fit into those
three boxes."

My head was spinning — I had no idea what or
how to pack. After all, I needed everything I had,
didn't I? Those three boxes filled instantly, and my
room looked exactly the same. Dad knocked on the
door. *More boxes, I hope!*

"Come in." I maintained my cold demeanour, and
he held out a small box, forcing me to look up.

"Um, this was your mother's. I think she'd want
you to have it."

With trepidation, I took it from him. He bowed
slightly as he backed out, closing the door with him
as if to say, *I'll respectively leave you two alone.* I sat
on the bed and placed the box beside me. My heart
crashed in my chest. *What could possibly be in here?
It better not be her green skirt and yellow sweater.* As

if it were a breakable ornament, I carefully undid the folds of the box and peered in; no clothes. I pulled out an open Kotex box with one pad missing. Neatly tucked inside was my mother's sanitary belt. I held it up as if it were a string of diamonds. I slipped off my shorts and underpants, stood in front of the mirror and stepped into the belt. My legs shook. My mother's belt that she had worn every month between her legs sat loosely draped around my slender hips. The intimacy overwhelmed me, like I was eavesdropping into her life that no longer existed yet should remain private. I imagined her wrapping the pad into the loops, pulling it up over her hip bones, using her hand to gently place the pad just so, securing it.

Pretending I was her, I wound a pad in and around and through the plastic loops, front and back. Then pulled up the belt and reached under to secure the pad where it belonged. It felt as if I had a pillow between my legs. *How can I move around with such a thing?* The belt was too big for my shapeless hips, however, I discovered my underpants held everything snugly in place.

I walked around the room mimicking Mum, laughing and talking, all the while being acutely aware of the goings on in my crotch. How did she do it without anyone knowing or seeing? Surely people knew she had that thing between her legs.

I further investigated the contents of the box. There was a small clay dish and two home-made wax-paper envelopes on top of her Bible. One envelope was labelled "Grace" and one "Marget." Inside the envelope labelled Marget was a lock of fine baby hair and what I assumed was my first tooth. It was difficult to imagine Mum actually going to the trouble to make these keepsakes. She must have loved me in that moment and had no thoughts of ever leaving me alone.

I then pulled out her Bible that, in life, sat on her bedside table. It was a reminder to believe in God because we were sinners. I'd occasionally see her making notes beside parables that spoke to her in some way yet failed to save her in the end. The Bible fell open to a thin letter written on light blue paper laying snugly between the pages. For a split second I thought it might be a real suicide note filled with loving words, an explanation of her actions. Something I could understand.

Sept 19, 1974

My Darling Laurie,

It seems I will not be coming your way after all. My yearning for you is immense, you are the love of my life, the one, the only one.

My daughter has taken seriously ill, she may not survive the year. Jane has made arrangements for us to take her to the Mayo Clinic. We leave in two days. My future is sewn up, I simply cannot leave my daughter in her grave condition, but my heart will always be committed to you and no one else.

I will love you forever but must say goodbye. I am so very sad and so very sorry.

Love always, Henry.

It may as well have been a suicide note. It explained everything. There were words of love, however, none for me. Henry's letter was the missing piece to the puzzle. I sat on the floor with Mum's sanitary belt around me as revelations of what had occurred that fateful morning came into view.

The first thing I noticed entering the house was Mum's coat and purse perfectly placed on the kitchen chair. Sept 23, 1974, the mail arrived before Mum left for the bus. A letter from Henry quickened her heart. She couldn't wait, she dropped her coat and purse, then frantically opened the love letter telling her when and where they would next meet. Henry — her lifeline, her sanity, her mania, her reason for living — ended it all. She died right there and then. She went upstairs with the letter, placed it in her Bible, wrote one line in her journal, swallowed her pills, lay down and waited to be released. My mother couldn't take it any longer.

Henry, you bastard.

I stood, took off the belt and pad and threw them away along with the remaining pads. I placed Henry's letter in her journal, put her Bible in the corner of the room and robotically packed my life into those three boxes. I was ready to leave it all behind.

Chapter 19

The Space Between Cars

Dad was nervous, impatient, in need of a drink. He sweated and paced. Made me nervous.

"The station's quiet," Dad sputtered, hands shaking as he passed paperwork across the counter.

"Yes, you're nice and early," said the man dressed like a storybook character in his engineer's hat and vest. "It'll pick up soon — there you go." He slid the tickets across the counter. Dad slapped his hand on top of them in an attempt to stop it from shaking. "You can board in half an hour. Go to Track 4, there's a café just over there," he said, pointing down the large marble room.

"Thanks, is there a washroom close by?"

Ticket man gave Dad a quizzical look. Seemed to be assessing if he needed to call for medical help. He looked at me and I gave him a reassuring smile. "Just down there," he said, pointing the opposite direction of the café.

After a bathroom visit, we plunked down on one of the long wooden benches and Dad commenced rummaging through his suitcase. I buried my nose in Nancy Drew's latest escapade. Maybe she could solve the mystery of my shattered life; I'd look for clues.

Dad and I boarded a train July 5, 1975, bound for Toronto. Despite loathing my father for ruining my life, I also felt sorry for him. It was as if he was a scared little boy who didn't know how to handle his wife, his children or himself. The complexities of life were too much for him. He knew nothing of Henry — or did he? Maybe he felt relief that another man had looked after this woman who was so hard to handle. So there I was, bitter and pitying but excited to see Grace. However, I wasn't sharing my excitement with Dad. I brooded and remained silent as we navigated down the train's narrow hallway to our cabin. *A day and a half in here with him — I'll suffocate!* "You'll sleep up here," Dad said, pulling a fully made bed out of the wall. "This," he said, placing his hand on the little sofa, "pulls out into a bed for me. There's the bathroom and there's the closet," he said, pointing.

I swung my overnight bag up onto my bed and climbed the ladder. After I stuffed my pajamas under the pillow, I turned on the overhead light and nestled down with my book. Dad washed the sweat off his face and hung a few things in the closet.

"I'm going to see what time the dining car opens for dinner. Do you want to come, you know, to see it?"

Without answering, I climbed down the ladder. He held the door open for me.

"Thanks," popped out of my mouth.

I might have been rebellious, but I wasn't rude. The train platform was busy with passengers lined up to board. Porters yelled; whistles blew. It was thrilling to step over the covered metal that held each car together.

"Do you want some candy?" Dad asked, stopping at the canteen for cigarettes.

I placed an *Oh Henry* bar on the counter. He paid and handed me the bar.

"Thanks," I said again.

I spotted the latest *Seventeen* magazine and thought, *I'll come back for that*. We were greeted at the dining car door by a man dressed in white and black. His skin was as dark as night.

"We open at 5 p.m., sir."

I could smell home-cooked food — was quite sure it was roast beef.

"We'll come back at five," Dad said.

It looked like he needed a drink — NOW. I knew the signs. I managed to get a glimpse of the sparkling room. White tablecloths, glistening cutlery and glasses of many sizes. I could hardly wait to get in there.

"I'm going back to our cabin," he said. He was hunched over, walking quickly, unaware if I had followed or not.

"Dad!" He stopped, hunched, looked at me. "I'm gonna continue to look around. I know my way back, I'll see you at five," I said, tapping my battery-operated watch.

He nodded. Twenty minutes later, we were speeding away from the city into the countryside as the train clickety-clacked under foot. It was exhilarating. I took my time walking back to our cabin, smiling at other passengers and pretending I was a lone traveller. I felt very grown up. Dad had pulled out his bed and crawled under the covers fully clothed.

"Are you coming for dinner?"

No response, so I grabbed my purse and left for the dining car. I was met by the same doorman, who warmly invited me in. I found my own table and waited for my roast beef dinner. The car filled quickly, so I needed to share my table with three men. They were pleasant enough and thoughtfully tried to include me in a juvenile conversation they figured a young teenage girl might enjoy. I smiled and pretended to be amused but was happy when they ignored me to talk business. I was left alone to gaze out the window.

At a table farther down the dining car, I spotted some kids that appeared to be my age. They were with their parents, of course, and I made eye contact with the girl. The men I was sitting with drank wine, then whiskey. It stunk and they got louder, so it was time to leave. I headed to the canteen for my *Seventeen* magazine and continued to wander. It was even more thrilling crossing from car to car with the train running. I felt daredevilish and wondered if the train company wasn't careless in letting passengers do this. I ended up in the observation car, took a seat and opened my magazine only to close it — I couldn't take my eyes off the view; I was spellbound.

Back in the cabin, Dad remained asleep and fully clothed. I got ready for bed, climbed onto my bunk, opened my magazine, closed it again, turned off my light and didn't wake up until I heard Dad calling out. I didn't know where I was or who was yelling, but I figured it out quickly.

"Dad!"

"Uh? What?" Dad said, waking with a start.

"You're yelling — having a dream. You woke me up."

"Oh, God — sorry," he said as he cleared his throat.

He went to the bathroom, splashed some water on his face, but was panting fast and frantic like a thirsty dog. *Is he sick?* I fell back to sleep. Dad's bed was already made when I woke. "Dad?" No answer. I dressed in the bathroom and was brushing my teeth when he arrived back.

"We can go to breakfast whenever you're ready," he said with a little knock on the door.

I didn't answer. Not sure why, but it had something to do with my life and him being at fault. He looked better, dry mouth, pale and skinny, but not hunched or sweaty. He didn't like crossing from car to car and he reached out for balance. I was used to it and skipped in front of him, showing off what he had missed yesterday. I was first at the dining car door, and I pretended to know the doorman, smiling like we were old friends. I went to the same table where I sat yesterday with the three strange men, and Dad followed. He guzzled his water before he sat down and indicated to someone by waving his empty glass in the air that he wanted another — quickly. A pitcher was brought to the table. Dad choked down a piece of dry toast while I had scrambled eggs, two sausages, and toast with jam. I was still showing off. I looked for the girl my age, but she wasn't there.

"Just going back to our cabin," Dad said, mouth still dry. Before I could respond, he was gone.

After breakfast, I stood in the fresh, open air between cars. I breathed in deeply and thought, *I could live on a train*. I spotted a little town off in the distance, a kid on a bike, houses behind him. And just like that, we were past it. The train whistle had blown to warn the town's people to stay off the tracks.

It was going to be a long day — we wouldn't arrive in Toronto until almost midnight. Dad stretched out on his bed and, once again, fell sound asleep. I picked up my magazine and settled down in the observation car, but I simply could not take my eyes off the vastly changing landscape. I lunched on my own — really good clam chowder. Had the table to myself. Spotted the girl, and she held up her *Seventeen* magazine. We smiled at each other, and she said something to her mum, who nodded. She walked to my table.

"Hi, I'm Linda," she said with a glistening mouth full of braces.

"I'm Maggie."

"Can I sit here?" she indicated to a chair. "You going to Toronto?"

"Ya, visiting my cousins." I left out the sister part.

"Oh, I just visited my cousins in Halifax — I live in Toronto."

How simple her life sounded. Nothing to hide, nothing left out. *My sister lives in Toronto with my cousins. I'm moving to British Columbia with my father because my mother died — of a heart attack.* Linda was talking, so I tried to focus.

"… these bell-bottoms," she said, pointing to a picture in the magazine.

I quickly opened to the page. "Ya, me too — they're groovy!" The word sounded foreign coming out of my mouth.

Linda had a hippy look to her. She slammed the magazine shut and said, "Don't you just love Carly Simon — she's amazing! And James Taylor? I just love them both," she said, opening the magazine again. So did I, but was having trouble keeping up.

"You're really pretty," she said, now looking at me.

"Oh, thanks — you too," I said but wasn't sure if she was or not. "I really like your hair." Which was true. It was long, wavy and full — like she had a ton of it.

"Thanks, I'd rather have yours, though. Have to iron mine to make it straight," she said as she pulled her mane into a ponytail, showing off her freckled face. When she let it go it exploded like a wild, angry animal with its hackles up. "Ugh," she said, adjusting her upper lip over her braces, "these things are killing me. Just had them put on two weeks ago — have to wear them for at least a year."

She had little elastic bands hooked inside.

"Do they hurt?"

"Kill," she said dramatically. "See," she said, commanding my attention, "you don't need braces — your teeth are perfect."

"Oh, thanks." I needed to go even though I had nowhere to go. *Standing between the cars in the cool air.*

"Do you want to go stand between the cars?" I said enthusiastically.

"Oh, no. I hate that. It's so freaky," she said dismissively flipping the pages in front of her. She looked at her mum and nodded. "Looks like we're heading out." She grabbed her magazine and leaned across the table. "Well, have a good time in Toronto. It's the best city in the world — you'll love it." She stood quickly.

"Oh, thanks, you too." *What am I saying? She's not visiting Toronto.*

"Bye," she said, joining her mum like they were best friends.

"Bye," I said to the back of her.

I needed air, so I stayed between the cars for a long time. Miles and miles of forest. I imagined the animals living in, around and under the trees. I leaned over the barricade that kept me from falling off the train, looked down at the speeding ditch, then up into the still sky. I held my face into the wind as we sped along; my eyes watered and the tears slid across my temples into my hair. *I'm coming Grace, as fast as I can.*

Just in case Linda was in the observation car, I went to our cabin, climbed the ladder and read. Dad snored, then rustled around fitfully, then snored again. This went on for an hour before he awoke, snorting and coughing. *Gross.* He stood, looked to see if I was on my bunk.

"Oh, you're here. Sorry for the coughing. I'll get cleaned up."

It sounded as if he was taking a bath in the sink. *Splish splash I was takin' a bath, long about a Saturday night,* I sang quietly. I laughed despite myself — *Am I happy?* Dad did well with his sink bath. His hair looked washed, he had shaved and smelled pretty good.

"You ready for dinner?" he asked, buttoning up a clean shirt.

"Yup, sure."

I climbed down the ladder, gave my hair a brush and applied lip gloss.

"Hello folks, come on in," the lovely doorman said, waving his outstretched arm.

"Thanks so much," Dad said. He sounded like himself, only better.

Our regular table was occupied by the three men I had dined with the night before. They nodded at me as I passed them. Linda and family had not yet arrived, and we took a table farther back on the other side of the train. The view was the same, which was important to me for some reason. I didn't know why, but having to sit at a different table unnerved me just a little.

"Mm, fish tonight," Dad said.

Fish was not his favourite. We waited. A pitcher of water was brought to the table. *Good memory.* We ordered iced tea and continued to wait.

"I finished my book," I said, finally breaking the silence.

"Nancy Drew?"

Well, he knew something about me. "Ya."

Our fish arrived. He poked at it a bit.

"The veggies look nice, let's see how the fish tastes," he said, taking a cautious bite. "Do you like it?"

"Sort of, the sauce is a bit strong — lemony," I responded.

"Didn't need sauce. Don't know why they put sauce on everything — don't need it," he said, scraping it to the side.

"Had roast beef last night," I said, plunking that piece of information in the middle of the table.

No response. More silence.

"I like that the scenery changes. Every time I look out the window, it's different," I said, deciding not to make things difficult.

Dad looked out the window as if he'd not noticed. He nodded and said, "The sun's setting. It's pretty. I think after dinner we should pack up and then just lay down until it's time to disembark. Sound okay to you?"

"Okay," I said. "I don't want to get off the train — I really like it."

Dad gave me a quizzical look and said, "We'll be back on a train for four nights soon enough — you'll get your fill."

That train is taking me too far away.

Dad stood between the cars for a smoke. I stood on the other side looking for the lights of small towns in the distance. The sorrowful train whistle blasted through the darkness of night.

"I'm gonna take a walk around, I'll see you in a bit."

"Okay, see you there," Dad said, flipping away his butt between his thumb and middle finger.

I passed Linda and family playing cards in the observation car. We waved to each other. *We'd not be friends even if we went to the same school*, I thought. After my ceremonious stroll, I went to our cabin. I was so excited to see Grace!

Chapter 20

Awkward and Upside Down

"Dad! There she is!" I yelped when I saw Grace.

She looked different but the same. Her hair was darker than I remembered and she looked older, healthier, happier. Then I saw a mirage — my mother in my aunt, her smile and wave, and the way she turned her head; it took my breath away. As if releasing a hallucination, I shook my head so the pieces inside lined up properly.

Grace and I locked eyes briming with tears and ran into each other's arms. It shocked me how I towered over her.

"You look different," I said, truly surprised. We dropped our embrace; our bodies didn't fit together the way they once did.

"Yeah, you too. I can't believe you're really here. You're so tall!" We hugged again, a little easier this time, and months of held emotions in our young bodies let lose. In unison we started sobbing;

together at last. All the animosity I felt disappeared. We were in this together.

But there was doubt.

Was she different? I grasped for memories. She was a little girl when I last saw her, and now she was not a little girl. What was to become of us as more years passed — me on one side of the country, her on the other?

My aunt now looked more like herself; it had been another fleeting moment. Dad and Uncle Brian shook hands, sharing pleasantries. Dad shaped up well, hadn't had a drink in almost two full days. I would keep his secret, along with the others.

"Oh goodness, girls, you're so happy to see each other!" Aunt Joyce said, nervously attempting to stop our tears and get us smiling.

"Okay, let's get the luggage and head for home," my uncle said, taking charge.

Grace and I made nervous small talk; thank goodness the luggage came quickly.

"Girls in the back, men in the front!" We piled into the wagon.

"Tell us all about the train!" Aunt Joyce chirped.

"I loved it — everything about it! Our cabin, my bed, the dining room, the view. I especially loved standing in the open space between the cars; it was amazing!"

I didn't bother saying I wanted to live on a train; they'd laugh.

"I enjoy train travel as well, Maggie. It's romantic."

Romantic … yes it was romantic.

"You two are sharing a room. Joy's sharing with Lacy while you're here."

"Okay, thanks, that's great," I said.

Grace and I shot a sideways glance at each other as if to say, *No Lacy talk.* It was our first sisterly connection; maybe she hadn't changed.

It was a two-night visit. Grace was right. David, now referred to as Dave, was really cute, every light in the house remained on most of the time, and country music played from early morning till bedtime. The house smelled of beef stew and banana bread. My aunt vibrated in anxious twittering motions that I reckon kept her weight under 120 pounds. Although she looked like Mum, she did not have Mum's alluring, sensual beauty. Joyce was hometown-girl pretty.

Grace was doing fine here; I could see that. She was doing better than when Mum was alive, proving that living with our aunt and uncle was a good move. This was a hard pill for me to swallow. Our first night together was wonderful. We snuggled in bed like old times. I was exhausted and fell asleep quickly, only waking when Grace stretched out either bonking me on my head with her elbow or kneeing me in the hip. The next morning when Grace was in the bath, Aunt Joyce came to our room.

"Can we have a little talk?"

"Sure, sure," I said, sitting up. *This is it. I'm going to be living here. She's going to tell Grace the truth and then we'll live together.*

"I just wanted to find out how you're doing. Gracie says you're doing well, that you've been babysitting.

I know you must not be very happy about moving so far away. I wanted to see if there was something I could do or say to make you feel better," she said with concern.

"Um, whatever … it's OK."

My chest hurt. Someone was screaming in my head, *PLEASE LET ME STAY!*

"Why don't you tell Grace how Mum died? Why don't you tell her the truth?"

I'd not planned to say those words, but there they were, like I had nothing to lose. She looked at me like I was evil.

"Oh, I'd never do that to her. She's had enough trouble for one little girl. Losing her mum and having to move away from her home — she's doing so well now." She put her hand on top of mine. "It took almost the whole year for her to get where she is today; I just couldn't ruin that for her. You understand that, don't you?"

"Sure, sure, I understand. Do you know who Henry is?"

I felt strong. I'd walked between train cars on a moving train.

"Henry? No I don't know Henry. Who's Henry?"

She sounded serious, but I wondered if she was lying. She took her hand off of mine.

"Mum was having an affair with Henry."

"Maggie!" she said as if I had the affair. "How do you know this?"

"I have a letter from Henry breaking up with Mum. I think that's why Mum killed herself."

How does that feel, Aunt Joyce?

She stood up, wrung her hands together and said in a much higher pitched voice, "Well, I think you should rip that letter up and throw it away and never think about it again. You don't know anything for sure, and it's long in the past now — it doesn't matter! It's over now, said and done."

I would never throw that letter away. It was evidence — the suicide note. How many little, insignificant secrets seep out in a lifetime while this enormous, life-altering story remains locked up? How does this happen? Weeks, months and years passed without one person letting it slip out in conversation. It never ceased to amaze me. Even as Grace matured, she never questioned how Mum died. With no history of heart disease, why would she just up and die from a heart attack? The nature of our mother's death went into the ground with her, and Grace learned, like the rest of us, to leave it buried. I would move across Canada and take the secret with me, leaving behind the lie for my sister to live with. This was my last chance, and I could see clearly nothing was going to change.

. . .

My aunt spent the day in the kitchen cooking up a storm like this was our last meal till we hit BC. I felt slightly off kilter from my conversation about Henry with my aunt, and I avoided eye contact with her.

"Maggie?" she called from the kitchen. "Could you set the table, dear? Got my hands full here. And before you do, can you help me drain this big pot of potatoes? You hold the lid and I'll tip the pot."

Mum did it this way too. With me standing right beside her, teaming up to protect the potatoes from falling into the sink, she said quietly into my ear, "I'm sorry I was abrupt with you about the letter you found. It kind of shocked me — to think of my sister having an affair — but I guess she did." She straightened up the pot, now fully drained, and placed it back on the stove. "I'm sorry I didn't talk to you more about it; it must bother you." She took off her oven mitts and looked right at me.

"It did. Well, I guess it still does, but I don't think about it much. But I wonder if that's why she —" I checked to make sure no one was within earshot and lowered my voice, "— did what she did."

She came close to me and spoke in a low voice. "There were many reasons your mum did what she did; no one thing can be blamed."

It felt like she was saying this for me to hear — telling me I wasn't to blame. I nodded, teary eyed. She hugged me and said, breaking the sadness, "Now set that table so we can eat."

It looked like Christmas dinner. Candles lit, best dishes, plates and plates of food, and a great big family — my family. Grace sat right beside me. I was now used to her face and she looked like my sister, except there were changes. Some awkwardness between us continued. It wasn't obvious what the changes were except she no longer came to me as she once did. She no longer needed me as she once did. I watched as she sorted things out with our aunt; things she'd once sort out with me. We no longer knew the intimate details of each other's lives, and there was no time to catch up. Grace and Joy were close as well. Joy relied on Grace as Grace once relied on me. Some chit-chat about British Columbia, schools and work brought Dad and I into the conversation, but so much was unknown about our future so we didn't have much to offer.

"Can I drive to Lund Harbour?" Dave asked.

Dave driving to Lund Harbour — when?

"We'll see," Uncle Brian responded.

"How long are we going to be there?" Lacy asked in a manner that let everyone know going to that little hole in the wall was the last thing she wanted to do with her summer.

"We're staying the whole summer, Lacy. Don't worry, you'll love it once you get there," her mother said encouragingly.

"Jesus," Lacy said, exasperated.

"Gracie and I are going to be in the same room, right Mum?" chirped Joy.

"Yes, dear. You and Gracie can share the double dormer room at the end of the hall."

Everything went silent. I saw lips moving but heard nothing. I looked at Dad, he remained quiet, head down. Grace kept eating, unaware that my heart had shattered into slivers of ice. I got up from the table, went to the bathroom, leaned on the sink to steady myself. *Grace curled up with Joy — sharing the bed. Not me. Where will I be? Thousands of miles away.* I was sweating, panting, felt dizzy. My heart pounded, I struggled to breathe, to stay standing. I slid to the floor or maybe I fainted — I don't know, everything went black. And just as quickly, I came to. I slowly stood, not knowing how long I'd been gone. I felt clammy and cold. I flushed the toilet, splashed water on my face, dried with toilet paper, took a deep breath and left the bathroom in a daze. When I returned to the table, Uncle Brian had everyone arranged for a picture using my camera so I'd have it for a memory. Everyone is smiling in that picture except me. Lund Harbour was not brought up again.

To my surprise, Lacy and I connected. She was funny, and sarcasm was her preferred method of communication; I liked it. I observed how she spoke to her parents and learned the techniques of pissing everyone off yet seemingly remaining fine herself. Hanging out with Lacy became easier than being with Grace, and this left Grace free to be with Joy. I felt conflicted, thinking I should spend all my time with my sister.

It was a tedious task going through photo albums with Grace and Aunt Joyce. Picture after picture of Mum as a little girl, a teen, and young woman.

"How beautiful she was — she was so sweet, full of fun," Aunt Joyce said, as if she hadn't killed herself with no thought of us.

My mind filled up with bitterness, resentment and secrets, and Grace could feel it. There was no life for us to reminisce about, and no new life for us to establish. It was a strange turn of events that my time spent with Grace felt like a chore. I think Lacy and I would have become friends given a chance. I think I would have told her about Mum, if she didn't already know. There wasn't enough time in this visit to broach that subject, not to mention she could not be trusted. That piece of information was just to juicy not to use to her advantage.

On our second night, Grace slept on a blow-up mattress and I in the bed; it was much better. As we tucked in, Grace said, "I can hardly remember Mum but I miss her. Does that make sense?"

"You're asking me what makes sense? Nothing makes sense to me. I mean, look at our lives. You live here, I'm moving to the other side of the world. Who knows when I'll see you or Aunt Joyce or Lacy again".

As soon as Lacy's name was out of my mouth, I regretted it. After all, my sister had shared how horribly Lacy had treated her and here I was aligning with the villain.

"Never mind," Grace said with hurt in her voice.
Shit.

"Don't be mad; everything's all upside down right now. I don't know where I'm going …." I said, my voice cracking.

The tears came at last. Grace slid into bed with me, only this time she comforted me.

Chapter 21

Going Under

Our train to British Columbia left at 18:15. Dad was surprised when I interpreted the time correctly, and I told him I learned the 24-hour clock in my candy-striping days. I couldn't help enjoying his attention. He did well with Uncle Brian — better than any time they'd spent together in Lund Harbour. Dad got right in there, all three of them tinkering with Dave's car; he knew his stuff. *Why can't we live here? There's buses in Toronto!*

Saying goodbye at the train station was torture. I was tired and scared. When would I see them again? Seemed like never. No one said they were planning a visit. No one said, "See you soon!" All I heard was, "Bye, safe travels — say hello to those big mountains for us!"

"Thank you, yes, thank you so much for everything," I repeated until they finally left, walking away back to their home full of family.

Grace and I happened to turn our heads at the same time, and we shared a look. *What was to happen to us?*

I felt a rock in the pit of my stomach as I climbed aboard. We settled in our cabin, beds opened, PJs on.

"Goodnight," I said.

It seemed like only seconds later when I heard, "Maggie? Let's get some breakfast."

"Mm?" I said, rolling over and realizing where I was and where I was going.

Dad was already dressed. I felt no excitement about being on this train. No desire to stand between the cars, drink water from the sparkling glassware, watch the forests and meadows speed past, taking me farther and farther away from everything I knew and loved. My stomach turned at the thought of the eggs and sausages I had once devoured on a train. Seemed a long time ago.

"Not hungry — feel sick."

"I'll bring you back some toast and juice," he said.

I heard the door click. *Did he just leave or is he back?*

"I've got an orange, a cinnamon bun and a pitcher of water," he said.

"Water please." I sat up, had to pee. "Actually I'd like a Coke," I said, heading to the bathroom.

"That's because your tummy's upset," Dad offered.

"Yes, I think it will help."

I ate oranges and drank pop the entire trip across Canada. I did not wash or bathe. I stayed in the cabin, sleeping or gazing out the window. The Prairies were impressive. Memories snaked their way around my brain, holding me hostage. Visions of Mum lying dead on her bed, of our little family home in Halifax, of Mum posing in picture after picture, of Lacy trying so hard to be tough, of cute Dave, of my last night with Grace. How natural it was to have her there, right beside me.

One cannot live on oranges and pop alone. By the time we arrived at the Vancouver train station, I was in bad shape and Dad was quite frantic about my condition. I could not keep feigning nausea. We disembarked; I was weak.

"Come sit down," he said.

We sat on a bench as we had done on the other side of the country a few days ago. He handed me an orange from his stash of fresh fruit in his carry-on bag.

"You steal that from the dining car?" I said with a laugh.

"Not really, we paid for them," he said, passing me a banana.

I shook my head. We sat while I ate an orange. It was a warm day, the air was fresh. I could see the mountains across the water. The lay of the land was foreign to me, but I had to admit that it was beautiful. Dad flagged a taxi and we headed to a motel on the North Shore. Our furniture would arrive within the week, so the motel would be our home until then. I'd lost a lot of weight, my clothes hung on me, but I simply could not eat; a little fruit and some dry Cheerios filled me up. I slept, watched TV and slept some more. I thought about writing Grace, but that's as far as I got. I had no strength, physically or mentally.

Dad started work that first Monday. He hadn't had a drink since leaving Halifax. When our furniture arrived, we moved into the two-bedroom apartment. It was a box with doors, a shocking lack of character in comparison to our family home. I didn't leave the apartment and continued to watch TV, eat oranges and Cheerios and drink pop. Dad was beside himself, but there was always a bowl of oranges on the table and pop in the fridge so at least I'd eat something. By mid-July I was skin and bones, and hospitalized.

. . .

"Maggie, what are you doing, starving yourself to death? Do you hear me?" Dad stood over my hospital bed speaking with a mixture of pity and frustration.

I ached from head to toe. I rolled over, being careful not to pull the needle out of my arm. My eyes remained shut. Dad sighed. I remembered Mum saying, "I feel like I've been hit by a truck," after she'd spent a month in bed. I now knew the feeling.

"Come on, Mags, you don't have to do this — you have to eat. Things will get better, you'll see. Just give it a chance."

"Leave me alone, Dad. Just leave me alone ..." I whispered, the sides of my throat stuck together.

He put a letter from Grace on the bedside table and left the room.

July 10, 1975

Dear Maggie,

It seems like a year since you were here. Aunt Joyce just gave me your new address. We're going to be moving to Oshawa. Uncle Brian says the house is to small for all of us and he wants to get out of the city. He will have to drive a long way to work but he said he can work from home to. I'll send you our new address. Lacy's really mad about moving, she's fit to be tied. I'm kind of sad to because I have to change schools and leave my friends, and I'm tired of moving. Aunt Joyce said that we'll be in the new house for ever.

I'm sorry you didn't get to come to Lund Harbour with us, it was different there for me, I kept looking for you and Mum. We came home early to start packing. Aunt Rose was there. She's really nice. She told us stories about picking wild berries in the field and baking pies in the big pantry. She said Mum and Joyce were two little monkeys. They ran under foot and stole the berries for the pies. But she winked at me when she said it. Aunt Joyce said she missed Mum not being there too. Remember how much fun they had together? Mum was so happy there with Aunt Joyce and all us kids. I really missed you and Mum being there so much, sometimes I felt like I shouldn't be there. Uncle Brian only came on the weekends like Dad use to. It's all so different now. I was glad to leave.

Tell me about where you live. Do you have a big room? What are you doing for the summer? Did you get a job? Tell me everything. We're getting a dog when we move because we'll have a big yard. I'm excited about that.

Lacy has a boyfriend. She's on the pill. I think maybe because you're the same age you got along better with her, but you're different than her.

Ok, write me back soon. Tell me all about British Columbia. It seems so far away, like I'll never see you ever again. How will I ever get there to visit, or will you get here? It makes me sad.

Love Grace xo

If I were able to cry, I would have — for Isabella, Jennifer, Julia, little Ellie, the smell of the Big House,

Penny, Mum, and everything lost. But my body was dry and weak. As if in a dream I heard a whisper.

"Maggie, wake up."

A young nurse gently put her hand on my head. She moved the hospital table in front of me and took the lid off a bowl of soup. Her name tag said "Brooke."

"I'll just roll your bed up and we'll see if this appeals to you," she said. "I didn't cook it, so I have no idea how it tastes." Brooke smiled warmly. "But it smells pretty good, so let's see."

She moved swiftly around the room.

"Do you think you might like to try some?" she asked, lightly touching the spoon. "I think its consommé, like a beef broth sort of thing."

With bleary eyes, I weakly lifted the spoon to my mouth and managed a sip. It was the best thing I'd ever tasted in my life. The salty, warm liquid exploded in my mouth, soothed my throat and slid like warm silk down to the bottom of my belly. Brooke watched for my reaction.

"Yeah, it's good, isn't it? I like consommé too. Take your time with it, though; if you eat too quickly you might feel sick."

Six sips was all I could manage before my head flopped back onto the pillow and I dropped the spoon, exhausted.

"You did really well. I'll leave your Jell-O here; you can have it whenever you like. I'll come back in a minute with more ice chips."

She glided out the door so full of life, and I fell asleep. I dreamt Grace and I lay head to toe in the hammock strung from two leafy trees out the side of the Big House. Our sandy legs touched. We laughed about something and Mum called from the back door, "Girls, come in for dinner! We're having soup."

During my two-week hospital stay, I was seen by numerous professionals. The dangers of heart failure from not eating were explained by one, the stages of grief by another, what and when to eat by yet another. Dad was given firm instructions that he needed to buy proper groceries and cook meals and make sure I stayed healthy. Did they also tell him to relieve me of this lie? Of course not because they didn't know. Although I never saw Brooke again, I wanted to be just like her.

Chapter 22

Navigating a New Life

Sept 23, 1975

Dear Grace,

I think you know by now I was in the hospital. I lost too much weight. I'm fine now. All I had to do was eat more. I started my period for real. I didn't fit any of my old clothes so Dad took me back to school shopping. He bought me tons of stuff, he kept saying he had to because nothing fit me. I even got two bras. Dad doesn't drink anymore, he just stopped. He's much nicer now. He says he likes his new job.

I don't really like where we live. It's an apartment. I guess I'll get use to it, but Dad said he's looking for a small house to rent. School's okay, I keep to myself, everyone seems to know everyone else. I think I'm the only new person. It's a big school so I got lost a few times at first but I know my way around now.

Everything's big here. Big trees, big mountains, big city, big school, everything is just bigger. It's pretty but I miss home, I miss Lund Harbour more than anything else. I'm seeing a counsellor, she's nice. I call her Dr. Beth. She told me too much has happened to me in a short period of time and it affected my body's chemistry and that's why I got sick. She said with the right food and support I'll get better. I still see her once a week. We talk about stuff and she helps me. We talk a lot about Mum.

Did you notice the date of this letter? One year ago today Mum died. It seems longer than that in some ways, and shorter in other ways.

You've moved too by now. Tell me all about it. Did you get a dog? Do you live in a house with a big yard? What's your new school like? I know your birthday is next month, what will you do for it? This is the second birthday I'll miss. Maybe Dad and I will call again, I hope so.

Write soon.

Love Maggie. xo

This letter had to be read with a fine-tooth comb six — maybe seven — times before mailing. I took big chances talking so much about Mum, but I had developed expert "keeping secrets" skills. Dr. Beth knew about Mum's suicide, about Henry, and about Grace moving with my aunt and uncle, but I even kept things from her. I dared not tell her about "the lie" or about Dad's drinking. Dad was now under the watchful eye of the ministry, so I couldn't expose his inability to do right by his children. However, just sharing partial events of my life helped, and I started to feel better.

"Where do you see yourself in a year?" she asked during one session, leaning in to listen as if she didn't want to miss a single word of what I'd say.

To my surprise, I was doing well in my future life a year away. I looked happy and I had friends around me; we were laughing as we walked the school hallway. It was the strangest thing, this future snapshot of myself that looked nothing like my present self.

"Well, um, I see myself doing okay. My hair is longer and I have friends." I thought I sounded stupid.

"That's pretty good — long hair, friends and doing okay."

She sat back and smiled at me, I think with relief. After all, my mother had taken her own life and I had come close to starving myself to death, so I'm sure she wondered what I had in store for myself in my own head. But in that moment, hope began to blossom like a desert flower. It was as unassuming as a bud on a prickly cactus that cannot be ignored once in bloom.

Amazingly, about six weeks into the school year, I made a friend named Natalie. Nattie is what she liked to be called. She was considerably shorter than me and had trouble with acne. Even though she walked like a duck, it was kind of sexy in a cute way. She was easy to be around, didn't ask too many questions about my life — none that I couldn't handle.

We'd go to her place after school and sing along with Captain & Tennille's "Love Will Keep Us Together," followed by the Carpenters' "Please Mr. Postman," over and over. We'd make toast with mounds of peanut butter and talk about who'd we marry, where we'd travel and how many kids we'd have. We spent very little time talking about our present lives, which suited me fine. Even though marriage, children and travel had not crossed my mind to this point, Nattie's enthusiasm for the topics tweaked my interest. She thought I was insane when I shared the news I would be a nurse.

"Grave — yard — shift, Maggie! It's called the GRAVEYARD!" she'd say to me, wide-eyed. "That's the last profession I'd choose. In fact, I have absolutely no intention of working at all. I've watched my mother drive herself into the corporate ground just to keep up with my father; her earning power is more important than her children."

Not much of what she said made sense to me, but I got the gist of it and figured she'd change her mind about not working at some point. The girl was driven, and I was quite sure she'd inherited her parents' genius. Living a "leisurely life," as she called it, just didn't fit the Nattie I was getting to know.

Life fell into a predictable routine, something Dr. Beth said was "Crucial for my well-being." Even though Dad and I avoided certain topics, cooking and eating dinner together every night became a highlight of my day. To his surprise — and mine — he enjoyed cooking, and food became our umbilical cord, our first authentic connection. He educated himself about spices and herbs, different cuts of meat, what vegetables to serve with what proteins, and he'd show me while we chopped, sauteed, baked, and roasted our tasty meals.

One evening we ventured into a lemon cream sauce recipe for our salmon. We turned and smacked into each other both attempting to get to the fridge.

"I'm as tall as you are," I said, our blue Scandinavian eyes meeting.

"Bloody hell, I must have shrunk," he said, winking.

We typically ate in silence, only talking about the food, what it needed or needed less of.

"Well, was I right about the lemon sauce?"

"It's good, but I still think not necessary," he replied as he scooped up the last bit of rice doused in lemon sauce. He caught me watching him. "I like it on my rice more than the fish," he said with a smile as he sat back and looked around, rather pleased with himself. "Dessert, Mags, we need dessert. I've read dessert is important for digestion, but I'm not sure if baking is my forte."

"I like baking — I baked cookies all the time with Jennifer and Julia …"

Memories flooded in.

After a pregnant pause, Dad said, "Yes, of course. I remember those cookies, they were delicious. One of those would be great right now. Write down what you need and I'll pick it up."

Dishes were also done in silence, but this night I asked, "How's work? Do you like it?"

"I like work, yeah. I work with some good people," he said, looking surprised and then pleased at my question. "I know the job, I like the hours. It's good. How about you? How's school? How's your friend, what's her name? Nancy?"

From this night forward, the antics of Nattie became a must discuss at the dinner table. She made us laugh, and we now had two topics: food and Nattie.

. . .

Although Nattie couldn't have cared less about her looks, she did, however, make me aware of mine.

We were trying on lipstick from her mother's stash, and I put on deep red and smacked my lips together.

"You have no idea how pretty you are, do you?" she asked. "It's amazing because all girls want to look like you: tall, slim, blonde, blue-eyed, no need for make-up. You don't see the guys look at you, do you?"

"What are you talking about? No one looks at me," I protested.

"Yes they do — you just don't care. Which is great, because you shouldn't care. They're all idiots and they just want sex anyway."

She turned off the bathroom light and waddled out. Boys and sex were the furthest thing from my mind. I was still feeling unsteady from the events of the past year, so taking on another new adventure seemed ludicrous.

"I'm joining the swim team," Nattie said. "Wanna come?"

"The swim team? I don't think I'm that good a swimmer," I said, picturing Grace and me dashing into the cold Atlantic Ocean, flapping our hands and racing back to the warm sand. It hardly constituted swimming.

"Well try. You never know till you try," she said as if it were settled.

Nothing stopped her from exercising her will, not even envied beauty.

"I don't even think I have a bathing suit."

"Let's find out what kind we need because I'm sure they have to be a one piece and not sexy at all. Like competitive swimmers wear, ya know?"

"Okay, I'll come with you, but I'm not sure if joining is something I want to do at this point."

In actual fact, I did join, and to my astonishment I could backstroke. It was no surprise to anyone that Nattie would take charge of the butterfly stroke. Her body was the perfect build: awkward on land, fast and powerful in water. The real test came when we swam against other school teams. No one beat me on our school team, but once I was up against other schools, I didn't have a chance. Nattie, on the other hand, whipped everyone's ass. She was a hybrid, half pit bull, half shark. The sound of that gun going off ignited an intense competitiveness in her, something that most of us would never experience in a lifetime.

Nattie had a way of opening my eyes to things that had not occurred to me before. The boys did look at me, but I just had not been looking back. Now I couldn't stop looking. No matter when I looked, there they were with smiles, nods, winks. I became self-conscious, flustered.

"Just ignore them. That's what you've always done, so just keep doing it," Nattie said.

"I wasn't ignoring them, I didn't notice them — there's a difference," I said to the genius. "It's not easy to ignore them; I wish you hadn't told me," I said, truly perplexed.

Nov 2, 1975

Dear Maggie,

Got your letter. I'm happy to hear you're better. That must have been scary. Aunt Joyce told me Dad found you on the bathroom floor, unconscious. What happened? Poor you. Are you better now? It's exciting you got your period. Some girls in my class have their period already.

I get a lot of Lacy's clothes just like I use to get yours. Then they go to Joy. I love our new house. Joy and I still share a room but I don't mind. We have a big yard and lots of kids in the neighbourhood. We all take a school bus to school. I like the school too. Moving wasn't as bad as I thought.

Something weird has happened I want to tell you and you tell me what you think about it. For some reason I called Aunt Joyce - Mum. It just slipped out. I was kind of shocked when it happened. She said that's because I hear everyone else call her Mum and she's taken on the Mum role with me and I just wasn't thinking and out it came, and after all she's Mum's sister.

She said it's perfectly fine, and that I could call her Mum if I wanted and Aunt Joyce if I wanted. It's been weird because now I don't know what to call her, but I'd like to call her Mum. Tell me what you think about that.

This year I'm having a birthday party. This house is so big I can have lots of friends from school. I wish you were going to be here.

We got a puppy, it's a golden lab, we named him Mango because he's the colour of a ripe mango. He's so cute, still a puppy so we have to make sure he doesn't eat our shoes and stuff.

Halloween was fun, we all went tricker treating in the neighbourhood then we had fireworks. All the families chipped in to buy them so we had lots. Did you go tricker treating? Lacy didn't go. She's really mad about living in Oshawa because she doesn't get to see her boyfriend.

I know what you mean about it seems longer than a year that Mum died and sometimes shorter than a year. Aunt Joyce says that one year is a milestone in the grieving process. Are

you going to call me on my birthday?
I hope so.

Write back soon.

Love Grace xo

Why wouldn't she call Aunt Joyce "Mum"? In comparison, Aunt Joyce mothered Grace in the last year more than our own mother did in her lifetime, or so it seemed in my head. *Go ahead, call her Mum.* And why was *she* telling me how Dad found me? First I heard of that. Typical that no one knows the full truth about anything in our family. Dad must have shared the gruesome details with Aunt Joyce and then — what — Aunt Joyce told Grace? Was I taking my last breath on the bathroom floor? I didn't remember going to the bathroom; what was I doing there? How long had I been there? I was disturbed that I couldn't remember what happened.

Chapter 23

Getting Control

It turned chilly on the deck quickly. The sun disappeared behind one dark cloud that floated randomly in a perfect blue sky. A sudden breeze kicked up, knocking over an empty watering can. A rainbow bridged the mountaintops right in front of me and, as a rainbow demands the attention of its viewers, I longed to summon those around to come see it, to talk about the rain that must be somewhere, the number of colours we can see, and the pot of gold at the end. There was no one to summon.

With Jeffery not home for dinner, the house told a story of how life would soon be with all my children gone. The nostalgia of their little faces and voices haunted the quiet. Was life easier then? I didn't think so at the time. On the contrary, it was harder, yet when I recall those days of mothering three blonde-haired boys, I fall into an illusion of perfection.

Days spent on my own while Phillip travelled overwhelmed me. In hindsight, I needed help; I was a single parent much of the time. Mind you, when Phillip was home, he gave 100 per cent of his attention to the boys. It's just that I had no time to develop a life of my own — or maybe I just wasn't interested in doing so. When Phillip was home, I went from being front and centre, full-on single parent to being somewhat abandoned, floundering and, yes, resentful. Resentment accompanied me everywhere.

The boys lived in a holiday atmosphere when Phillip was home, even on school days. They raced home to find out what Dad had planned for them — a game, an outing, or building something. Then, just like that, he'd be gone and old Mum was left to hold down the fort and make life work. *Blah, it wasn't easier.*

At the time, Phillip and I saw Jeffery's reluctance to join in with his brothers as an age difference thing. "He's the baby," we'd reassure each other. More than once, I'd turn in the kitchen to see his little face looking at me like he had done something wrong. He just didn't want to be out there with the boys, he wanted to be with me or by himself. As time went on, it became clear to me that Jeffery was most likely gay. This was something Phillip refused to discuss with me, and this concerned me most.

. . .

"Dad, can you grab the cookies? The timer went off and I'm doing the dishes!" I shouted from the kitchen.

"Got it, got it!" Dad scrambled to get the oven mitt on. "Don't want to burn these beauties," he said, licking his lips.

We sat with a cup of tea and the freshly baked ginger cookies, dunking, dipping and slurping our way to sugar and ginger heaven.

"Dad?"

"Yeeees?" he said, mocking and teasing at the same time.

"How long was I lying on the bathroom floor before you found me?"

I kept my eyes on my tea and cookies. He dropped his hands, sat up straight and looked at me, surprised.

"What brought this on?"

"I want to … I *need* to know. How long?"

"Awhile — no one knows for sure because I was at work and you were home."

"So it could have been eight hours?" I wanted the story.

"No, not that long; they said maybe three," he said, looking at me sheepishly.

"Was I dressed?"

"In your pajamas."

"What was I doing in the bathroom?"

"Don't know — maybe you were going to the washroom, but you hit your head on the sink."

"I did? I didn't know that."

"You had a bruise and a headache, mild concussion. It wasn't the worst of your predicament. Your heartbeat was slow and weak. Scary," he said more to himself. He abruptly got up from the table and dumped the remainder of his tea in the sink. With his back still turned to me he said, "That was the scariest day of my life — scariest of all my scary days; that was it."

"I bet," I said with a hint of redemption in my tone.

He was lost in reliving the moment. "The ambulance driver said you were close to your last breath," he said slowly, as if in a trance. "They could hardly feel a pulse — it was weak and slow, maybe sixteen beats per minute. Your eyes were sunken."

"Okay Dad, I got it," I said, dumping the rest of my tea in the sink.

I turned to leave but he caught my hand. Still not looking at me, he squeezed it. *I was close to dying.* I wanted to cry but not here, in front of him.

"Sorry I scared you," I whispered, so close to tears.

He let my hand go and I went to my room. We never talked about it again, didn't need to.

. . .

It seemed to me that Grace and I said all we needed to say in our letters. There was no need to talk, but a phone call was made as planned for her birthday.

"Hi Grace, happy birthday!"

"Thanks, Maggie."

Silence

"Did you get a birthday present?"

"Ya, I got a brand-new winter jacket."

"Oh that's great! What colour is it?"

"Blue."

Silence

"How's Mango?"

"Great! Here Mango, come boy, come on, say hi to Maggie. Mango, come!"

I waited while Grace summoned the dog to the phone as if the dog and I would have a chat.

"Mango, come girl. Oh, she's not coming. I'll get a biscuit, hold on."

"That's okay Grace. I better let Dad talk to you now. Have a good birthday, okay?"

"Okay. Okay, bye."

It was painful. We were officially estranged, a word Dr. Beth used, and now I knew what it meant. Estranged felt like loss.

When my parents arrived home from the hospital with little newborn Grace, we all sat together on the sofa in our living room. Her little face was so perfect I couldn't believe it. I instinctively started to unwrap her blanket to see more of her. When her arms released from the swaddle, they stretched out as if she wanted to hug me. When I touched her hand she wrapped her fingers around mine so tight that I was amazed at her strength. She was my strong sister Grace. I bent to kiss her cheek, so soft and delicate. Soft and delicate and strong Grace.

"Can I see her feet?" I asked Mum, not taking my eyes off the live doll in front of me.

Mum pulled her foot out of the newborn sleeper that was once mine. Her foot was the sweetest thing

I had ever seen. Her tiny little toes spread out as if to greet the world. I kissed the bottom of her foot and her eyes opened. She knew it was me.

"I love her," I said.

"And she loves you too," Mum said, bonding us for life.

Now where are we? An atomic bomb secret and miles of land between us.

I listened as Dad talked awkwardly to his youngest daughter, repeating the same questions I had just asked her. He then spoke briefly to Aunt Joyce. It would be a long time before we'd speak again.

Dr. Beth helped me stay focused on "the present," a new concept that she loved. She pointed out that I could do nothing about what had gone on in the past. This both terrified and relieved me at the same time. I wanted to change the past; I wanted it to be different. Dr. Beth said the closest I would come to changing it would be to stop rehearsing it in my mind. Rehearsing it guaranteed it would stay the same.

Dr. Beth Miller wore her thick, red hair in a loose ponytail. Her skin was the colour of rich cream, eyes light brown, almost yellow. The reddish-orange rims of her glasses matched both her hair and eyes. She had a perfect smattering of freckles across the bridge of her nose. I can't remember why, but she mentioned once that she had just turned thirty-six. There were no family photos in her office that I could see, but she wore wedding rings.

Going to visit Dr. Beth was something I looked forward to. Just being in her office relaxed me.

The walls were a soft, light grey, the chairs vibrant colours of reds and greens. There was one piece of artwork: a meadow of poppies bending in a breeze. All the wood furniture was white. She had a small fountain on a shelf that made trickling water sounds. My chair faced a large window with a view of the Lions Gate Bridge and Stanley Park. She sat in front of me but slightly to the side, just the right amount of distance between us. There was a small table close to me with fresh flowers and tissues, which I used every time. Her desk was behind her, and a floor-to-ceiling bookcase was on the far wall behind her desk. *Has she read all those books?*

"Shall we have our touch in?" she asked.

This is how each session started. I liked the predictability.

"I got a letter from Grace. She told me Dad found me unconscious on the bathroom floor."

Saying the words out loud almost made me cry. Dr. Beth waited silently — safe space, as she referred to it. I loved just sitting, quietly, until I felt ready to speak.

"I asked Dad about it and he told me I was close to dying."

More safe space.

"I didn't know I was that sick. I can't really remember how I got to that point," I said, blowing my nose.

"What's the part that scares you the most?"

"That I almost died."

More tears.

"Yes, that's a scary thought."

She waited until the penny dropped. *It was just a thought.*

"It's okay to feel the emotion of this as it's not about shutting down your feelings. You just don't want to be run by them. Think the thought, feel the feeling and change your thought."

"Why can't I remember that?" I said, smiling and blowing my nose again.

"It's practice, that's all; you'll get it. And you'll discover that our memories of events become distorted. An event starts out the size of a little seed, and as we continue to think about the event, we add layers and layers of feelings — like resentment, victimization, guilt and so on." She paused. "And this is new information for you Maggie. You're trying to make sense of it — quite normal."

I loved hearing Dr. Beth say the word "normal" to me; most of the time I felt anything but.

"Look at something right in front of me," I said aloud in an attempt to stick it in my brain.

"That's it — look at something right in front of you and describe it to me."

"I see how the Lions Gate Bridge disappears into the trees, and I see a freighter going under the bridge, and it looks like the freighter's going to hit the bridge."

"Excellent, you've got it — nicely done."

Dr. Beth told me all about anorexia nervosa. "There are many reasons why a person develops this. In your case, I believe, with the death of your mum and subsequent changes in your life, you felt a loss of control."

"But I just couldn't eat; I felt sick at the thought of food?"

"It's complicated for sure; many people lose their appetite when upset about things and some people eat more. You tend to lose your appetite, so it's a good thing to know about yourself. You can watch for signs and take precautions. When you notice you're upset about something, you can eat small amounts often throughout your day, amounts you can tolerate."

I nodded; it made sense.

Chapter 24

That's the Way I Like It

Christmas that year was a trifle better. We put up a few decorations, although I found Christmas lights sloppily draped around apartment windows depressing, still do. Aunt Joyce sent a box with several gifts for both Dad and me. In comparison, our gifts to them were lacklustre. Pretty writing paper with matching envelopes and stamps from me to Grace, and a fifty-dollar bill from Dad, unwrapped, shoved into a manila envelope.

Grace sent me five rolls of film for my camera and a picture of her standing in the front doorway of the Big House that led into a large, glass-enclosed wraparound sun porch. Orange and yellow lilies lined the walkway leading up to the door. As with all pictures from Grace, I studied it, dissecting each morsel. I longed to be there. Mum continued to emerge in my sister. We were so different — Grace, dark and full-bodied like Mum; me, fair and lanky, like Dad.

An invite from Dad's colleague for Christmas dinner saved the day. Only a slight anxiety slithered into my belly when Mr. Driscal refused to accept Dad's decline for a drink.

"Oh no Mike, I never touch the stuff," he said, to my great surprise. "Don't handle it very well you see."

And that was that. I smiled at him, he nodded. I was the only kid there, but everyone spoke to me like an adult and made sure to include me in the conversations. They wanted to know about Nova Scotia, like it was an exotic destination. No one had been to the Maritimes but all wanted to go one day. I thought this gave me an edge — something I'd not experienced before. I felt grown up and relaxed.

Two Christmases without Mum under my belt. In the New Year, the ministry deemed Dad a fit parent and closed our file, which meant my visits with Dr. Beth would end. I gazed around her office, exactly as I had done my first visit, and took my chair.

"How do you feel about our sessions ending?" she asked me, looking younger with her hair cut in the latest shag style.

I didn't want to be rude and say I was fine not seeing her again, but I was. She picked up on my loss for words.

"I find it is usually the perfect time when sessions end."

I nodded.

"Is there anything on your mind that you'd like to talk about?"

"Can I come see you again if I want?"

"Any time Maggie. Absolutely any time."

I have little recollection of what we spent the hour talking about, but, as usual, I left her office feeling better, even normal.

"Normal is a concept," Dr. Beth always said. "We all have concepts of what we think is normal, and concepts change as we age and live life."

As I left her office, I did indeed feel prepared to live my life.

. . .

Nattie and I remained close friends. We were an odd couple in appearances, but our personalities fit well. I almost told her how Mum died and the whole sordid tale that transpired after, but just thinking about it sucked my energy away. There'd be too many questions and too many hours spent trying to resolve the unresolvable. My mother was not a standard topic for us, where as her mother, Alison, was a constant in our conversations.

Nattie resisted her mum's achievements and go get-'em attitude. In reality, she was exactly like her mum. They never fought. They did, however, heartily discuss, share differing opinions, debate possibilities and challenge options; it was entertaining to watch. The benchmark ending of these vigorous dialogues would be Alison saying, "Well Natalie, you know what's best." She'd then leave the room. Nattie felt validated, and I thought Alison didn't mean a word of it, but she knew when to quit; she was one smart cookie.

Her father was just as much a high achiever and was a partner in a law firm. Nattie said that Alison had to compete with him to prove that she was capable of earning as much dough as any man.

"Why couldn't she be happy raising her children? It's an important job. Isn't it the most important job in the world?"

It was a rhetorical question. And what could I offer anyway? Nattie had an amazing mother, and I could only dream of such a relationship with my mother. And, of course, I did. It occurred to me that no matter how parents parent the child, the child will end up complaining about it to some degree.

Dad and I moved into a two-bedroom house at the end of February. Mum's birthday, February 2, came and went, notarized by a two-minute conversation between Dad and me at the dinner table.

"She would be thirty-nine," Dad said with a sigh that indicated he thought it a shame for a vibrant woman to end her life so early.

"Do you miss her?" I dared ask.

Surprised by the question he sat up straight. "That's an interesting question."

I waited, "safe space."

"To be honest, not until I stopped drinking," he said slowly and quietly. "Didn't give myself a chance to miss her. It's not easy," he said, shaking his head at things he wasn't going to share. "Do you miss her?"

"Ya, I miss her."

Silence.

"I miss her laugh."

Silence.

"I miss Grace more."

He wasn't expecting that. He lowered his head, didn't want to talk about it. I let it go.

Not unlike our Halifax home, this new (old) house had character. Boxes that had been left packed since leaving Halifax because there was no room in the apartment were opened. It felt like Christmas. We took our time finding the right resting spot for each piece that was so full of Laurie Holm. I'm sure Dad also felt her presence.

Things were going well for me. That is, until one day I arrived home from Nattie's house to find a woman in my kitchen doing dishes. She didn't hear me come in, so I stood still and watched her, like an eavesdropper. She stood five feet tall, the size of a child really. She wore an old-fashioned, multicoloured skirt cinched at her tiny waist with a wide elastic belt under which looked to be a crinoline. Her blouse was tucked in tight, and high-heeled shoes matched the red bow in her hair. Her hair was dirty blonde, dry, thin, over backcombed and over sprayed. I cleared my throat and she turned around; her narrow face was lined, making her look older than I expected — older than Dad.

"Oh, Maggie," she said, taking off the long, yellow rubber gloves.

Where'd she get those?

She stuck out her hand to shake and said, "You don't remember me, but we met at my brother's house on Christmas. I'm Mike Driscal's sister, Trish."

She paused, waiting for the pin to drop in my head. I did remember her — her sharp features

— and I remember trying to guess her age. And yes, now that she mentioned it, I remembered her talking to Dad in a flirtatious way. I shook her hand.

"Yes, I remember you." *But what are you doing in my house?* "Is Dad home?" *Or do you have a key?* At that moment, Dad came in from the back lane.

"Well, I see you two have reacquainted yourselves."

Dad shot me a familiar look as if to say, *Be nice, say the right thing. You have no control over this, so just be still and learn to live with it.* Amazing what can be said with a look. This explained Dad's random, short disappearances and long phone conversations of late; it was all about Trish. Physically, they were as mismatched as Nattie and me. Dad was six-three and Trish almost a foot and a half shorter. It was fine with me that he had a lady friend, however, I took great exception to her nosing around my kitchen. Dad should have known that.

My concerns were short-lived. Trish had her own place, had never been married and never intended to. Now that we'd finally met, Dad began spending more time at her place. He, of course, kept in touch with me through little notes taped to the fridge: *Dinner's in the fridge, stick it in the oven 250° for 15 – 20 minutes to warm up. Invite Nattie over if you like. Call me anytime.* The man had learned his lesson; I guess finding his daughter unconscious on the bathroom floor, twenty, thirty minutes away from death changes things.

It bothered me somewhat that Dad was an idiot drunk when married to my mother and that Trish got the best of him when the mother of his children got the worst. *It's in the past. Don't rehearse it. Present time — the man is happy — I like Trish. Excellent!*

February in Vancouver was nothing like February in Halifax. Halifax would be dealing with yet another winter storm while Vancouver hosted a banquet of early spring flowers, cherry blossoms included. It turned out that Trish was as welcome a presence in my life as those flowers. She did not muzzle into my kitchen; in fact, she said on many occasions, "I think I've died and gone to heaven" while eating dinner prepared by Dad and me. She hated cooking, loved eating and willingly did the dishes. Once in a while you come across a person that seems ageless. It has nothing to do with their appearance — it's how they adapt or embrace the changing world. These people don't resist new inventions or new ways of doing things. Trish was one of these people in every way, except for her wardrobe. In that respect she was in a league of her own, with her poodle skirts and crinolines. One night after dinner, I mentioned I wanted new Levi's.

"Slacks don't look good on me, do they Jack?" Trish piped up.

"I like your skirts," Dad replied.

I wondered if he really cared one way or the other.

"I'll wear them next time, you'll see what I mean," she said to me.

She was right. She was so tiny that the full skirt gave her substance that jeans stole.

"Have to buy them in the young girls' section —
they do nothing for me," she said, looking down at
herself.

I didn't want to insult her, so I borrowed Dad's
line. "I like your skirts."

She laughed; she knew exactly what I was saying.
I just loved being with Trish. Maybe because she
never had children she travelled a different timeline
than women with children. She was both a strong
adult presence and a fun-loving teenager all tucked
into her little frame.

Women with children had "in your face"
reminders that the years were flying by. One day
you're up to your eyeballs in diapers and screaming
kids wishing *this part* would just be over, and the next
day it would be over. Just like that, you're old and you
better get on with doing those things that you said
you wanted to do all those child-rearing years.

On nights that Dad did the dishes, Trish and I
cranked the stereo and danced to "Jive Talkin'" and
"That's the Way I Like It," singing at the top of our
lungs. She'd kick off her shoes, grab my hands and
jive me around the living room like a pro, her skirt
twirling. We'd then collapse on the sofa, laughing
hysterically and completely out of breath. After a
minute or so, she'd place the needle carefully on
the vinyl, stretch out her hands to me and off we'd
go again. I didn't know it, but Trish let me trust
being happy. I could not have done it without her
permission.

Chapter 25

Sorting Things Out

Jan 9, 1976

Dear Grace,

Sorry I've taken so long to write you. Thank you for the film. I take lots of pictures. This is a picture of Nattie and me at her place after school. We hang out there most afternoons. Her parents work and she has to babysit her little brother who doesn't need babysitting at all.

I'm glad you like your new house. The picture of you in front of the Big House is really nice. Has anyone told you you look like Mum? I miss Lund Harbour and the Big House most of all. I wonder if I'll ever get there again, it's so far away now, but sometimes I have dreams about it.

Christmas was okay, better than last year. We were invited out for dinner so that was nice. Dad likes to cook, surprise surprise. He still doesn't drink at all. He's like a totally different person. Nattie thinks he's neat and funny, she can't imagine him drunk. Sometimes Nattie sleeps over and Dad makes us breakfast.

I don't mind if you call Aunt Joyce, Mum. She's like your mother now, right? I'll call her Aunt Joyce though. What do you call Uncle Brian?

So far there's been no snow here. It's so different. Christmas without snow was weird. There's snow on the mountains and lots of people ski.

I have to keep buying new clothes because I'm growing so fast. Dad says I grow an inch taller every night. I'm taller than any other girl in the school, and taller than most of the boys too, I don't like it.

I'm getting good marks in school. Nattie is fanatical about doing homework so we do it together. It does make a difference. How about you, how are your marks?

That's about all for now – write soon.

Love Maggie xo

I slipped the letter into the mailbox to be transported to a girl I once knew. To a girl that once owned my heart. I was once her defender and protector. Now I was someone she would not recognize on the street and I had no claim over her; I played no role in her life. I was a reminder of a life she once lived, now a vague memory to us both.

Any time I broached the topic of my sister with Nattie, the end result was always the same, as if she had no time for it.

"It's done, Maggie; there's nothing you can do about it. Don't waste your time — it's probably for the best anyway," she'd say curtly.

What Nattie was really saying was, "Think about it the way I think about it," so I'd retaliate with, "Nattie, you sound just like your mum."

This incensed her, but, just in case I was right, she'd soften a bit.

"I bet when you two see each other again, you'll pick up right where you left off."

"That didn't happen when we were together in Toronto."

"Of course not. You were on your way out here and they were going to — what's the name of the place? Lund Harbour?"

"Ya, Lund Harbour." All of a sudden, I felt exhausted. "You're right, there's nothing I can do about anything right now. Do you want to sleep over this weekend?" I said to change the subject.

"Sure, as long as we make time to work on our project."

"Of course, we're gonna get an A+ on that thing!"

February rolled into March. Days got warmer, trees continued blooming, and rain fell profusely. The state of people's bashed up umbrellas was a mystery to me. Also astounding were the number of people wearing cotton sweatshirts while walking in torrential downpours without umbrellas! *How can kids sit in school all day in a soaking wet sweatshirt?*

By this time, my swimming career consisted of watching Nattie, and she continued to destroy her competition. I preferred being dry and warm anyway. From the onlooker's point of view, I had stability, routine, day-to-day predictability. So why did I sense dread? I'd take account of all that was right in my life, and I no longer compared Grace's life to mine. Yet, history dictated that I was living an illusion and the *real life* of Maggie Holm would soon emerge. Maybe when Nattie was away. Maybe when Dad and Trish weren't paying attention. With supports gone I was easy prey.

Practicing Dr. Beth's thought-stopping skills offered a moment's reprieve, but the doom in my belly was relentless. Days and weeks passed uneventfully. Nevertheless, I did not "branch out" as Nattie said I should.

"It's not right that you just come and watch me swim. Don't you want to get involved with something?" she said impatiently.

"Sure I do, I just don't know what yet. I'm gonna get a summer job. Are you?"

"Hell no — don't you know that once you start working you will NEVER stop. That's it. You'll get a taste of that money and you're hooked."

"I like working. I miss babysitting and making money. I want a job for the rest of my life. What's wrong with that?"

It wasn't easy sticking up for myself when conversing with Nattie. It also shook up my equilibrium; couldn't she see I needed downtime? I just couldn't be on the go every minute of the day. It struck me then how little she actually knew about my life prior to meeting her. Sharing how Mum died was out of the question — the girl had far too much to say about everything and I just didn't want to hear it. She never witnessed Dad drunk. She even said to me once when I mentioned Grace that she kept forgetting I had a sister.

What was I to her? What was she to me?

. . .

The phone rang, but I let the machine pick up.

"It's me, Trish," she said as if I didn't know her voice by now. I chuckled. "I know you're not home, just leaving a message. I'm gonna visit Jack later today, thought I might pop by after, you know, if that works for you. Think Phil's away; would love to see you and Jeff. I'm aware of what day it is, just thinking of you. Let me know either way. Ta-ta for now."

As close and loving as Trish was and still is, she never did assume the position of being my mother. She was an anomaly and said that some of the decisions she made, like never marrying or having children, ended many relationships with girlfriends over the years.

"Of course they wanted to be with other women that had children. I sure wasn't going to hang out in a park full of screaming kids, so relationships ended. It took two of us, but my feelings did get hurt — can't deny it."

I secretly bought her Mother's Day cards but was afraid to give them to her; afraid she'd not accept them and I'd be hurt. For many years, I struggled with her "mother role boundaries" and took it as personal rejection that I wasn't daughter material. Now I realize the woman was simply living her life on her own terms for whatever reasons. She'd been as stable as a rock, and faithful to Dad, Grace and me to this day. She is as much a wife and mother as anyone I've known. It was Trish that came to my rescue time and time again without hesitation or hysteria. One time in particular solidified our lifelong bond.

Halfway through Grade 10, my emotions caught up with my hormones. Up until then, my only experience of menstruation was a monthly bloody nuisance. Prior to Grade 10, the smiling, nodding, winking boys lurking around the corners of the school were more repulsive than attractive. Then I saw Coal — even his name made me swoon. Coal Mathews, Coal Sebastian Mathews. *Maggie Mathews* had a nice ring to it, I thought. Nattie didn't think so.

Coal was born years after his two older sisters, who were now both living on their own. According to Coal, he was a "pleasant surprise" for his parents. I didn't know what that meant other than he was a pleasant surprise and I would make sure to tell our children that they, too, were pleasant surprises; I liked the sound of it.

Coal, the quintessential tall, dark, handsome Grade 11 male, wore glasses that set him apart from the others. Behind those glasses were light green eyes, clear like glass. Our first kiss took place under a tree on the way home from school. I was cold and he held his coat open for me to join him up against his warm body. He smelled of school and soap. I could hardly breathe with passion. He took off his glasses, shoving them in his pocket, then looked deeply into my eyes. I was swallowed up into the green. He was taller than me — not many boys were. The kiss was the first time for me, not for him. At first, it was a soft, mouth-closed connection. We each pulled away slightly and then went back for another slightly open-lipped kiss. Again, we pulled away, but then there was a full-on open-mouth, tongue-touching union. My knees buckled. I wanted to lie down. It was only a matter of time.

Chapter 26

A Day in Mid-August

Nattie was incensed that I had succumbed to the likes of Coal Mathews.

"Are you out of your mind?" she asked as if I was actually out of my mind.

In truth, I clearly was. Coal Mathews' name was written a hundred different ways on every square inch of every notebook I owned.

"Do you know how many girls he's had sex with Maggie? If you knew, you'd be disgusted."

I had no intention of having sex with him, and he didn't want me for that anyway. But I was intrigued by the fact that he had experience. *Where are these girls now? He doesn't want them, he wants me — he's chosen me.*

"Nattie, how come you say you want to be married, not work, let your husband take care of you, but everything you do is about getting good marks and ignoring boys?"

I felt a new sense of confidence now that Coal Mathews' tongue had been in my mouth. Nattie looked exasperated.

"You just don't get it, do you?"

"What? What don't I get?"

"I'm not just going to marry some dumb sex-craved asshole with a Grade 2 education. I will work, obviously; I'm not going to marry someone right out of high school. I'll work in a really great high-paying job and most likely go into law. I'll meet an educated man where I work or where I network. We'll marry, have children and so on …"

She seemed to lose interest in her own life plan as she laid it out in front of me like fake peanut butter on white bread.

"What's network?" I responded, thinking about Coal.

"Networking is where you meet people that are in the same business or industry as you are and you talk about your work and other people that share the same interests or employment opportunities as you," she said like it came out of her mother's mouth.

"Oh," I said. I didn't understand a word, but I pictured a group of nurses talking about other nurses.

I began to see Nattie in a different light. She was brilliant, no doubt about that. And yes, she would meet another brilliant person to share a life with, but right there, in her bedroom, watching her organize her desk for the evening's homework, I felt sorry for her.

"I've already been told I'll get to any university I want on a swimming scholarship, so I'm taking advantage of that, of course," she said, shuffling books.

"Yeah, that's so great," I said, realizing that everyone struggles and doubts.

Nattie hung onto her future plans to keep her stable, and why not? If I knew anything, I knew to hold onto those people and things that offered stability. Did Nattie have more faith than me in those people and things? Most likely. Faith is not part of reality for a girl whose mother's suicide rips the earth out from under her and drops her into a hole with no bottom.

Amongst our approved topics of conversation, Coal was not one of them. What had been a perfect arrangement between two friends was now deficient. It was a natural parting of the ways. Nattie spent her time swimming and studying. I spent my time improving my necking with Coal, which consisted of receiving and giving hickeys. We were interrupted more than once with, "That'll be enough of that, you two. Move along," said by a "jealous" teacher, or so Coal would say. I was slightly embarrassed about my hickeys when I wasn't with Coal; they were out of place somehow. It was Trish who addressed them. The newspaper lay open on our kitchen table where she sat. She gazed at it and absentmindedly said, "Who's neck art are you wearing"?

"What do you mean?" I responded, honestly forgetting about the latest blood sucked into the tissue of my neck.

Trish raised her head and tapped the side of her own neck with a disapproving look.

"Oh, oh that … my turtleneck was … uh … too tight."

I wanted to evaporate. She'd never looked at me like that before. I wanted to say, "I'm sorry," but the words wouldn't come out. She went back to her newspaper. The very next day she handed me a book all about sex and contraception. It would have been extremely helpful had I read it, but good grief, I wasn't having sex and I had no intention of having sex probably until I was married — or at least engaged. And I loved Coal so much for never pushing me or even talking about it. And we never did talk about it, even that summer.

Nattie's dedication to us doing homework together had paid off and I was an honours student at the end of Grade 10. I had a clear plan for my grades eleven and twelve years that would lead me straight into nurses' training. I landed a summer job at the local recreation centre that was running kids camps and Coal worked for the municipality, weeding the city gardens. This meant we both had every evening and weekend together, except when he went away with his family. At which time I awaited his return.

It was a hot mid-August day. At the end of a long hike in the Demonstration Forest, Coal and I arrived at a popular swimming hole. It was busy. We spoke very little, which wasn't unusual, but agreed to find a less populated space. He pulled his beach towel from his backpack, placing it just so on the tall grass in our secluded spot. He then laid my towel beside his.

"Let's go for a swim," he said, sweat permeating his clothes.

I removed my clothes and showed off my new bikini.

"Holy shit," Coal said with a smile as he ripped off his T-shirt.

He grabbed my hand and we ran to the water's edge. He didn't hesitate, just dove under. He then walked straight out, picked me up and walked us both in, me squealing with delight. Our bodies touched, skin to skin, wet. We kissed above and below the water. It was intoxicating. I was intoxicated.

He led me out and indicated to lay down on the towels. He lay beside me and carefully dried my face. He started kissing me, my neck — a slight tug on my skin.

"Don't do that, I don't want a hickey." My voice sounded stark and out of place.

He moved along quickly. I thought of Trish. He was at my collarbone, shoulder, just above my breast, back to my mouth while he untied my bikini top and placed his hand on my bare back. No one had ever rested their open palm on my back as if they loved me. I succumbed to it.

Then he slowly moved his hand across my ribs to just under my breast. I thought I might faint with pleasure. He then cupped my breast in his hand and circled my nipple with his thumb. Till now he had only "felt me up" over my clothes; this was nothing like that. He stopped kissing me. I opened my eyes, he met my gaze, he then sat up.

"What's wrong?" I asked.

"I don't have anything."

"You don't have any what?" A fleeting thought crossed my mind that maybe he didn't have a penis.

"Safes."

"Oh," I said. "Well, we'll just do what we're doing then."

I sat up to meet him, mostly so I could cover my breasts. I had no thought of going all the way anyway; second base was as far as we'd go.

"Oh geez," he said, laying me down and resuming where he left off. He sucked my nipples and threw me into a frenzy. He placed his hand just above my bikini bottoms and then slowly under the rim; my legs instinctively parted. His finger slid easily inside and I rose to meet it, wanting more. He then untied the bikini strings. I lay completely naked under the warm sun, his eyes on me. He slid off his swimming shorts and maneuvered his body on top of me. He was wet and cold; I didn't like it, this was too fast, I didn't know what was happening — didn't know how to stop it. I was confused and afraid. The feeling of his erect penis touching my thigh was odd, almost hideous. He continued kissing me but wasn't paying attention. He struggled to support his body on one arm, trying to kiss me while guiding his penis into me with the other hand.

"no," I whispered, placing my hands on the front of his shoulders in an attempt to push him back.

His weight and size held my legs apart. And with that, my insides ripped open like a truck had rammed up inside me. I yelled out in pain. Coal put his hand over my mouth and said, "Shhhhh!" I couldn't breathe, and I violently shook my head from side to side until he took his hand away.

"Don't yell," he said as he continued to shred my insides seemingly without concern.

I smashed my lips together to keep noise from escaping. Tears streamed down the sides of my face. Finally he stopped and then kissed the tears off my temples. He felt heavy on top of me. I took a deep breath in, coaxing him to get off. He lay on his back beside me, his penis now soft with traces of blood, my blood. I was cold, shaking, numb. I sat up, saw blood between my legs and on the towel.

"Are you okay?"

I couldn't look at him. I felt raw. "I'm cold."

I reached for my bikini and kept my back to him. My hands shook as I attempted to sort out the strings. He put his hand on my back. It was warm.

"It only hurts the first time," he said, turning onto his side and raising himself up on one elbow. "Come lay beside me for a while."

I looked at him over my shoulder. He had covered himself with his towel. Not so scary now. I was wet between my legs and didn't know what to do with myself. Coal reached for his T-shirt and said, "Here, put this on. It's hot from the sun." I remained sitting with my back to him. I didn't want anything from him, but I was cold and needed to cover myself quickly, so I slipped his warm shirt over my head.

"Here," he said, patting the towel beside him. "Lay down here for a while beside me."

I lay down on my back and stared up at the unforgiving sky. It saw everything, I felt ashamed. Coal blocked my view with his face. His hair was messy, his skin blotchy. He kissed me, but it was different.

"You okay? It stopped hurting right?"

It occurred to me that, due to his age, he had most likely had sex with only virgins. He was well versed in the experience.

"I'm fine."

I remained on my back, looking at the sky. He laid on his back beside me.

"You'll see, once you get over the first time, it'll be good. You'll like having sex."

Oh God, I'm never doing that again.

"I think we should get back," I said.

"Why? Your dad's not home and it's still early. Why don't we go for another swim?" "I'm still cold, I don't want to swim. But I'll wait here in the sun if you want to. Then we can go home, okay?"

"Ya, sure, okay."

Cole easily slipped his bathing suit on, stood and headed for the water, which he again entered without hesitation. He was a strong swimmer and did methodical crawl strokes to the other side of the swimming hole where he got out to sit on the rocks. In the meantime, I used my towel to clean myself and assess any damage.

Everything looked as usual, maybe a little reddened. It was the inside that told a different story, along with confusion about what had just happened. Of course, I knew we had had sex, but something was terribly wrong. For some reason, I thought of Nattie.

I managed to get my bikini tied up, it was mostly dry. I finished dressing, brushed my hair and started to feel calmer; a slight recognition of my former self rallied. I rolled up my towel to hide the evidence like a crime had been committed, only I was hiding the evidence from the perpetrator.

Once the dirty little secret was out of sight, I walked to the water's edge to wade. Coal looked pensive as he sat on the rocks, and I wondered if he regretted what he had done. I didn't want him to feel bad; I mean, obviously, I let it go to far. I splashed my hands in the water to catch his eye. As if I had woken him out of a dream, he looked up at me, quizzically concerned. I smiled at him, *All better*. He waved in relief and swam back to me.

The truth of what had just happened was already tucked away in the "secrets" part of my brain. The only way to keep it there was for him to be my boyfriend. And as it turned out, Coal was right; it didn't hurt after that, and it was good. I liked having sex. We proved this to each other every single time we were together — mostly at my place after Dad and Trish left for the night. They never knew. Coal arrived after they left and was gone by morning. He climbed out and in his bedroom window so his parents knew nothing either. Secrets abounded.

Chapter 27

Life Lessons

It was Trish, the closest to a mother I had, that I told. Would my own mother have been available for me? I couldn't imagine it. Like ether, she continued to vanish into emptiness.

"What's up, honey pie?"

I had Trish's full attention. Wasn't sure if I wanted it. *Maybe I should wait to see if it goes away.*

"Okay — what's the matter?" she asked, taking a step closer seeing the weight on my shoulders, my hands shaking. I cried at the sight of them. "You can tell me anything, you know," she said in a much more serious tone. I looked at her and she nodded. "Anything."

"I'm pregnant," I said, attempting to hold in a volcanic sob that escaped anyway.

She went pale and said, "What makes you think that?"

"I'm late and I'm sick in the morning." I dropped my head. "I'm sorry." Another loud sob. "I didn't read the book you gave me — till ... after. If I did, this wouldn't be happening. I'm so sorry."

Trish sat down and tapped her fingers on the table, not looking at me. I'd never seen her this way: focused, determined. I remained quiet and kept a distance. I'd caused a lot of trouble and she never wanted to be a mother in the first place.

"I should have guessed," she said more to herself. "I could see what that boy was up to."

At one time I'd have defended Coal, but I didn't dare, even though I wore a bikini, giving him the wrong message.

"Should have got you on the pill." She was thinking out loud.

"I could have got myself on the pill — doctors will do that," I said. "I read that in the book."

Still looking straight ahead she asked, "Does he know?"

"Yes. He thinks we should get married."

I was terrified that Trish would agree.

"Oh for heaven's sake!" she said, standing up, lips thin, colour returning to her face. She slipped her high heels off as if they distracted her from thinking. "We'll need to talk to your father."

My eyes widened. "Please, no! I really don't want him to know," I said, panicked at the thought.

"Of course he needs to know — you're his daughter."

Not mine is what she was saying.

"I beg of you — don't tell Dad." *Could I not have a secret of my own?*

"This is a drastic thing you're asking of me, young lady."

Trish was angry — at me. I'd never seen her angry at anyone. I dared not say one word. She sighed and looked to the heavens for guidance, her face lined with concern, jaw tight. I felt guilty; she didn't deserve this.

"I'll make a call. You'll need to see a doctor quickly. Depending on how far along you are will determine if you can have an abortion or not. And if not —" she looked at me abruptly, "you'll be having this baby and giving it up for adoption." She paused, and I could feel the gravity of the situation, "And abortions are expensive; I don't have that kind of money."

"How much?"

She didn't answer.

"Coal has some money," I said.

She looked at me with fire in her eyes at the mention of his name.

"He's been saving for a car," I said sheepishly.

"Good, he'll pay for this!"

In more ways than one.

The appointment was made, and it was to cost $5000. Coal saw his car fly out the window. If I was early stages in the first weeks, the procedure would take place right then and there.

"This will all happen after hours. You'll be visiting the doctor in the evening, and he'll want his money before he does anything. And who's going to look after you ... after?" Trish said, shaking. I had put her in a terrible position.

"Coal will take care me and he can stay here the night. He can sleep on the couch. I'm sorry — I don't know why. I just don't want Dad involved."

I was talking fast, so scared. Why was I concerned about disappointing him? I didn't want to deal with his reaction. He was unpredictable. I'd never seen him really angry, but I didn't want to be the one that sent him back to the bottle.

"All right," Trish relinquished, "but just let me say this: If anything happens to you, I will never forgive myself and I will never be the same."

That's something a mother would say, I'm sure.

"And God knows what your father would think of me."

"I'm sorry — I've made a mess of everything."

Trish did not offer comfort in her usual way, meaning she agreed. I had made a mess of everything.

Coal picked me up at eight. It was already dark, the fall fast approaching. We drove in silence to a small office building. An older man was waiting for us at the door.

"Hello, Maggie, come in. I'm the doctor and I'll be examining you this evening." He looked at Coal. "Do you have the money?"

Coal handed him the $5000. He may have had tears in his eyes. The doctor counted it quickly. I felt sick and cold. Coal put his arm around me, I shifted slightly and he dropped his arm.

"You have a seat right there," the doctor said, pointing to a chair. "Maggie, come with me, please."

I followed him down a dimly lit hall into a small, bright room. There were no documents on the walls indicating his name and that he was, in fact, a doctor, but I trusted Trish explicitly.

"Leave on your top, but take off your pants and underwear please. Put this gown on backwards, lie down here and put this blanket over you. I'll be back in a minute."

Even though Trish had done a pretty good job of coaching me, I was terrified; this was the real thing. I read about women dying from having abortions. And this was no blanket, it was a paper sheet and offered me no comfort except for hiding my naked lower half. There was a faint knock on the door and I started to say, "Come —" but he just walked in anyway.

"Okay, Maggie. Do you know what to expect during this procedure?"

I opened my mouth to answer, but he grabbed my ankle and said, "Just put your foot in the stirrup here, right here."

I couldn't see where my foot was meant to go, so he tried to direct it into the stirrup but I wasn't letting him. Eventually I surrendered and the cold metal bracket hit the bottom of my foot.

"Now the other foot here. Yes, that's it, almost. Right there, good."

My legs were spread open and it felt somewhat like preparation to be tortured. The doctor lifted the sheet to expose my privates right at eye level to him. I was horrified. The sheet folded over on top of my knees, keeping the goings on down there out of my sight, thank God.

"Okay now, just slide down the bed a bit here, now. Yes, that's it, just a bit more now, yes. Keep coming Maggie, almost there. Okay, a bit more, just keep sliding down, only once more. There, that's perfect. Okay, I'm just going to examine you."

This meant his fingers of one hand would slide inside me while he palpated my belly with the other hand. Being poked and prodded by a stranger was horrible. I felt so alone — completely alone — enduring something I knew I was too young to be going through. *You have no choice. It's your own fault.* I dared not cry; the guy had no time for that. I wanted a secret of my own? Well, I got it.

The doctor with no name was saying words to me that I could not interpret, but they required affirmations that I understood.

"This will feel a bit cold and uncomfortable; do you understand?"

"Yes."

Trish had told me I'd have a D & C if early enough in my first trimester. It seemed I was early enough. The speculum was cold and unforgiving. I floated to the ceiling. I saw myself laying on the bed of paper, feet in stirrups, the top of the doctor's head as his hands worked between my legs. He continued to talk the entire time, explaining everything he was doing. What it would feel like, why he was doing this and that. I politely affirmed after each statement.

I was scraped clean, the baby material scoured away. Two visions entered my brain simultaneously: my mother lying dead and Coal's hand over my mouth, "Shhhhh." I wept silently.

Coal jumped to his feet when we rounded the corner. He was so young, just a boy. Dr. No-Name asked to speak to him privately. I was to wait in the waiting room, and I sipped tea from a thermos prepared before I arrived. Ten minutes later, they reappeared. Coal looked sheepish and afraid.

"Maggie, thanks for waiting. Come with me, please, just for a minute; bring your tea."

I stood and followed obediently. Coal sat down and shut up obediently.

"How are you feeling?"

"Okay," I said, nodding reassuringly.

"I've informed your boyfriend there's to be no sex for a month."

"Oh, there'll be no sex at —"

"You must watch out for infection and bleeding. You'll know something is wrong if there is an offensive odour or yellowish discharge. You MUST contact me right away at this number." He handed me a small piece of paper with a number scrawled on it. "I will call you in the morning at 8 a.m. Will you be available to answer the phone?"

"Yes," I answered because that's all he wanted to hear from me. And I'd be damn sure I'd be there to answer. This guy meant business.

"Okay, Maggie. You should be okay now."

Code for "You are no longer pregnant."

Coal quickly stood again when we entered the waiting room — as if his life depended on his behaviour. The lights had been turned off. Coal was a shadow figure. Dr. No-Name opened the door wide and stood still, silently indicating for us to leave quickly and quietly.

The night air was freezing. It was strange sitting beside Coal in this parents' car waiting for heat. Heat was the thing we needed most, but to talk about heat seemed trivial considering what had just happened.

After a long silence, Coal asked, "Was it terrible?" His voice was hoarse and scared.

"I guess so — kind of terrible."

I didn't want to think about it and sure didn't want to talk to him about it. I felt guilty. Guilty for getting pregnant and dragging him through this and using his money for an abortion. But not guilty enough to accommodate his feelings.

"You look okay," he said, smiling like he could jump me if I was into it.

I wanted to jump out of the car, but I found some words.

"Maybe you love me. Maybe I love you. I don't know. But this was terrible. It was terrible for me, for Trish and for you. And for the potential baby." Tears choked in my throat. Coal gripped the wheel, bracing for what he knew was coming. "I need some time. I need a break. We need to break up."

I couldn't believe I actually said those words, but they were true. I wasn't mad, I was sad. It was a loss. Another loss. He said nothing. I dared to glimpse at him in the oncoming headlights. Tears were streaming down his cheeks. I stayed on my own that night and cried myself to sleep.

. . .

The stench of urine assaulted my nose upon entering the extended care unit where my father now resided. I spotted him sitting in his geriatric chair, his hospital gown falling off his bony shoulder. Something from lunch was congealed in his spiky white whiskers. His sticky, cold hands gripped the table in front of him as if he were taking off in a rocket.

"Hi Dad," I said, bending to kiss his scaly bald head, but changed my mind before making contact. No response. A bad day. "Let's get you fixed up a bit for Trish," I said, slowly pulling the chair from behind.

At the slightest movement, Dad gripped the table harder and attempted to let out a yell, which sounded like a whisper.

"It's okay, Dad. It's Maggie, just Maggie," I said in an attempt to trigger a memory. This meant nothing to him. Emptying catheter bags, cleaning dentures, washing people's bottoms was nothing for me, and doing this for my father felt natural.

"Let's put on your blue sweater, Dad. It'll bring out your sparkly blue eyes," that were now a dull gray. His lively eyes had disappeared incrementally as Alzheimer's laid claim to his mind. "Come on there, old fellow, lift your arm up so I can pull this sweater on." He resisted, then let a punch fly, connecting squarely with my left breast.

"JESUS DAD!"

He looked at me as if to say, *Come on then, try me.* Tears spilled down my cheeks — they always seemed so close to the surface. After regaining my composure, I bent down to eye level, keeping just the right amount of distance.

"Dad, it's Maggie, it's me — remember me, Maggie? Come on then, it's okay, I'm not going to hurt you. I just want to put this sweater on you, Jack."

I kept cooing to him, and he lifted his arm with less resistance. I attempted a shave, put his dentures in and propped his baseball cap on his head. He was ready.

By the time Trish arrived, he was sound asleep in his chair, top denture resting peacefully on his lower lip. Trish stopped in her tracks to admire his outfit.

"Oh Maggie, he's so cute. This could not have been easy to do," she said, looking pleased.

"Well, it's my own fault, but I should have a good bruise on my left breast by this evening. Really, I'm fine," I said, rubbing my breast with one hand and waving away her concern with the other.

"I'm sure on some level that he appreciates looking dapper," she said, reaching for my arm to comfort and acknowledge my sacrifice.

Trish had not changed that much over the years. She was a similar version of her younger self, a bit shorter, tinier frame, hair thinner and pure white. But her fashion had changed. She loved leotards and long sweaters in various colours. She called them her "daytime pajamas." Taking a seat on his bed, she launched right in, wasting no time. "What's your plan — do you have one?"

She, of course, was referring to me telling Grace the truth about Mum's suicide.

"Sort of." Mum's angelic vision and my graveyard visit had contributed to a sense of ease I couldn't explain. "I'm going to kind of wing it. I don't know how it's going to go. I know I'm telling her, but I don't know exactly what I'll say or how I'll say it. I know I won't fight with her. I'm just winging it." I shrugged.

"Sounds just fine to me," she said, looking for signs of Jack awakening.

"Ya, I feel relaxed. I hope it's not the calm before the storm, but it feels different. I guess we'll see."

"Jack, wake up honey. It's Trish, and Maggie's here too." she said, gently rubbing his arms in an attempt to stimulate some life into his body. She then pulled out her iPod, placed the buds in his hairy ears and selected "Jack's Favourites" from her playlists. His lower jaw involuntarily slammed shut on his upper denture. It must have hurt because he grunted and opened his eyes.

"Hi Jack," Trish said, putting her smiling face squarely in front of his. "Are you enjoying the music?"

He closed his eyes and we shared a knowing look that said, *It's such a shame and so sad*. She held his hand and admired it. The hand that once held hers.

"Well, fiddly-dee," she said, sniffing back a tear.

In ways, it was if my father had lived his whole life with a touch of Alzheimer's, never really communicating or connecting with anyone in a deep way. Without food and cooking, I doubt we'd have found anything much to talk about. He and Trish shared something only the two of them understood. I know Trish felt frustrated with him at times for not talking to me about certain things that I had to find out on my own. Yet Trish herself seemed to need very little in the way of meaningful conversation. I never got the impression she felt she was doing without or settling for less. I wondered if Dad's passion for love and life burned with Elsa. Did he ever laugh out loud with delight as he picked up his young bride to spin her around in his arms? I hoped so and doubted it at the same time. What you saw is what you got with my dad.

Chapter 28

Interlude at Summer Camp

Coal was sworn to secrecy. Trish had an amazing power over him that I admired and wanted to emulate. She told him he was not to breathe a word of our having sex, the pregnancy and subsequent abortion or there would be "consequences." In confidence, she told me she didn't have a clue what she would do, but he didn't need to know that. Coal was terrified to even look at me, but on occasion I caught him staring, and what would have once sent me running into his arms now repulsed me.

Girls at school, pretending to be my friends, would sympathetically ask me about Coal. *Why had I broken up with him? What happened? Was I okay? He's such a jerk. Didn't he know what a good thing he had with me?* They reeked of bullshit. They soon tired of my evasiveness, and my refusal to engage in the gossip bored them. Like the vultures they were, they turned their attention to Coal, who was now … available.

Trish suggested I go on the pill to regulate my periods. Even though I didn't have a boyfriend nor did I want one, after what I put us through, I willingly went on the pill. In the summer between grades eleven and twelve, I met Jo at a kids' summer camp. He was a first-year university student, handsome, rugged and fun-loving.

It was wonderful to be close to another human again. No wonder sex is so popular with teens. Never mind the raging hormones, it's the closeness, the sense of touch. Why are we not touched after the age of twelve when we need it most? How many fathers stop embracing their daughters because of their own screwed up issues. Other than a peck on the forehead, holding my hand at Mum's gravesite and grasping my wrist when telling me about my near-death experience, I cannot recall Dad touching me at all.

Two months of summer camp gave Jo and me little time to establish a relationship. Soon after we had acknowledged our attraction to one another with flirtatious eye contact, he invited me to join him for breakfast the following morning. He arrived at the dining hall before me and waved me over to the back corner where we'd have some privacy. I spotted another couple already paired up, giggling and sipping coffee. We had forty-five minutes before the place would be jammed with rambunctious ten-year-old kids.

"Good morning, Maggie May," he said, testing me out to see if I'd accept his nickname for me.

"Good morning Jo, how'd you sleep?" I said, sliding in beside him.

He'd dished up plates of food and set the table.

"I slept well, and you?" He looked at me square in the eyes. "You're tall," he said as if I didn't know.

"Yes, yes I am — take after my Dad's side —Swede."

"Ah, well I now know something about you. What would you like to know about me?"

"Well, let's see. What brings you to summer camp?"

"Nice one. Hate to say it, but I need the volunteer hours for my program; going into pre-med all the way across Canada, Dalhousie in Halifax."

My heart sank. *He's leaving.* "That's where I'm from — moved to BC a few years ago."

"Really? What brought you to BC?"

"My father's work." He sensed a shift in my demeanour, my smile gone. "And what brings *you* to summer camp?" he asked, knowing it was a safe question.

"I love kids; I'm happiest being around them," I said, still recovering from the news of a pending loss at the end of summer.

"Ya, I love kids too — plan to specialize, pediatrics."

"Pretty sure I'll go into nursing," I offered, picturing us working together in the same hospital. *Maybe this could work.*

"Ahh, beauty *and* brains. How about going all the way?" he trailed off, realizing what he had just said. We shared a smile. "No, I meant, why don't you go all the way to get your MD?"

"You wanna pay for it" I asked, taking a bite of my toast with jam. *Let's just see what happens. Present time. What's in front of me.* He looked at his watch. *Jo's in front of me.*

"Five more quiet minutes. I think we're hitting it off, Maggie May."

I nodded in agreement, still chewing.

"Shall we dine right here in this very spot this evening?" He flashed me a smile.

Go for it Maggie.

"Thank you, Jo. I accept your invitation." I flashed him a smile right back.

We spotted each other throughout the day with our group of kids heading to the lake or looking for pinecones or shaping clay pots. We shared a smile knowing we were on each other's mind no matter where we were or what we were doing. When the day was finally over and the kids in their bunks in the capable hands of their cabin leader, we met for dinner as planned. He beat me again — the table set, water poured.

"Hi, let's get our food, I'm starving," he said.

Strange, I should be hungry but my stomach is full of butterflies — no room for food. But I'd eat!

"Gosh I love camp food. Made right here, fresh!" Jo said, slurping spaghetti.

"How'd your day go? Great bunch of kids, eh? Some so shy and others full of beans."

"Really good bunch this time around. So far no bullies," he said, slowing down and watching me twirl a small mouth-sized bite around my fork.

"Mmm, this is good spaghetti. My sister used to pronounce spaghetti 'sgapetti.'"

"Cute," he responded, watching his rolled-up spaghetti fall off his fork. I cracked up. "You having fun there, Maggie May. Wanna do something after dinner?"

"Like what?"

"Well, depends."

"On what?"

"If you'd like to make love — with me?" he added with a smile.

"Wow, I've never been asked that before," I said, taken aback.

"Have I insulted you?"

"No, of course not. Just the opposite, just surprised — to be asked."

"If you're not asked, Maggie, then you're not with a gentleman. Wise words from my mother."

"Very wise Mum."

We then sat in silence. The writing was on the wall. Jo was leaving. It's as if we'd broken up before we even began.

"I think you might be feeling pressured. We can wait — and we don't need to at all, if that's what you'd like."

Where did this guy come from? I tore off a piece of garlic bread with my teeth and said, "Well, this *is* our first date — a little fast, wouldn't you say?"

"That is true, and under normal circumstances I'd not be so forward, but I'd really like to get to know you and spend as much time with you as I possibly can."

"Because you're moving to Nova Scotia?" There, I said it.

"Kind of hard to make love when we're opposite ends of the country, but I have no intention of ending what appears to be a blossoming union."

Union? What does that mean? More silence. I looked at him, was very attracted. He looked at me, smiled. Then I smiled. There was no turning back. I sipped the last of my coffee.

"So you'll write me and we'll talk on the phone once a week?" I half-heartedly said, laying down some ground rules that let him know this was more than a summer fling for me.

"At least once a week," he said reassuringly. "And a trip home at Christmas."

Why couldn't it work? Kiss him. I kissed him.

"Okay," I said.

He kissed me and tenderly put his hand on the side of my neck. He had a gentle touch, and I fell under his spell. We dumped our dishes into the bucket, Jo grabbed a rag from the kitchen staff and wiped down our table, reached for my hand and off we went to his cabin. As we walked, Jo established a few ground rules of his own.

"Are you on the pill?"

This wasn't his first rodeo; I once heard someone use that expression, think it was Nattie, about Coal.

"Yes," I answered, "to regulate my periods," I added, not wanting him to think that I slept around.

His eyebrows went up. "Don't be offended, but have you had sex before?"

Wow, this guy left no stone unturned. "Why is that important to you?" I decided to match his comfort level with the topic.

"Good question," he said, smiling. "If you're a virgin, we'll not be engaging in any love making."

"Why not?" I persisted. *Inexperienced, might fall in love?*

"No one's ever asked me that — not sure I even have an answer. Not comfortable being someone's first, I guess." He looked at me as if he was surprised I'd asked him a question that he didn't have an answer for.

"So you've never been someone's first? Interesting that it doesn't matter to me if you're a virgin. What if I was your first?" I asked, very feministic like.

"I'd be thanking the Lord above for sending me an angel."

Flattery.

"But just in case you're wondering, I'm not." He winked. "Oh, should also let you know that I use condoms — STDs — want to keep you safe."

I nodded. *He's thought of everything.*

He was nothing like Coal. Coal and I only had sex as common ground in our relationship whereas Jo was worldly, inquisitive, interested and interesting. He lived life to its fullest, seemingly absorbing the best it had to offer. He had the kind of personality that made me feel like the most important person in the world in his presence, giving his full attention to me and only me.

Love making was its own entity, the complete opposite of sex, in my experience. It came as a pleasant surprise that he was happy and content to lie together, spooning, afterwards. It was then that he'd ask me questions, it seemed, at my most vulnerable.

"Tell me more about yourself. What was life like for you in Halifax? What's your sister up to?"

I froze. He noticed. He lifted his head off the pillow in an attempt to look at my face. "Okay ... not a good question. Let's see, you ask me something."

I didn't like this game. "I have to pee, sorry, be right back."

He was up and dressed when I returned. He put his arms around me and gave me a reassuring kiss. I smiled and dressed in silence.

"I'll walk you home," he said, opening the door for me.

He had a wonderful way of lightening the mood, but I knew his inquisitive nature would not let me off the hook. We rendezvoused in his cabin almost every night for the entire summer. I got closer to telling Jo the truth than anyone else in my life up to that point, except Dr. Beth. Every night together felt like the first; making love was like that.

"I want to lie on your hair; I'm gonna pull it over my pillow, but don't let me hurt you, though." He used his fingers to comb my hair across his pillow, then slowly lay his head down. "Feel okay?"

"Uh-huh."

"Your hair smells delicious."

"You must like that campfire smell,"

We lay in silence with our eyes open. He wanted to talk.

"How'd your Mum die?"

"It was a tragic death, Jo. I don't want to say more than that. It was sudden, unexpected and tragic."

"Got it. I'm sorry that happened to you. You were young."

"I still am."

He pulled me closer and tenderly kissed the back of my shoulder. I had never felt so cared for, or about, by a man. I sensed this was truly him, sensitive and attentive; he'd be a wonderful doctor. But we never spoke about us as a couple. When he talked about his future life plans, I was not included in his story. So when I talked about my future, I didn't include him, although I would have willingly. As the end of camp fast approached, I started to panic. He seemed so aloof. The exact opposite of my panic.

"Mmmm, I can't believe this is our last time together," he said, pulling me close for one of many last kisses.

He didn't say, "Until Christmas."

"Me too."

I silently wept. I had come to love him, of course.

"Oh, don't be sad, Maggie May. Wasn't this the best summer of your life? It's been my best summer ever. No one can take that away from us. You have a special place in my heart, you always will."

He might as well have put his hand over my mouth and said, "Shhhhh."

I wanted to scream, "WHAT THE FUCK ARE YOU TALKING ABOUT? WHAT DOES THAT MEAN? YOU'RE FULL OF SHIT!" But I didn't. I just panicked inside, heartbroken again. If he knew, he didn't let on.

Our final kisses goodbye were unbearably painful for me and, I believe, a dutiful pretense for Jo. Maybe he was full of shit all summer. I was relieved I'd not told him everything. There were promises of letters and phone calls, but his words held no truth; he spoke them to the wind and they blew away.

To this day, when I think of Jo the MD, he hasn't aged. He's climbing some mountain in some far away, exotic place in the world, telling some girl she will always have a special place in his heart. But she'd be on the pill and he'd wear a condom; no diseases and no kids.

Chapter 29

What We Inherit

The new school year started at a hell of a pace. Past experiences, like I'd forgotten to finish something important, crept into my thoughts. The constant reminders of what I once had were relentless: a mother, a home, a friend named Penny, a sister, and Jo. The reminders came to me unannounced with a shock as if forgetting them for a moment meant I could lose them all over again.

My course load was heavy, sciences and math. Nattie's discipline with homework continued to stick with me and I worked hard. Even though I was approached to join various school clubs, I kept to myself. It seemed to me with each involvement with another person came the burden of heartbreak. I had lost too much, and I was clearly grieving the "relationship that never was" with Jo.

I worked part-time at a stationery store. It was stress free: Show up to work, stock shelves, ring in people's purchases and go home. The routine of dinner together at home with Dad and Trish was something I looked forward to. Trish was an expert at getting me to talk. In her non-threatening way, she'd seek my opinion about something. "What's your opinion about private schools versus public?" she might ask, and before I knew it I'd be spilling my guts. How I felt about a teacher, the kids in my class, my grades, future plans, graduation, worries, fears, anxieties ... that woman was a genius. Even though Dad contributed little to the conversations, he'd listen, nod his head or crack a smile; I had his attention. After these shared dinners together, I felt better. The weight of the day's events evaporated, and this allowed me to focus on homework. Dad was one lucky man.

May 22, 1979

Dear Maggie,

I was cleaning out my dresser drawers this morning and found my writing paper that you gave me for Christmas, so now I'm writing you. Aunt Joyce said we should try to keep writing even if we don't have much to say. I know Dad and Aunt Joyce talk about once a month. I don't know if you know I was sick. I'm okay, don't worry, I'm getting better. Apparently I was depressed, or am depressed. I'm on medication. No one knew what was going on with me. I just couldn't get out of bed, I slept all the time and wasn't eating, so I ended up in the hospital for a week. I remember the same thing happened to you. I see Dr. Weller he's a psychiatrist. It's already hard for me to remember, but Aunt Joyce told me that Mum was depressed too. I remember her sleeping a lot. The medication seems to be helping. My periods make it worse even on medication I just stay in bed for 2 days. No one at school knows.

I missed a lot of school so have to go to summer school. I don't mind. There'll be smaller classes and kids I don't know. Lacy is really nice to me now. She's changed a lot. She visited me a couple of times in the hospital. She said she was sorry that Mum died and that she wasn't very nice to me when I first moved there. That made me feel better. She's moving out after she graduates with 2 girlfriends. She's got a full time job lined up as a bank teller, she wants to go into accounting but she wants to work for a year before starting university. Dave went to Dalhousie, I miss him around. He'll be home for the summer. I know you're starting nurses training in Sept. That so great. You always said you wanted to be a nurse and now you're going to be one.

Dad calls Aunt Joyce when I'm not home. He didn't even call me when I was sick. Is he mad at me? Aunt Joyce said it's because he feels sad that we're so far apart. It doesn't make sense. I hardly remember him anymore. I have a hard time remembering both Mum and Dad. Dr. Weller says this contributes to my depression.

It feels good just talking to you again, even if its writing. Maybe I can call you on your birthday. I can't believe you'll be 18! Do you have any plans for it? Write me back soon.

Love

Grace xo

"What's this about?" I asked, placing the letter in the middle of the table.

"What's that?" Dad looked puzzled.

I picked up the letter and read, "*I know Dad and Aunt Joyce talk about once a month. I don't know if you know I was sick. I'm okay, don't worry, I'm getting better. Apparently I was depressed, or am depressed. I'm on medication. No one knew what was going on with me. I just couldn't get out of bed, I slept all the time and wasn't eating, so I ended up in the hospital for a week … Mum was depressed too. I remember her sleeping a lot."*

"I told you, Jack," Trish mumbled as she slowly turned and left the room.

"Just when were you planning on telling me?" I said, holding up the letter.

"Soon. I was waiting to hear more concrete news."

"Like what, Dad? She told me all there is to know. Why would you keep this from me?"

"I didn't want you to worry. She's fine, Maggie; she's being looked after. There's no need to worry about her. She's not going to do anything … bad."

"How do you know that? And so what! You should have told me. I'm not a child anymore, and Grace of all people should know the truth about Mum. She said she has the same mental illness that Mum had, and look what happened to Mum. How is Grace supposed to deal with that? Does this Dr. Weller even know the truth? It's nuts! And why don't you talk to Grace? Why do you call when she's not home? She thinks she's done something bad and that you don't love her."

As usual, Dad had nothing to say. I grabbed the letter and left the room. Trish was looking out the living room window, hands in prayer mode to her mouth, listening. I shot her a look that implicated her in this scheme too. Why was I the only one that could see what should be done here? I was completely trapped in their web of deceit.

Or was it my web of deceit that they were trapped in?

June 7, 1979

Dear Grace,

It was so good to get your letter. And thanks for telling me everything. I'm so sorry you have this to deal with. But I'm happy to hear that you're getting help from Dr. Weller. I guess Mum didn't get the help she needed for her depression. I know what you mean about kind of forgetting Mum, (and Dad for you). It's weird how that happens. Even you, when I'm writing you I picture you 11 years old.

When does summer school start? How often do you go? It's good to hear that Lacy visited you and that she's nice to you now. I knew she had it in her. I've got to say, I'm kind of mad at Dad right now. He should have told me you were in the hospital. I don't know why he doesn't call you, I'm sorry it makes you think he doesn't care about you. I know he does. He told me that you were getting good care and he didn't want me to worry about you. That bugs me because it's like I'm a child.

His friend Trish should have told me. She's like a big sister or something. I tell her everything. She's really nice, you'd like her. But I'm kind of mad at her too for not telling me. Maybe Dad told her not to.

I started smoking. Don't tell Aunt Joyce PLEASE! I've met some friends at school and we hang out in the smoke pit. They drink on the weekends but I don't. I did once and didn't like it. I threw up. One guy, Nick, brings a flask with rum in it to school. I really don't hang out with them except in the smoke pit, except Nick invited me to graduation with him. I told him I wasn't going to graduation and he said he would pay for everything if that was a problem. I don't want him paying but I'm thinking about going. I don't like him as a boyfriend, but I think he likes me. Trish and Dad said I "must go" to my graduation, that I'd regret it later if I didn't go.

I still listen to the Toronto weather report and think of you in the sweltering heat. It's pretty nice here, warm, it rains a lot in the winter. I'm getting use to it.

I don't think we'll be able to talk on the phone on my birthday because of work and the time difference. I like work. We sell all kinds of stuff for parties and celebrations, and balloons too. I'm going to keep working all summer. I'm saving like crazy for a car. I don't have my license yet because I don't have anything to drive, and I really don't need to drive anywhere. But I want a car.

Keep writing me because it's obvious that Dad isn't going to tell me how you're doing. I get sad just before my period too. I think most girls do.

Love Maggie xo

I was treading on thin ice again. Not only talking a lot about Mum, but in relation to her depression made it extra tricky business. I didn't want to talk to Grace on the phone. The previous calls did not go well. With Dad and Aunt Joyce hovering over us, we weren't able to say what was really on our minds. Writing letters was our best method of communication and I promised myself I would keep it up from here on in.

As usual, my frustration with Dad, Trish and Aunt Joyce subsided, as if all feelings, good or bad, have an expiration date. Happiness doesn't last; in fact, who even knows when they're happy? It's the absence of happiness that's in our face. Misery is potent with awareness. I read this somewhere; it made sense.

After all, I needed these people in my life, and I knew Dad was never going to change. Trish, as usual, did the best she could to celebrate occasions, such as my birthday. Her big gift to me was a home-made cake. It was a well-known fact that she did not like cooking, but she liked baking even less. So to have her make me a cake was really something. This special treatment was explicitly for Dad and me, on birthdays only. We had begun to develop our own family traditions over the few years together. These traditions were, and still are, a blessing to me.

. . .

Trish and I wheeled Dad back into the main hall. Well, I wheeled Dad and Trish held onto the handle for support. She wore her salmon-coloured pumps that matched her leotards, with a long, blue pullover sweater that came down to her knees.

"Trish, you look lovely today. And who's this handsome fellow?" my favourite care giver said to my semi-conscious father.

"fHi, Melanie. Just to let you know, he's not going to like having this sweater taken off. It may come to blows," I said.

"Ah Jack, you wouldn't take a swing at me, would you?" Melanie said, tenderly rubbing Dad's back. "How are you today, Trish?"

Trish looked vulnerable; her hands trembled as tears filled her eyes. "I miss him." She averted her watering eyes towards her Jack.

"Of course you do," Melanie said, taking her hand.

I wasn't sure if my heart or my breast hurt more. We all stood for a moment around Jack. It was like a healing ceremony, each with a hand on him and on each other. I had a strong sense his time was coming to an end; I think Trish did too.

"Thank you, Melanie. You're a dear," I said, squeezing her hand before letting it go.

"Trish, let's get a cuppa."

The mixture of her broken heart and sparrow like face gave the illusion that she could blow away in a light breeze. But she was steadfast in the conviction of who she was. Solid to the ground even as her little feet clicked clacked down the halls.

"Yes, that would be nice, dear," she said, stuffing her tissue under the cuff of her sweater.

The hospital café was perfect. We settled in our seats by the window and allowed the afternoon sun to sooth our bones and melt away the lingering remnants of the ECU. The feeling of satisfaction for visiting my father settled nicely into my body, along with the relief that it was over.

"I don't think he'll make it home for Christmas this year. What do you think?" Trish asked, lightly testing the heat of the cup with her tongue before taking a sip.

It was a loaded question, as it would be up to Phillip and me to make that happen.

"Ya, it's hard to tell right now. It's been a while since he's been on his feet. That's really the determinant."

Silence.

"But let's wait and see; maybe we can figure something out."

"Alzheimer's sucks," Trish said, placing her cup firmly in its saucer.

I stifled a smile at her use of the word "sucks" and the velocity at which she said it.

"Yes, it does — it just sucks. I believe he'd be doing well without it. He's strong and healthy in every other way." She shook her head as if ridding it of unpleasant thoughts. "When's the last time you spoke to Grace?" I asked, changing the subject.

"Yesterday — seemed fine; just taking the neighbour's dog for a walk. Having her place painted before Lacy arrives."

"Ya, she mentioned that a while ago. Is it coming together? Does she have a painter? I'm looking forward to Lacy's visit," I added.

"I think so; can't remember the dates she's got lined up," Trish said, looking a bit weary at having to remember such things.

"We talked about her staying with us while it was being painted, but we've not spoken in a while so don't know if that'll happen."

"Oh, I think she's counting on it," Trish said with direct eye contact.

"That's good then. I thought maybe she might have changed her mind." I felt both dread and excitement rolled up into one confusing ball of emotion at the prospect of having her living with us. It could go well or be a disaster. Much like being in the presence of Mum. And who knows what would happen after she hears the truth?

Tea, right in front of me. Pick it up, taste it.

"She's not said anything to me about changing her mind. She doesn't tell me when you two are at sixes and sevens."

I felt a tinge of guilt for burdening Trish with my various dramas: Grace, Phillip, the boys, etc. I made a mental note to stop doing that.

"Sixes and sevens, I love that. That's exactly what it is. And after I speak with her today — well after today — I'm hopeful that we'll be at twos and fours."

We clinked our cups, and she smiled and nodded.

August 19, 1979

Dear Grace,

> *The summer is almost over and I haven't heard from you. Dad told me you're doing okay and passed summer school. He said that you all went to Lund Harbour for 2 weeks but I think you're home now. I want to hear all your news!*

> *As you can see from the picture I ended up going to graduation. Dad came with me for the dinner dance part. We had a father daughter dance. It was okay. He seemed nervous. I got the dress from someone Dad works with. His daughter*

graduated last year and she just lent it to me. I really liked it, what do you think? I saw Nattie's parents there. Her Mum congratulated me on graduating and going into nursing school, she's nice. Nattie and I talked a bit, she's going to UBC into criminal justice then into Law, and as planned, all on a swimming scholarship. She was funny, still trying to talk me out of a nursing career, but in the end wished me well. She's got a really nice boyfriend, he's on the swim team at another school, they met somehow through swimming.

The after party was at someone's house. I heard it got out of hand and the cops came. I was kind of with Nick because I didn't know a lot of the people there. Anyway, Nick got super drunk and barfed all over the floor. That's when I left.

I worked all summer, didn't take any holidays and I didn't do much so I saved all my money and I have enough to buy a car. Dad's helping me get a good deal through his work friends. I think I'm getting it this coming week end. I have driving lessons scheduled for Sept. I'm really excited! I'll be driving back and forth to the hospital, Vancouver General, every day. Training starts the day after labour day. It's 3 years. I'm going to keep my job for weekends as long as I can, for the money.

Can't wait to hear from you, write soon.

Bye for now,

Love Maggie xo

p.s. I quit smoking, I never did inhale.

As it turned out, Grace wasn't doing so well. The medication was difficult to regulate. Apparently, Aunt Joyce had her hands full. Her youngest, John, now fourteen, had cravings for designer clothes, music and girls, with little to no interest in school, not unlike his older sister Lacy at that age. On top of it all, Uncle Brian had a cancer scare. Some surgery and mild treatment did the trick, but it all had an effect on my aunt. While Uncle Brian took the kids to Lund Harbour, Aunt Joyce went to a spa somewhere in Florida. To this day I have no idea if this actually happened or if she had a breakdown. It was amazing that they managed through it and were still together and in the same house. They had married well.

Chapter 30

Open to Receive

Sept 23, 1979

Dear Maggie,

For some reason I'm more sad about Mum today than the last 5 years. I'm home can't get out of bed. It feels like Mum died last week. I try to go to school but I end up coming home at lunch time. Aunt Joyce is tired. I hear her talking to Uncle Brian. I think I'm a problem for them.

I can't remember the last time I saw Mum. Did I say good bye to her that morning? I guess so, I just can't remember. Do you remember what you did? Did you see her, dead? I never asked you. All I remember is coming home and you sitting still in the living room waiting for me. And then you telling me Mum was dead. That's all I remember. I feel bad because Aunt Joyce has been so nice to me all these years. We had a fight, and I still feel so bad.

I've kind of lost my friends too. They all go out together to movies, I just don't want to go out. Aunt Joyce makes me call them, and makes me go out, and sometimes I do feel better when I do, but mostly I just want to come home. I don't feel like laughing. She said that I wouldn't feel any better if I moved to Vancouver. She said that I'll just take my depression with me where ever I go. I don't know about that, I think if I came to Vancouver, and lived with you, I'd be better. I feel better just thinking about it. Anyway, we fight about that. I've been calling her Mum, but now I call her Aunt Joyce again. She's not my mother, I just wanted a mother. But I think it hurts her feelings that I stopped calling her Mum. I think if I came to Vancouver to live with you and Dad I would be fine. You said Dad doesn't drink anymore so he could look after us both. Maybe you could talk to Dad about it. I ask Aunt Joyce to talk to Dad about it but I don't think she does. You're right that they do what they want and we don't have a choice in what happens to us. I'm going to write Dad and tell him I need to come home. I'm not happy here. And you tell him too, maybe if we both tell him it'll work. Let me know what he says.

Love Grace xo

Nursing school had me spinning, and Grace's problems lurked in the shadows of my mind. As soon as I took my head out of the books to eat or pee, there she was, pleading to come home. I managed to push her back into the shadows and carry on, feeling drained with guilt, but I needed to focus. I had assignment after assignment, and the amount of information to learn in just the first month was astronomical. My admiration for doctors increased exponentially, and seeing so many females go into the profession inspired me. I loved everything about it.

Dad was teaching me how to drive my new-to-me 1971, four-speed, mustard-yellow, two-door Vauxhall Firenza. I heard him telling Trish that driving with me was the closest he'd ever come to wanting a drink in years. Made me giggle, which surprised me. I'd come to trust his sobriety.

After getting my license, Heather, a fellow classmate and I, carpooled to the hospital each day. We shared enthusiastic conversations about diseases, medications, bodily functions, childbirth and dying. She was spunky with a good sense of humour. Talked a lot about her year of travels around Europe with her identical twin sister Rachel, who was getting her undergrad to be a teacher. Even though I was envious, I really did love hearing her stories, one funny adventure after another. Heather was 5'10", we were almost eye to eye. Brown hair, poker straight like mine. She taught me the trick of sleeping with my hair pulled into one big ponytail at the top of my head wrapped around a large roller (that she gave me). The result in the morning was a head of full-bodied hair with a slight curl at the bottom. She was also slim, with long legs; She was stronger than me, with broad shoulders. Her front teeth slightly protruded and she had a large nose. Her best and most charming features were her deep dimples that were visible whether smiling or not.

Heather knew my mother had died at home when I was thirteen, and the nurse in her wanted to know more. Heading over Lions Gate Bridge one day, she softly asked, "How did your mum die? You never told me."

I inhaled and said, "Strange circumstances." *Where did that come from?*

"You mean it was never determined — no autopsy?"

"No, there wasn't," I said too abruptly.

Didn't stop her, though.

"Oh, okay. That must be kind of tough on you. Not knowing how or why she died."

Heather knew something was up. It didn't make sense that a woman dies in her home and no one investigates the cause.

"I've grown to accept it," I said, hoping she'd accept it too.

Picking up on my curt response, she took a sideways look at me. I kept my eyes straight ahead, so she let it drop. Another friendship with boundaries and limitations. Topics for discussions included our studies, travel, hair, fashion, boys, music, TV, future plans, and her family. Enough to have fun together, but never enough to develop a full-on, trusting, deep relationship. Unlike Nattie, Heather wanted more. She liked me. She wanted to know the parts of me that came before we met, the parts she missed. I know this because I wanted to know those parts of her. I loved hearing about her and Rachel. Her stories helped me understand how she ticked and why she thought about things the way she did.

Summers at Lund Harbour were easy to talk about. Stories that told of a happy mother, a large, loving family and my closeness to Grace. But somehow our conversations always came back to my mother's mysterious death, leaving me scrambling for words that came out vague and nondescript. I could never oblige with a straightforward answer, and it created a sense of dishonesty. Like all my former friendships, Heather and I fell into a rhythm directed by me. And I was having trouble keeping my sister's problems in the shadows; talking about her shook them out like flapping sheets on a clothes line.

"Dad?"

"Ya?" he answered to his newspaper.

"What do you know about Grace wanting to move here with us?"

He and Trish simultaneously dropped their papers in their lap as if to say, *Here we go!*

"I got this letter from her today," I said, holding the evidence out to view. "And she's really not doing well. She thinks if she moves here with us, she'll get better?"

"Yes — I know. She has good and bad days. She probably wrote that letter on a bad day."

He pretended to resume reading his paper. Trish stayed with me but did not speak, as usual. Unfortunate given that she was the voice of reason.

"Well?" I directed my sarcasm at Dad, who then dropped his paper again with a bothered sigh and looked to the heavens for escape. His exasperation no longer intimidated me.

"Please don't bother sighing. I need to write her back and tell her *something*. What do you think about her moving here with us? What does her doctor say?"

"Okay, look," he said, resigning himself to the conversation, "here's what I know." He cleared his throat, and I sat down. "Joyce says that her mental illness — manic depression, they call it — will be something she'll have to deal with for the rest of her life. But with the right medication, she should be able to lead a happy, healthy life and that's what the doctors are trying to figure out — the right medication and the right dosage. It would make no sense for her to move here. It would disrupt her progress. She would have to change schools, and that's hard at the best of times. You're busy with school and I'm busy with work."

He shot Trish a look as if to include her in his business. Everything he said was right. I knew it, but how was I to write it?

"She never should have gone to live with them in the first place. If she had stayed with us, her doctor would be here and it wouldn't be an adjustment."

"Come on, Maggie. Don't go there." He pushed the leaver on his recliner to drop the foot rest, stood and headed for the kitchen. "You want some tea, Trish?"

"No thank you, Jack, I'm fine," she said methodically, each word enunciated as if to say, *You are being rude leaving in the middle of an important conversation.*

I followed Dad into the kitchen. "Have you talked to Grace or Aunt Joyce lately?" I asked, managing to soften my tone. "She and Grace are fighting about her wanting to move here. I think Aunt Joyce is tired." *Tired of looking after your kid.*

"Yes, I know all this. Joyce and I talk a couple times a month. She thinks it's best I not talk with Grace right now because she'll hound me about moving here and, as I said, that's not a good idea." He turned and gave me a look that said, *You do know this, don't you?*

"Ya ya, I know what you're saying. I don't think it will help her to move here, I know — but not talking to her is not helping either. You have to tell her yourself."

The kettle screamed as if to say, *Stop the insanity!*

When had I stopped missing Grace? Time, distance and secrets had eroded us, and we couldn't bond or support each other over this hellish tragedy. I continued to hold Dad and my aunt responsible for this. They made their beds, now they can sleep in them.

· · ·

"A text from Phillip," I said, responding to his personal text tone, "Reminiscing" by Little River Band. Trish started mouthing the words. "Ah, he's got a few hours in Toronto, then heading back." I squinted to read the small print without my glasses. "Will be home ... around 1ish ... good luck; wink emoji."

"Will he sleep for a few hours now before flying home?"

"Knowing Phillip, he'll get himself to a driving range and hit some balls. He says it releases tension," I said teasingly.

"How are *your* golf lessons coming along?"

Trish wasn't going to engage in any forms of gossip, never did, never would.

"Ha, well, slowly. Of course, it would help if I actually practiced. It's true what they say, it's a bloody frustrating game."

"Is that what they say? I thought it more a social game. Very nice when couples play together and women friends play together; I like that idea." Trish was on her third cup of tea. "Not to mention the accessibility to playing golf year-round in our fair city," she said, sweeping her hand towards the window that showed off the spectacular day.

"I know what you're up to. You want Phillip and me to be golf buddies."

I had put too much milk in an already cold cup.

"Oops, you're onto me. Yes, I do, as a matter of fact. I know how hard being with the same person for so many years can be. I'm still devastated that my dear brother was dumped. He's a good man, I don't understand." Trish shook her head with confusion.

"Phillip's not going anywhere," I said reassuringly, but I wanted to change the subject. "I had a visitation this morning."

I sat back in my chair while pushing the tea cup away. Trish put her cup down, giving me all her attention.

"What do you mean, 'visitation'?"

I smiled at her seriousness. "From Mum. She appeared in front of me, like an apparition."

I didn't look at Trish but waited for her response. "And?"

I sat up straight, feeling the excitement of finally sharing this experience. "In my car this morning — outside school. Gosh, I'm going to cry saying this out loud." I took a deep breath, slowing my speech. "I got to school early, the car was warm, I hadn't slept well, so I rested my head and closed my eyes for a minute, ya know? And I kinda went into that place between awake and asleep. And there she was — like an angel — I mean, really, just like an angel, dressed in flowing layers of white cotton, just how you'd expect an angel to look."

Trish nodded, listening intently.

"She came really close to my ear and whispered something to me. I couldn't hear what she said, and in my dreamy state I asked her to repeat what she said. I told her I couldn't hear her — and she just faded away." I twirled my tea cup around, still puzzled. "You know, it's like she comes to me for a reason, she wants to tell me something, but I can't hear it. What's that about?" Trish sat quietly, patiently. "What do you make of that, the whole thing?" I asked pleadingly.

She cleared her throat as if to choose her words carefully. "I think it's fascinating — and wonderful. We know so very little about — anything, really. I wouldn't question any of it." She sat up straight and looked right at me.

"But why? What was the point, after all these years, if I couldn't hear her 'message'?" I said with quotation fingers.

Trish slouched as if she had been onto something but forgot what it was. But then she seemed to retrieve it. Sitting forward, she said, "What do you think she said to you? No, no, I mean, What would you have *liked* her to say to you?"

I was a bit stunned at the question. *What would I have liked my mother to say to me? Gosh, where do I begin?*

"I have no idea. She didn't say much to me when she was alive, so I have no idea what she'd say to me now that she's dead."

These words came out more aggressive than I'd wanted. I'd forgiven her, I knew she loved me. *What am I afraid of?* Trish sat quietly, very Dr. Beth like. And then it came to me.

"'I love you,' I guess," I said out loud.

"Those *are* lovely words," Trish said more to herself.

Then, like magic, I heard Mum's voice. *I'm sorry I caused you so much pain. It will be okay — everything will work out. I love you.*

"Trish," I whispered, "I just heard her. She said she loved me, she said she was sorry, she said it would be okay." I sat, transfixed. "It was her voice, her own voice. How is that possible?"

"We don't know the mysteries of the afterlife, we just need to be open, like little children. You were open, so she could enter." I looked at her and blinked as if that would help me understand. "It's a known fact," she said, nodding with certainty.

"Deepak, Eckhart, Wayne?" I asked a bit teasingly.

"Pema Chodron, I think. Or maybe A Course in Miracles; they all say it in different ways, and you're living proof it's true." She looked at me wide-eyed as if to say, *Can't argue with that.*

And she was right, I couldn't. I shook my bewildered head.

Chapter 31

Lost on Sage Island

Oct 10, 1979

Dear Grace,

I've taken a while to write you back, sorry. Has Aunt Joyce talked to you about staying with them a little while longer? Dad and I talked about you coming here to live but he says it's not the best thing for you to do right now. It's not like when we lived in Halifax.

I'm super busy with school now. I'm in school all day and then I come home and study every night until I go to bed. There's so much to learn. I'm loving it, but it takes all my time. I think I'm going to have to quit my job because I'm missing study group that meets on Saturdays.

I always wanted you to come home in Halifax, I never wanted you to leave in the first place. I'm not sure what's best. What has Aunt Joyce said? Every time I talk to Dad about it he just says the same thing, that you have security where you are. I guess you do with your doctors and Aunt Joyce.

I forgot the 23rd this year. I remembered on Sept 24th but not on the 23rd. Trish said that was normal, and a good sign that I was moving forward.

I know it's a bit early for your birthday card but I hope you like it. It came from the stationery store I work in. It reminded me of you and me the time we got stranded on Sage Island. Remember how terrified we were? I still get spooked thinking about it.

Anyway, I hope you're feeling better. Do you have any birthday plans? Write me back soon.

Love Maggie xo

It had been a long time since I begged Dad to let me speak to Grace on the phone, and that year I *really* didn't want to. I had joined the ranks that thought it best that Grace live with our aunt in Ontario. Poor

Grace. I now had also rejected her. It's not that I didn't mourn the loss of my little sister, but my thoughts were of a time long ago. Childhood. I loved this little chubby-cheeked, bright-eyed creature. She'd reach for me and I for her. But she was gone. Seemed like another lifetime.

When I saw the card, my memory was tweaked. Grace was five and I eight. We were in Lund Harbour. When the tide went out, we could walk from Lund Beach to Sage Island. A walk across the meadow, down the bank and onto Lund Beach led us over to the island. Picture perfect, like out of a holiday destination magazine; we were a bunch of happy kids skipping through tidal pools. Our loving mothers strolled barefoot, their own childhood memories awakening as the perfectly rippled sand squished between their toes.

Once on the island, the conversation was always about getting back before the tide came in and the dangers of getting trapped — or worse — washed out to sea with the force of the incoming tide. It was all folklore, of course, passed down by parents who needed their children to obey. These were heavenly times, with our bodies at play and minds at rest. We'd collect sand dollars, periwinkles and seaweed. We'd search for the bones of those that got swallowed by the rip tide, never to return. Bones were difficult to find in the layers and layers of bleached white shells that made up the island shoreline; it was completely different than the soft white sand of the mainland beaches.

This summer, a new rule was made that David, the oldest, could accompany the youngsters across to Sage Island if the adults didn't want to go. However, this particular day, Grace and I — or, if I'm honest, *I* — decided it was time for us to venture out on our own. People had said that it was possible to walk around the entire island and get back to the mainland while the tide was out. It was a hot day and, at my bidding, we headed to Sage Island.

"Come on, Grace!"

"Wait up, Maggie!"

"No, you have to run to catch up!"

"You're walking too fast. Slow down or I'm going back."

I stopped.

"Okay, let's get over there — come on."

As it turned out, it was impossible to walk around the island because the other side of it was rocky and covered in sharp brambles and bushes. I, nevertheless, was on a mission and insisted we keep going, bare feet and all. By the time we found a small path that cut through the middle of the island, our feet were torn to shreds, we were both crying hysterically, and, yes, the tide was in. The sun was already setting when we hobbled out of the woods onto the Beach of Bones, where we sat in mortal fear of becoming part of it. Our hysteria continued as it went from dusk to pure blackness. Somehow yelling, "HELP!" only terrified us more; our tiny, frantic voices vanished in thin air.

Finally, we saw a light waving back and forth on the other side. A man yelled, "Stay right there!" Then the light disappeared up the bank. As I watched the light disappear, I thought maybe we'd be left there for the night as punishment. But no, we'd been found. Our hysteria subsided and I knew as soon as everyone was over the relief of us not being dead, I was going to get holy hell. Our teeth chattered as we sat on the Beach of Bones waiting for the light to reappear over the hill and down the bank with the screaming voices of Aunt Joyce and Mum attached to it.

"Maggie, Grace — oh my God, we're coming to get you! Stay there — oh my God — thank God you're safe! Stay there, don't move!"

We piled into an old flat-bottomed rowboat that required Mum to bail as fast as she could while Billy, a neighbour, rowed with all his might to get us to shore before we sank. We had been missing for four and half hours. We sat sipping chicken noodle soup with saltines while they interrogated us.

"How many times have you been told about the tides? You know how dangerous that is — what's wrong with you, Maggie?"

Mum was furious.

"Sorry, I wasn't thinking."

Mum huffed, then growled.

"It was my idea too," Grace piped up.

"No, it wasn't," I said directly to Mum. "It was my idea. I thought we had time to walk around it."

Mum shot me a look, so I shut up.

"All I can say is I'm relieved you're both home safe and sound. I bet you'll never do that again. And it's a good lesson for us all — don't take any chances," said our aunt in a much softer voice.

Dave then said, "The worst that could happen is you'd have to sleep over there and then come home the next day when the tide went out."

"Or cross in the middle of the night when the tide was out," Lacy contributed. "That'd be damn scary, though."

"Be damn scary sleeping over there all night too," Dave said, wide-eyed with the thought.

"Okay, enough of that talk. Everyone's here safe and sound," said Uncle Brian. "Let's get ready for bed."

Was Mum really as upset as she appeared or was this a show for her sister? After all, Grace and I had been left on our own for days. The scolding felt harsh. I, too, had been terrified, wasn't that enough? It was our aunt who filled our cups with loving words that night.

"Hi girls, can I tuck you in?" She said, tucking us in. "I'm so happy you're home safe in your beds, together, like two peas in a pod. I think today might have been the most scared I've ever been. Honestly, if anything ever happened to either of you … well … I just don't know what I would do. I love you so very much. Seeing you lying here makes me the happiest auntie in the whole wide world."

She kissed each of us as she forced the blankets under the sides of our bodies, starting from our shoulders down to our toes, as if we might fly away if she didn't.

"Goodnight, my darling scallywags."

We lay in silence. The presence of what was missing, our mother, overwhelmed us both. We were terrified for our lives, and, yes, I was stupid for taking us to the island, but could I not be scolded and loved at the same time?

"I'm sorry I made you go over there," I said to Grace. "Mum shouldn't be mad at you, it's my fault."

"Why was she so mad at us — it's like she doesn't even care we didn't die," said Grace.

"She's not mad at you, just me. She should come and tuck you in; this is all my fault."

I started crying and could hear Grace was too. This is how we fell asleep.

My mother didn't say one word to me for three days. I spotted Aunt Joyce looking at me when Mum deliberately spoke to Grace and not me when she said, "Grace, make sure you make your bed before you go out to play." Obviously, she wanted us both to make our beds. My aunt and I made eye contact and I knew that she knew.

Chapter 32

Lost and Found

The next year flew by. With the presence of Trish, and Dad's continued sobriety, my home life had never been more stable. My studies consumed me, and I could feel the gray matter expanding in my head with the amount of information I was taking in. My mother's suicide and subsequent secret of such no longer controlled my every word and move. And even though "strange circumstances" does not explain a death in the mind of a medical professional, for the most part, no one questioned me further.

Without Heather forcing me to attend all parties and social events, I would not have met Rafe, a second-year intern. It was the nurses' fall kickoff party held at a downtown disco where I was freely dancing with a group of schoolmates. I spotted him watching me from the sidelines, and he tipped his glass in acknowledgement that I'd seen him. He headed towards the dance floor.

"Rafie! Come dance with us," several girls squealed, inviting him into our dance circle — not that he needed inviting.

Other than a few dates, I'd not had a boyfriend since Jo, if Jo was even that. Rafe and I hit it off right away. We met up between shifts and lectures for food and/or sex. Our time together was peppered with stimulating conversations about diseases, treatments, complications and everything else that happened to a human body. He helped me with my studies and I with his. We were a solid item until the summer break when he joined forces with Doctors Without Borders, a noble and relationship-wrecking undertaking. Rafe thought he'd return in the fall, but he didn't. He encouraged me to join him in Sudan, stressing the need for nurses. He'd sponsor me, we'd be a team. The content of our letters shifted from sexually romantic to needy and explanatory. Me needy, him explaining, then him needy and me explaining. He knew little of my past struggles. Why would he? I'd shared nothing. In his eyes, I was put together well, mentally and physically stable and healthy. Why wouldn't I join him in hell to fight the good fight? When he called me, I could feel the sweltering heat as he spoke. Could see his sweaty dusty face.

"Your training will always be there, Mags — it's not going anywhere. Think of how much you'll learn and experience being here; you can't pass up this amazing opportunity."

"It sounds amazing," I'd respond, not wanting to be a disappointment.

"It *is* amazing! Hard, yes, but so worth it."

"Tell me the hard parts."

"Well, you've seen the news, seen pictures — the conditions are horrible, tragic. All the more reason to come here to help. We have it so damn good in the West. We have no idea how good. People are in need. I'd just love to have you with me — you know — love to share this experience with you."

I felt sick hearing words like horrible and tragic. *No, I will not go there.* Rafe was mid-sentence, something about us being a team, when I said, "Rafe —"

He stopped talking.

I whispered, "I'm not coming. I'm sorry, I can't explain it. I just know I'm not."

I cried. Our relationship was now over. Another loss, another disappointment; I cried for it all.

If I'd had Rafe's upbringing, I'd be gone in a heartbeat. He lived a modest life but wanted for nothing. He had healthy relationships with his two loving parents, younger sister and brother. Went to the same schools all his life. Other than losing his best friend in a car accident in Grade 12, he spoke of no other tragedies. He actually told me once that his home was peaceful, which allowed his siblings and him to grow to be curious about the world. His younger brother was following in Rafe's footsteps, his sister was gearing up for a master's in counselling. I did the best I could to make my chaotic past seem only slightly challenging at worst, and he seemed to understand how difficult it would be for a thirteen-year-old girl to lose her mother.

After that phone call, the time between letters expanded. I wrote about my studies, he about the latest outbreak that took so many lives. Ten months after he left Canada, the letters ended altogether. I heard he moved to the States to complete his internship. That was the end of Rafe, except for how he rose like a holy vision in my mind, taking my hand and leading me to a makeshift hospital in a tent where we'd treat the wounded and suffering, all the while sharing loving, knowing looks that said, *We are heroes and we are in it together till the end.* Real romantic Hollywood stuff.

Grace's letters had also stopped. She would tell me years later that she felt betrayed by Dad, and that my refusal to help her move to Vancouver — where she was certain she would recover — hurt deeply. Dad offered snippets of what was actually going on for her, or maybe he withheld information from me on purpose. Either way, I had stopped pushing for it. The once indestructible connection between my beloved sister and me was broken, reduced to a memory.

Dec 19, 1979

Dear Grace,

> *I haven't heard from you for a while. I asked Dad if you could come and live here, I tried. But you know what they're like. When Aunt Joyce and Dad decide about something, that's it, there's no changing their minds.*

Look how fast time has gone already. Why don't you just finish school there and then move out here. You can get a job here. Then maybe you and I can get an apartment together, like roommates. I'll be finished training by then, and you'll be finished school so we'd both be working, so we could afford it.

I hope you like my Christmas card and pictures. That's Heather and me in our uniforms, and the other one is the whole class getting ready to catheterize a plastic penis. Nurses are a fun bunch of people!

My life is study study study, practice practice practice, then exams exams exams. The odd social get together, but mostly I've got my head in the books. Don't even have time for a boyfriend.

Please write me. Did you get my birthday card? Isn't it like the time we got lost on Sage Island?

I'll talk to Dad again about you moving here.

Hope you're feeling better.

Love Maggie xo

Just like every other letter to my sister, I read it many times more from habit than worrying about the secret slipping out. This letter was evasive and crafty. So much not said, and at the same time yelled, *I have no time for you! Stay where you are!* How sad. I didn't even want to tell her about Rafe. We had stopped sharing intimate details about our lives. I knew nothing about her other than she wasn't well. All she knew about me was I studied all the time. What was to come of us?

. . .

"Think I've had enough tea; you wanna do a little window shopping?" I said to Trish as I gathered up our cups.

"That would be nice. Do you have time to look for gloves? I can never find any nice plain ones my size. I'm sentenced to a life of wearing children's clothes," Trish said, shaking her hair-sprayed head atop her extra petite body.

The day had grown warmer. Except for the fall colours and light, it could have been the middle of summer. Trish tucked her arm in mine as she had done for a few years now. We looked like mother and daughter, and I dared to finally say it out loud.

"Sometimes I wanted to call you Mum." It was a day of telling long held secrets, it seemed.

"Did you." she said rhetorically.

"What would you have done if I called you Mum?"

She seemingly took what I was saying in stride. Trish was not easily thrown.

"Well — I don't really know." Her little face looked puzzled — as if it had never occurred to her. "I always thought I was."

This surprised the heck out of me, I needed to clarify. "You thought of yourself as my mum?" My heart was racing with excitement.

"It just felt like I was — you know — your mum."

I could have picked her up and spun her around, but instead I secretly teared up.

"We never talked about how Mum died."

"No, Jack didn't want to upset you — it wasn't my place."

"Of course, that makes sense."

I would not go into how it would have helped me to talk to her about the suicide and to call her Mum. We walked in silence; I think she had regrets too. I squeezed her little bony arm that was tucked in mine and said, "I think we did a great job, all of us."

She nodded and tapped her fingers on my arm.

"I've always loved you, and I should have told you that!"

I felt her frail body leaning up against me. *What a sweet thing to say.*

"And I've always loved you — and I should have told you too!" I said with just as much punch, while holding in tears. "They'll have gloves in here," I said with a big sniff.

"Grand!"

Chapter 33

For the Love of Grace

"It's not the first time she's disappeared."

Dad was on the phone with Aunt Joyce.

"What do you mean 'everything'? All her clothes? What makes you think she's coming here?"

"Well, let me know the minute she gets home — call me right away …"

"I know, I understand, but let's hope not."

He put the phone down with a sigh and yelled, "FUCK!"

I'd never heard Dad say a swear word, never mind the F-bomb! I waited from the bottom step, out of sight, as he dialed the phone.

"Hi — just talked to Joyce. She's gone again; Joyce thinks on her way here."

He was talking to Trish.

"Four days ago — longest she's ever been gone. No, she's positive she's on her way here."

I couldn't hear what Trish was saying, but guessed.

"Have no idea — maybe bus …"

"No no, she's got studies. Maybe Joyce is wrong …"

"Yeah talk later."

Dad sat next to the phone in the little alcove at the bottom of the stairs.

"Is Grace on her way here?"

Dad jumped. "Oh – I didn't see you there … Joyce thinks so."

He rubbed his face in his hands; I'd never seen him this unglued.

"She's on a bus?"

"Don't know, we just have to wait and see. Don't worry about this, you have studies to focus on."

I didn't bother saying that she could be dead somewhere; he was rattled enough, and I'm sure, was wondering the same thing.

Two weeks later, the police put out a missing person's report, my sister's face was on the news. The phone rang the next day, and Dad had a quick and quiet conversation.

"She's on her way," he said, putting the phone down.

Thank God she's alive, "When will she be here?"

"Don't know, didn't tell me where she is. She's fine, not missing — don't worry — but she's coming here." He looked worried and scared. "She's not good, you should know this. She refuses her medication and she drinks too much. Joyce said she's been challenging to live with for the last two years. Disappearing for days … I'll call Joyce, let her know."

I could have said so much, most of it accusing, so I kept quiet; he was agitated enough.

Two weeks later I was memorizing the structure of the myelin sheath when the doorbell rang. I ran downstairs, opened the front door and as if adjusting to a strobe light, I blinked. There was Grace.

"Hi Maggie, gonna let me in?"

She was heavy, smudged eye make-up, looked rough. I would have walked right by her on the street. I guess I was staring. Her eyes met mine as if to say, *Don't judge me.* I held the door wide open for her.

"Come in," I said weakly.

She walked by me, looking straight ahead.

"You in shock?"

"No, I knew you were coming …"

She gave me a sideways glance. Dad rounded the corner with a look of both relief and exasperation.

"Hi Dad," she said, dropping her backpack on his chair.

I could see him debating whether to give her a hug or not; he decided not.

"I'm glad you made it. I'll let Joyce know you got here safely — she's been worried," he said, emphasizing "worried."

Grace seemed nonplused by her aunt's worries. Dad called Aunt Joyce, and I could hear the sigh of relief across the country. Her duty was done; she had fulfilled her end of the agreement and she owed us nothing. I reckon if she had any guilt feelings for ignoring her sister's mental illness, she now felt redeemed. Grace was now our responsibility.

"Is this all you've got?" I picked up her worn pack with a broken strap.

"Everything I own or need is right in here." She took it out of my hands and patted it like a pet. "But I wouldn't mind a bath and doing some laundry. Probably stink, eh?"

"Oh, sure, of course. Come on, I'll show you."

The burden of all she'd been through was in that pack. It was more friend to her than any person. She was desperate. What had it been like for this young woman to cross Canada by herself, hitchhiking? I envisioned her sleeping under trees in bus stations or in people's backyards. Washing in gas station bathrooms, using paper towels.

"I can't believe you're here," I whispered.

There must have been too much tenderness in my voice; she'd have none of that.

"Surprise, surprise," she said sarcastically, looking into her pack for nothing.

"I'll show you around ... our sleeping arrangements. You said you hitchhiked? The whole way? Where did you sleep at night?"

"Geez, you sound like Joyce. Hitching was fine — no 'weird' stuff. I slept wherever. There's always places you can find. Hey, this is a cool house — like the one in Halifax, sort of. Lots of rooms, this your room?"

Her cavalier attitude was unsettling. I wanted to hug her as if she was eleven again, but that girl was nowhere to be seen.

"This is my room, and Dad's there. One bathroom but two sinks, so that's good."

Eggshells crackled under my feet, my gut tightened.

"Cool, okay, so I'll have a bath, good?" she said impatiently.

"OK, would you like me to throw some laundry on?"

She stripped down with abandon. She was fleshy, looked good — curvy, like Mum. She tossed her clothes on the floor in front of me.

"Thanks, this'll take a while. Gotta wash my hair, it's a big deal, too thick."

"There's a blow dryer under the sink, if you need it."

I felt dismissed as she strutted to the bathroom, not looking back, not looking to see if Dad could see her, not seeming to give a damn about anything. I picked up her clothes, heavy with body oil and dust. *Grace is home.* I caught a glimpse of myself in my full-length mirror. I'd changed, too, but there was something deeply disturbing about the changes in my sister. *Will I ever find her?*

In preparation for Grace's arrival, Trish gave us a single bed that we put in my room. I cleared a dresser drawer and some closet space for her belongings. Even though everything she owned fit into a backpack, once unzipped, they exploded like fire works, over the floor, her bed, on top of the dresser, everywhere except the closet. *This is not going to work.*

"I can't share a bedroom with her, she's messy and noisy; I can't study," I whispered to Dad over toast and coffee.

He nodded. Two days later, he moved in with Trish. I think it was more an escape than to accommodate me. Grace stayed in my old bedroom and I moved into Dad's. It had a big, bright window, under which I put my desk. I bought a bean bag chair and a floor lamp, which created a comfy space to study. Our bedroom doors where shut most of the time, which actually made me sad but did help me focus on my work. *Maybe this will work.*

Even though our mother's natural beauty could be seen in Grace, beauty, it seemed, was not her priority. Her skin was rough, like her attitude; her hair was dry and in need of a cut. Heavy black make-up circling her eyes in addition to rings and studs outlining her ears combined with ill-fitting clothing kept her unemployed. Our honeymoon period, such as it was, ended with a testy conversation that had been brewing in my head for weeks.

"Grace, could you take out the garbage and pick up a few groceries today? Here's the list," I said, stuffing food in my lunch bag.

"Sure," Grace said absentmindedly while opening a can of pop.

"And if you want more pop, you're going to have to buy it because I don't drink that stuff."

"Yes, you do — I've seen you drink pop before. And I don't have any money — there's no jobs around here."

No one's going to hire you — look at yourself!

"Where have you looked?"

"What the hell, Maggie? Fuck off."

She headed for her bedroom. That conversation provoked the first of many disappearances of which I learned to expect but never became accustomed. They took their toll on my emotional health. *Will I find her dead?*

To prove the statement "people don't change," my father refused to discuss her behaviour, encouraging me to ignore her. He provided groceries and money for necessities. No good ever came from complaining about Grace, so I eventually stopped. My sister's tortured existence joined the other secrets stored in my "never to talk about" file.

Unbeknownst to me, living with her illness was slowly breaking my heart. With every drunken binge, the dreams of our reunion that I held so tenderly in my mind for years dissipated bit by bit. Frustration and disgust trumped any compassion I might have felt for her every time she emerged from her bedroom with some random guy. Luckily, the daily chaos around me never affected my schoolwork or marks, and I continued to give Nattie full credit for this.

I graduated with honours, and despite the fact that Grace was not present at my capping ceremony, I enjoyed the moment. After the pomp and circumstance of convocation, Dad and Trish treated me to a fine dining experience and presented me with my own engraved stethoscope that says *Maggie.* I still have it. Grace was not mentioned the entire evening, although, during moments of silence, thoughts of her shrouded us in concern and sadness. It was a bittersweet night.

My hard work paid off, and I earned entry into a pediatric preceptorship which would commence the following September. Vancouver General hired me straight out of training, and my career was launched.

Living with my sister continued to take a toll on my mental health, and Trish could see it.

"What are your plans for the summer?"

Trish had stopped by with Dad to drop off groceries.

"Work," I answered, putting away cereal, frozen peas, milk, coffee, pasta sauce and peanut butter. "Why do you ask?"

"Is there a bulletin board where nurses can advertise things for sale or carpooling or roommates — that sort of thing?" she asked while sorting a cupboard of crackers.

"Yeah, in our locker room. Why? You looking for a new roommate?"

She laughed, "funny girl – I'm sure you've thought of rooming with another nurse?"

She kept her head in the cupboard. I stopped what I was doing.

"Who'd look after Grace?"

"Your dad and I."

How does she do that?

"I'll check the board tonight and put up a note."

Move out with a roommate. I could smell freedom.

Three months after my conversation with Trish, I moved into an apartment with Debbie, a fellow graduate and employee at VGH. I'd not paid much attention to Debbie during training. She kept to herself even more than me. She was average height, long, brown hair in a low ponytail, brown eyes that lay too far apart from each other. A long, thin nose sharply divided her face and seemed to complement her thin lips. Like me, she wore no make-up.

We were like kids in a candy store setting up our shared living space. It was our first home away from home. We hit thrift stores, second-hand furniture stores and dollar stores, managing to secure a coffee table, sofa and lamps all under $100. Salvation Army dishes, glasses, pots and pans, a kettle, a toaster and a blender completed the kitchen. Trish's old TV sat on a wooden crate draped in a tie-dyed cloth. Left side of the fridge was mine, right side hers. Top linen closet shelves mine, bottom hers. Bathroom same as the fridge. It was walking distance to the hospital and a bridge away from Grace.

Debbie and I worked opposite shifts, the perfect set up to maintain a healthy roommate arrangement. We were both clean, quiet and respectful of each other's space and belongings. Our work schedules were written on a shared calendar that hung in the kitchen; this I considered mannerly and is a custom I continued while raising the boys. On the evenings we were home together, we'd eat in front of the TV to watch *Night Court*, *Cheers* or *M*A*S*H*. Our conversations were limited to TV shows and work.

After our families' initial viewing of our apartment, not one other person was invited in. It was our sanctuary.

If not working, Debbie dutifully visited her parents for Sunday dinners along with her two older sisters in their extremely large home in the British Properties. She knew the bare bones of my past life — mother died, sister moved away, now lives here, Dad lives with his lady friend. I knew approximately the same amount about her family. I was never invited to join Debbie, either for dinner or for a summer swim in their pool. One might have taken her for a stuck-up snob, but I knew better, I knew the signs. She had a secret.

Chapter 34

Love is Love

"I hate to admit it, but I'm pooped," said Trish as we wandered aimlessly around the store. "Think I'll just head for home now. I'm reading an excellent book that will put me right to sleep. I'm like a cat, you know. I'll curl up on the sofa in the sun and doze right off."

"Sounds delicious," I said, remembering my doze in the car just this morning. "I'll walk you to your car."

We walked in silence. Trish was tired, I could feel her frailty.

"Despite my dear Jack, it's been a lovely afternoon. Not often I drink four cups of tea. And I love my gloves — they're perfect for driving, look how they grip the wheel!"

"A good find." I leaned into the car window to kiss her cheek. "Enjoy your book or nap, whatever comes first."

"They kind of come together." And then, with a twinkle in her eye, she said, "Thanks for the wonderful conversation."

She fired up her Volvo. Her CD player blasted "Purple Rain" by the one and only Prince. She turned and winked at me.

"Toodle-oo, darling! Say hello to Grace for me!" she said while pulling out into traffic with no signal.

Dealing with Trish's driver's licence would be the next hurdle on my to-do list of unpleasant things. *She thought of herself as my Mum.* This washed through me like a guarantee that I'd been loved all along.

. . .

When I lived with Debbie, I'd call Dad once a week. The conversations were pretty much the same.

"Hi Dad, how are you?"

"Oh, you know, getting on, but fine. How are you and … er … Doris? You need anything? Place okay?"

"Everything's good, Debbie's fine. Don't need a thing, thanks. Have you spoken to Grace lately?"

His answers were either, "Saw her today — last week — will see her tomorrow."

"How'd she look?" I pressed for more.

"Oh, you know — the same."

"Any more pieces of furniture missing?"

I shouldn't have said that — too upsetting for him. The TV was either stolen or sold, no one knew. I quickly spoke so he didn't have to respond. "Could you ask Trish if she'd like to have lunch with me on Wednesday? I'm off."

Living over the bridge and away from home meant I had to make the effort to keep in touch.

"Okay, I'll ask her; she's in the bathroom right now, I'll have her call you. How are you? How's work and ... er ... Doris?"

It was official, he was forgetful; not a good sign. *Thank God for Trish.*

"All good Dad, have Trish call me. My dinner's ready, we'll talk next week."

Nothing had changed. Even though Grace and I weren't living together, she continued to disappear for days. I thought it was because of me; apparently not. I'd given up calling her, she never answered the phone. It was when I crawled into bed at night, exhausted, that my mind found a loop that was impossible to turn off. *I'm ignoring her — She could be suicidal or dead in an alley — Where does she go? Who's she with? What should I do?* Hours ticked by as I tossed and turned. *Present time — what is right in front of me? GRACE!*

. . .

The day Phillip and I met on the VGH pediatric ward, Grace was in the Lions Gate Hospital psychiatric ward. The two times I visited her proved unhelpful. She was agitated and easily triggered. The secret lie stood like a brick wall between us. How was she to be properly treated? I felt like a cheat, withholding vital information that would contribute to her well-being. The visits were short and little was said.

At the same time, there was a readiness in both Phillip and me. A readiness for partnership. Intuitively, I knew to tell Phillip about Mum's suicide and the subsequent fallout of our family's life after the fact, including my own mental illness and brush with death. I had to be straight and honest. Take it or leave it. He was not deterred. He took it all in stride, offering a listening ear and head nods to demonstrate understanding. Sharing the secret lie with Phillip was easy, as if it was no big deal. Had I only assumed it was a big deal? Had I made a mountain out of a molehill?

If Phillip knew that his passionate love for me was greater than mine for him, he didn't care. The love I felt for Phillip was a trusting love. Although incredibly charming, I never did fully fall under his spell, as he fell under mine. This imbalance appealed to me. Like a steel-toed boot, Phillip offered me protection against any possible hurt. He was not a Jo or a Rafe — and certainly not a Coal. He wanted marriage, children, a life together in a house — right here, with me.

We were driven by a force that said *The time is now.* He liked that I enjoyed my work because it meant he could be gone for a few days flying and I'd not be home, waiting. We were compatible, reliable and committed. He was quickly ready to tie the knot and I could see no reason to delay. We moved in together. However, breaking up the perfect roommate team of Debbie and Maggie was not easy. To my surprise, Debbie cried when I told her.

"I saw this coming … I don't know why I'm so emotional. Of course you and Phillip need to be together. But we're such good roommates, aren't we?" she said, taking my hand.

"Ya, we are. Both clean and quiet, not easy to find in a bunch of nurses. I'll miss you too," I said, not nearly as emotional but taking hold of her other hand.

Everyone needs a place they can rest their hearts and minds. Debbie never did share her secrets with me, nor did I with her. But we created a peaceful living space where we both could rest, demanding nothing of each other. She was nowhere to be seen on moving day. *I'll connect with her at work, bring her a thank you card, maybe we'll go out for coffee.* Great ideas but none of that ever happened.

Phillip and I qualified for a mortgage. Using our savings as a down payment, we bought a fixer-upper bungalow on West Granville Street between the airport and VGH. It was almost too perfect, but I trusted it; I trusted Phillip. One night after seeing *Ferris Bueller's Day Off*, we walked out of the dark theatre and into the first snowfall of the season. Snow is rare in Vancouver, so we felt light-hearted. Phillip pretended to drop something, got down on one knee to pick it up and opened a little box.

"Maggie Holm, will you marry me? Please?"

There were no butterflies or skipped heartbeats, but the end of yearning washed me clean and I realized I truly loved him, dearly. I bent over and kissed him.

"Yes," I said, holding his face in my hands and smiling deeply into his eyes.

Some moviegoers who were filing out of the theatre clasped their hands over their hearts as people do when overwhelmed by love. Their enthusiasm inspired me: I was the lead female in a romantic comedy. We passionately kissed — cut!

It was a traditional church wedding, small and adequate. We had spent the day before decorating the church hall for our reception. Excitement waned as I teetered atop a ladder stringing paper hearts to the dingy church hall ceiling. I scolded myself for being in the position of having to do my own decorating. *Will I always be in some sort of effort, trying to string pieces of my life together while precariously balancing?*

The big day went off without a hitch. With the lights low, our décor looked fantastic; everyone dressed up and danced. The champagne flowed, humorous speeches were made, and I had a very nice father-daughter dance alongside Phillip and Fiona. Phillip's single friends were all polished up with high hopes of snagging a nurse, which the room was full of, although Debbie wasn't there.

I tried not to, but I couldn't stop checking to make sure my sister wasn't drinking. She was into her sixth month of her second attempt at sobriety, and I could tell this occasion was difficult for her. When Phillip spotted me checking, he'd sweep me onto the dance floor, where I remembered that I was a bride and he was my groom.

"Your speech was wonderful," I yelled to him over the music.

"I've been rehearsing for weeks!"

I laughed, picturing him in front of a mirror, "Hello everyone, for those that don't know me, my name is Phillip (pause) and I'm the lucky bugger that is married to this gorgeous woman sitting right here beside me (pause) Eat your hearts out fellows, she's off the market (pause). I want to thank (people) but mostly Jack and Trish – thank you for trusting me to look after your lovely daughter, and I promise to do just that. You've done a wonderful job of raising her, thank you …"

"Did you see both Trish and Dad tear up?" I yelled, gyrating to the music.

He shook his head, didn't notice.

"Very sweet referring to me as her daughter!" I yelled.

He smiled. "Should we get ready"?

"To leave?" I said, surprised. "Not yet — having too much fun."

"Let's change and dance some more."

I nodded, good idea.

"You want to come with me and help me change?" I said to Grace

My bridesmaid was sitting alone at a table in the back. She nodded, putting down her fruit punch.

"Great wedding," she said, unzipping my dress.

"Thanks, do you want to change, too, you know, out of your bridesmaid dress?"

"Na, I'll keep it on."

I wanted to tell her to look at all the single men out there and ask one to dance, she looked beautiful.

"Sexy going away outfit," Grace said, eyeing me up and down.

"Too sexy?" I felt self-conscious.

"Nothing's ever too sexy."

I tugged on my top. *Maybe too much cleavage showing.*

"It's fine, forget what I said. You'd look sexy in a paper bag, can't be helped," she said, shrugging her shoulders like looking sexy was such a shame.

"Okay, I see your point." I gave her a quick hug and her arms reached lightly around my waist. It took us both by surprise.

Later that night when Phillip and I were off our tired feet, stretched out in our king-sized bed in the Four Seasons Hotel, I said, "It was fast, but it was a bona fide hug." I couldn't remember the last time I had touched her. *I guess in Toronto, saying another goodbye at the airport.*

By the time I was pregnant with Brian, Grace had relapsed again, badly. When she surfaced for her fifth attempt at sobriety, I was already pregnant with James. We had moved into a larger home, close to the schools in a wonderful neighbourhood on the North Shore. I accepted a new casual position at Lions Gate Hospital, floating from floor to floor where I discovered the enjoyment of nursing adults.

In my mind, this was simply another dry spell for Grace. She would inevitably slide down the rabbit hole again, pulling all loved ones with her. But as it turned out, I was wrong; she was indeed ready to be well. An alcoholic seizure scared her straight. After she detoxed, she was moved to the psychiatric ward again where she was properly diagnosed and medicated for bipolar disorder. Doctors and therapists worked with her and for her, and it felt different this time. She stayed on her medication, but I'd not put the cart before the horse, I knew better. After she managed sobriety for one full year, I took notice that this was the longest she'd ever gone. One year turned into two. She was twenty-six years old when she finally put the bottle down for good. How many times had I heard "The addict has to be ready"?

Yet, the big secret remained just that — a big secret. With each passing year of Grace's sobriety, my guilt and anxiety increased about keeping the truth from her. It's impossible not to connect her struggles with her not knowing the full story of her life. Missing pieces of one's life are like drunken blackouts. It was as if she had been on a search for something unattainable, translucent, not tangible but as real as the burning sun, mysterious and out of reach. Grace was no longer drinking to escape the void. She was learning to live with it, sober.

I was convinced that her alcoholism was the only cause of our sisterly demise. If only she were sober, I could tell her everything and we could finally pick up the pieces and rekindle our sisterhood. However, she had been sober for a long time and doing well, and I still kept the secret.

"She's vulnerable, I don't want to upset the apple cart," I said to Phillip over pizza and beer.

We hadn't talked much about Grace lately; no need.

"So you're afraid she'll start drinking if you tell her how your mum died?"

It sounded stupid when he put it that way.

"As a matter of fact, I am."

"I don't think so. She's a Lund — you're made of strong stuff."

"Not my mother," I reminded him.

"Your mother wasn't treated," he reminded me.

No, Mum wasn't treated; unfortunate.

I thought about an Al-Anon meeting I attended a long time ago where there was a lively discussion about enabling. A woman was adamant that she was not enabling her husband's drinking so she could have an affair. She claimed she'd not be having an affair if he didn't drink. Yet she made sure there was alcohol in the house in case "guests popped in unannounced." Of course, he would drink it. *Why am I remembering this?* I remembered being confused. I agreed with the woman, but I didn't think it was smart of her to have alcohol in the house.

"As long as your husband drinks, you can continue on with your affair," the facilitator, Sue, said.

I remember the woman protested and stood to leave but then sat down again as if catching herself having a temper tantrum. Sue didn't stop. She addressed the whole group.

"This is important for you all to hear. The act of enabling and the problems it causes is why you're here. You can't stop the addict from drinking, BUT you can stop enabling the addict to drink."

She turned back to the woman, who'd composed herself. Using a soft, caring voice, Sue said, "If your husband stopped drinking today, would you end your affair?"

Everyone looked at the woman. It was a rhetorical question. Sue went on, "Tell me this: Does your husband know you're having an affair?"

"No, of course not; I'm very careful. I don't want to hurt him."

"If he did know, do you think he'd talk to you about it?"

All eyes on the woman again. It was like watching a tennis match.

"I would think so, why wouldn't he?"

"Because as long as you keep having an affair, he gets to drink. AND as long as he drinks, you get to keep having the affair."

The woman, wide-eyed, began to cry. I understood but thought it sounded a bit far-fetched. But today, it all made sense. As long as Grace drank, I didn't have to tell her the truth. I'm literally mad at her for not drinking because now I have no excuse. *Holy shit!*

Chapter 35

The Whole Truth and Nothing But

It seemed my whole life had brought me to this moment. I had lived it out in my head thousands and thousands of times, alone with my burden. Not so today. Something would change today. I buzzed Grace at 6 p.m. sharp. I was now excited, with a smattering of terror. My heart pounded against my ribs like bongo drums. Journal and letter in hand, the secret would soon be revealed.

Everything will be okay. Okay, Mum, here it goes.

"That you, Maggie?"

"Yup!"

She buzzed me in. In typical fashion, she left her apartment door ajar for easy entry.

"Hi!" she shouted from the kitchen. "Come on in, have a seat. I'm just putting the pizza in the oven."

So far, so good; she sounded upbeat.

"We having our usual, Mediterranean?"

"Ya! I looked at the others thinking we should branch out," she said, appearing around the corner and removing her oven mitts. She lowered her voice, "But this is our favourite, right?"

My sister had recently taken up group fitness classes, and she looked toned. Her skin glowed and she looked better than ever.

"Mediterranean all the way," I responded. "Like your hair — different colour?"

"Did this yesterday, myself, highlights. What a friggin' rigamarole, but I think they turned out okay. Saved myself a hundred bucks."

She was in a good mood. Was I going to obliterate it all to hell and back?

"Good job, they look great. How was work?"

Grace ran a recovery house for women.

"The best kind of day. Super nice woman discharged, her whole family was there to pick her up, all so supportive. How was your day, how's Josh?"

She had her back to me while doing up dishes.

"As it turned out, Josh was sick today so I had the day off. It was a gift from Mum."

A picture holds a thousand words, and Grace's face was ten pictures worth of words. I had never acknowledged Mum for anything good, out loud *or* in my head. I couldn't help but smile ever so slightly.

"What's going on? What's so funny? Have you been drinking?"

Oh, now I really wanted to laugh, but I'd not be careless with the space between us; it was delicate, to be respected, not to be squandered.

"No, no, sorry," I said, pulling myself together. "I need to tell you something, Grace. I've needed to tell you this for many years, and I just ask that you hear me out."

"O … kaay, let's sit."

She indicated for us to sit in the living room. She sat down in the armchair and put her hands in her lap as if to say, *I'm all yours, sock it to me.* I sat across from her on the sofa. Just as I started to speak, the lamp went on behind her.

"Timers," she said.

Or Mum's joined us. I nodded and swallowed.

"It *was* Mum you saw on the wing of that plane, and it was Mum you saw in your bedroom with Lacy."

Grace's mouth dropped open and she raised her hand in a gesture to stop the proceedings.

"Hear me out, Grace, please, just hear me out. It'll be okay, I promise, but I just have to say this, now."

"Okay, okay, fine, go on," she said, sitting back but not fully relaxed.

"I'm sorry for being hard on you. I'm sorry that I wasn't there for you in a way that a big sister should be." I paused and sat up straight so my emotions had more room. I took a deep breath and Mum's words came to me: *I love you.* With that strength, I carried on.

"When I came home from school, when I was thirteen and you were eleven, I saw Mum's coat and purse draped on the kitchen chair. She should have been at work, and I felt a sense of dread before I even knew there was something *to* dread. She didn't answer when I called her, so I went upstairs into her room."

I'd never spoken these detailed words aloud to anyone. This story, this real-life, gritty, shitty, tragic story lived in me and me alone. I had her full attention, she looked concerned. And even though she was now an adult, I wanted to protect her from this pain. I doubted myself for just a second, but I knew I had to go on.

"Mum was lying on the bed, dressed for work. She had on her green wool skirt, do you remember the one?"

She shook her head.

"It looked nice on her. And her yellow sweater. Anyway, as you can imagine, I was shocked and confused. Then I noticed an empty pill bottle beside her bed."

"Oh no, Mum killed herself? Mum committed suicide? Is that what you're telling me?" she said, her voice a bit frantic.

I moved down the sofa, closer to where she was sitting in her chair across from me. I reached for her hand, her cold, trembling hand. I spoke softly, just as I had done forty years earlier when telling her that Mum died of a heart attack.

"Uh-huh, that's what I'm telling you. Mum took her own life."

DING! The timer went off, pizza was ready. Neither of us moved. Not wanting the pizza to burn, I said, "I'll get that — be right back," and headed to the kitchen. *Oh my loving God, I said it, don't leave her.* I hustled back into the living room. Grace sat motionless, eyes staring at the floor, mouth slightly open.

"The pizza needs to cool a minute," I said, sitting down to wait for the questions.

"Why?" she asked, looking up at me.

For a second I thought she was asking why I lied to her, but, of course, that wasn't it.

"There were a few reasons. Undiagnosed mental illness, for one. Mum needed care that she didn't get."

I didn't want to lump Grace and Mum in the same boat. Although they clearly were, this had to be something Grace acknowledged on her own.

"Oh," she said hazily.

"When Dad and I were packing up for Vancouver, he gave me a box of Mum's belongings. Her Bible was in the box, amongst other things."

I thought of Mum's sanitary belt, how it hung on my hips. I wanted to cry. *I was so young. Present time, Maggie — what's in front of me.* I swallowed, took a deep breath and looked at Grace.

"There was a little clay dish sitting on top of her Bible," I said, retrieving the dish from my purse. "Inside, there were two wax paper envelopes each with our names on them."

I handed her the clay dish with her keepsake inside. She took it from me, unfolded the wax paper and looked at a strand of her fine baby hair and her first tooth.

"You have one?"

"Ya, mine's at home. You should have had yours too, but I didn't know how to explain it all to you. You'd already moved when Dad gave me the box."

After gently examining her hair and tooth, she folded them back up and placed the little dish on the side table. She looked at me, dazed. I waited, *Safe space.*

"Then I looked through Mum's Bible and found a letter from a man named Henry."

"Henry?"

"Ya, I don't know who he is or where Mum met him or where he is now; nothing really, except he and Mum were having an affair. I say 'affair' because he was married and, of course, so was Mum. He and Mum had a plan to get together and he broke it off in his letter. Apparently, he had a sick child that needed his attention and he no longer had time for an affair."

After all these years, I was still mad at him, still looking for someone to blame. I shook it off.

"It wasn't Henry's fault, of course; he was doing the right thing for his family. But the way I kind of figured it out, is that Mum got the letter before leaving for work. It was the straw that broke the camel's back for her, so to speak."

"You don't know who he is? Where he lives? Where the letter's from?"

"There was no envelope with it, just the letter, no address. I've put Henry out of my mind, really, because I kind of see him as a distraction for Mum. He knew nothing about her. Mum could turn on the charm — that's what he saw. I remember a red-haired man at Mum's funeral; he sat alone, didn't come to the reception. It might have been him, but I don't know — or care, really."

And I was hoping that Grace wouldn't care either. Looking for a scapegoat solves nothing and only hardens the heart.

"So Mum didn't die from a heart attack." She paused. "I've been telling people that all my life and it's not true."

She looked up at me and I shook my head.

"I'm sorry, Grace. I wish I could take it all back, for both of us. It's been the shits for me having to bear this GD secret all my life. I begged Dad and Aunt Joyce to tell you, but they actually liked the idea that you didn't know. They wanted to protect you, as I did, that's why I lied in the first place. But it wasn't fair to either of us."

She shifted in her chair. Shifting was good. I went to the kitchen to cut the pizza and give her time. *I said it and we live. She knows the truth.* Part of me couldn't believe it. It had taken less than fifteen minutes. Fifteen minutes out of a lifetime.

"You okay?" I called to her.

"Ya," she said, barely audible.

I was suddenly hungry but doubted she was, so I cut the pieces small in an attempt to make them more appealing. The presentation looked good: small plates, napkins, knives and forks, sparkling water in her best glassware on a big wooden tray placed on the coffee table so we'd not have to move. Grace leaned right in, mindlessly grabbed a plate, two slices of pizza and a napkin. No fork or knife necessary. Thank goodness she ate; food and sleep were necessary when coping with tragic news. We ate in silence, giving her time to assimilate and make sense of what she had just heard. How her life was shaped around what she thought to be true. All the pieces hadn't landed yet. What was to come? On her third piece she asked, "Is there a suicide note?"

"In a way, yes. It's just one line."

I fished the journal out of my purse, slightly annoyed I had left the letter from Henry in there. Didn't want to stir that pot more than necessary, so I slipped it into my purse. Grace examined the journal and stared at Mum's printed name as if the letters themselves might help her understand.

"I've never seen this."

"No, I hid it from you. Even though it was in my sock drawer all along and I always secretly hoped you'd find it so I could — or someone would — tell you the truth. But you never did." I shrugged.

Grace gingerly lifted the front cover open just as I had done forty years ago. A quizzical look crossed her face as she read the words out loud.

"'I can't take it any longer, this day, September 23rd, 1974.' This is it? This is all she wrote?"

"Uh-huh, that's it. I know, it's so empty; at least that's how I describe it."

"Ya, empty," she said, flipping through the empty pages.

"My whole life, no one told me. Everyone knew but me. I looked like a childish fool all my life, needing protection from the big bad truth."

"I'm so very sorry. I should have told you a long time ago. Time passed and, well, here we are now. It's shaped my life too. This deep, dark secret all my life. It's kept me from getting close to people. It's been hard on my marriage and the boys …"

Shit. I dropped my head in resignation.

"The boys know?"

"That was my mistake. They overheard me talking to Phillip, I didn't tell them on purpose. I'm sorry. Trust me, they've been on my case to tell you for years. They don't get it. They don't get how afraid I've been of you being so mad at me that you never speak to me again." My throat tightened and I took a breath. "And I've just had to let that go — finally — so I could tell you."

Please forgive me. I wanted to cry but held on.

"No one thought you a fool. At some point, I think we all realized we blew it, but time just kept marching on. You get so used to living with a burden that it feels normal, but it's not — it's so confusing."

She nodded and sat very still, again staring at the floor.

The pizza was now cold. I cleared the coffee table, leaving the water. I quietly placed the dishes in the sink, lowered my head. *I did it.* I wept with relief. Gazing out the little kitchen window, the sun now fully set, I could see the hint of our approaching winter. I inhaled deeply. *So this is what it's like to feel free.*

"Maggie?"

Grace stood in the doorway. She opened her arms to me and I moved into them as if our lives depended on it.

"I'm sorry," she said.

As if making up for a lifetime, we held our embrace. A river of emotions flowed in our tears, love being the underpinning of them all. *She said sorry to me?*

"I've missed you so much, Grace, you have no idea."

"I know," she whispered, "because I've missed you."

"Why did you say sorry to me?"

We headed back to the living room.

"You were a child and you found Mum dead all by yourself. You lied to protect me, and I'm sorry you had to keep this secret all your life."

"My God," I said through more tears. "You're the only person that's ever said that to me. The person I lied to."

She then said, "I was so confused. I couldn't understand why I was given away. What had I done that was so bad that Dad didn't want me home with you?" She blew her nose, remembering those painful feelings. "And then he just stopped talking to me, and you stopped too."

More silence.

"Even when you came to Toronto, Dad kept his distance. I tried a couple of times to be close to him, but he'd just move away like I was … poisonous."

She was crying hard. I sat motionless, never having heard this before, never even imagining that she'd have felt this way.

"I thought you were mad at me too. I wanted to spend time with you, alone, to talk, but it seemed you wanted to be with Lacy. I remember waiting for you to come and get me, take me to our room. You never did," she said, resigned to her childhood sadness and confusion. "I wanted to come with you and Dad to BC. I thought when he saw me, he'd change his mind and take me too. But he hardly spoke to me, like he didn't even like me."

I slipped into Grace's shoes, imagining how her little girl self felt, and cried too.

"Of course, I've dealt with all this in therapy, but the trauma's still there," she said, blowing her nose again.

"God, I'm an idiot. I was so envious of you, living there with a big family. You told me you were homesick, so I figured that was natural — of course you'd be homesick."

"I've felt like a problem all my life — well, since being given away."

Silence.

"I knew you didn't want me to go, but it seemed you didn't want me home either."

Silence.

"Aunt Joyce tried so hard, and I felt horrible being homesick. I tried not to be. I'd hear her and Uncle Brian talking about me; I was a problem for them too."

She stopped and looked directly at me. "You know, I never knew Dad until after I got sober, and even then, he didn't seem to want me around much."

I nodded and said, "Yes, that's Dad, a very isolated man. "But," I paused, not wanting to dismiss what I had just been told, "saying sorry doesn't seem enough — it's trite, really. I mean I am sorry, Grace, truly. I'm embarrassed how wrapped up I was in myself — in the lie. When you first left, I was beside myself thinking about you not being with me so we could comfort each other. Then in your letters you sounded like you were doing better — it was so screwed up."

"On top of all that," Grace said, "I couldn't figure out what happened to Mum, like she mysteriously vanished. I knew there was a secret."

"What do you mean?" I asked, surprised.

"It sounds stupid now, but I was only eleven. I thought Dad might have killed her."

I looked at her, trying to put that piece of information in its rightful spot. Then she giggled, and soon we were both having a good belly laugh.

"I knew, though, something was off. This makes total sense to me now. Even when I was so depressed — suicidal — there was so much whispering behind my back. I just always thought they were talking about what a burden I was, how to get rid of me. I had a psychiatrist and therapist, but I didn't share much; I really didn't know what to share. And neither of them told me about Mum's mental illness or suicide — nobody!"

"I know, it baffles me too. How a secret so big and known by so many people … I desperately wanted someone to tell you. Aunt Joyce or Dad, like right away, but they decided it was for the best you not know. But when I got older, I should have told you — no excuse."

We sat quietly.

"Will you come with me to see my therapist?" she asked. "She keeps suggesting she see us both for a few sessions. Never thought it a good idea, but maybe now?"

"Sure, I'll do anything for you — for us."

"Sometimes when I'm in a session, stuff comes up that I'm so mad or sad about, like stuff I didn't even know that I cared about. I blame my drinking — for everything."

"Just recently, I realized that I used your drinking as an excuse for not telling you the truth, but when you stopped, I just had to stay mad at you. I was a coward."

By 11:30 we had chipped the tip of the iceberg, reframing our life stories with "What ifs." It was clear we had both suffered from our mother's death, although I knew in my heart that my sister suffered more. Her stories were heartbreaking, and her subsequent alcoholism made total sense; a young body can only handle so much pain.

"I apologized to Dad and Trish years ago for my behaviour when I moved out here. What a shame; I was such a mess. Lucky I'm alive, really. Still so much shame and regret, but I'm getting there. But I'm sorry I was — the way I was."

Silence.

"Thanks, but no need to apologize to me. We both have shame and regret, and I feel terrible hearing how you felt when Dad and I were in Toronto. I'm sorry for that. Pretty wrapped up in myself having to move to BC, I'd say."

Grace let out a loud, contagious yawn at which time we agreed to resume after school tomorrow; she'd make tea. We hugged at the door, something that we'd now do the rest of our lives, we were sure of that.

I started up the car, chilly in the cool night. Before driving away, I texted Trish: "ALL GOOD :)" Still couldn't believe I actually did it. There were no more tears, no more rehearsing, no blaming. I didn't even tell her about Mum visiting me. *I'll tell her tomorrow.*

"I can tell her tomorrow, at her place, for tea," I said out loud as if it was a natural thing for me to just have tea with my sister and talk about Mum coming to me as an angel AND telling me she loved me. *Oh my God. Unbelievable. And here it is, Dr. Beth, right in front of me.*

Of course, when Phillip saw me waiting up for him at 1:00 a.m., he braced himself for a night of Grace and Maggie drama.

"Well?" he said.

"I have great news," I said, smiling from ear to ear.

. . .

"Good morning, Trish," nurse Peggy said with surprise seeing Trish at 8 a.m. "What brings you here so early in the day?" Peggy looked Trish up and down; she'd never seen her in a full skirt and crinoline before.

"Oh, it's a long story, but I've got a happy ending to share with Jack and I just couldn't wait one more minute," Trish said, pushing past Peggy to get to Jack, who was comatose.

"Jack," Trish said into Jack's ear. "Jack, dear? Jack, wake up, dear, I have something very important to tell you, some very good news," she said with a bit more determination, shaking his shoulder. Upon hearing Trish yell at Jack to wake up, Peggy went into Jack's room.

"You know, Trish, it's been proven that even when a person is sleeping or in a coma or unconscious they can hear what's being said to them."

She saw the writing on the wall *and* understood the importance of the situation. Trish stood, staring down at her beloved, so far away. Peggy gently moved in front of Trish and lowered the side rail. She then brought a chair close to the bed for Trish to sit. She brought Jack's hand over to rest close to the edge of the bed, and as she brought Trish's hand up to hold Jack's she said, "Tell him the good news, he'll hear you." She then quietly closed the door.

"Jack, it's me. I know it's so early and you're still sleeping …" She leaned in closer to his face, holding his hand in both of hers. "Your girls have found each other again!" She knew the importance of this information, and her words caught in her throat — the words she was so happy to share.

"Jack, Maggie and Grace …" he moaned, his hand twitched.

"Oh good, you can hear me. Maggie and Grace have talked — about everything," she said, giving his hand a knowing squeeze on the word 'everything.' "You don't need to worry anymore — they've talked and they've forgiven, Jack. They've forgiven everyone and everything. You can be happy now. Oh fiddle-dee-dee," she said, looking for her tissue to wipe her tears.

Three days later, after only one visit from his girls, Jack died. It was September 27, 2014.

Chapter 36

A Smile From
Across the Room

It was the week before our Thanksgiving celebration. I sat in my armchair in the living room writing a grocery list that would no doubt be left at home. There would be nine of us around the table, and I was actually excited. We would be meeting Brian's new girlfriend Katie. After Phillip completed dish duty, he joined me, giving me a peck on the top of my head as he passed, something I now embraced. He gave me a smile that said, *I like this. I'm happy to be home, with you.*

It was at times like these that I detected the remnants of the wall. The wall of distrust, the wall of abandonment, the wall of skepticism. It could bring me down quickly, and I was once again thirteen staring at my dead mother. *This is why I'm still in therapy.* I smiled back at Phil. He picked up the paper and flopped into his chair with a contended sigh.

"How's your group going?"

"My women's group?" I asked as if I belonged to many groups.

"Ya, how's it going?"

"Why do you ask — she asked curiously."

"What do you do there?"

"We take off all our clothes, light ten candles and dance around them, chanting."

"Hardy har."

"Last meeting, we practiced smiling as a method to pull out of a negative mindset. Interestingly enough, it works. It's rather Dr. Beth like, only she used looking at things right in front of you. So now I do both and so does Grace."

"Still can't get over you two."

"That makes two of us — it blows my mind."

He had sunk into his paper and I got back to my seating plan and topics for dinner conversation. *If you could choose your own name, what would it be and why?*

Jeffery, now wanting to be referred to as Jeff, stepped into the living room so quietly that when he said, "Mum," I jumped.

"OH!"

"Sorry," he said, clearing his throat. His face was pale.

"What, dear? What is it? Are you not feeling well?"

Phillip dropped one corner of the paper to take a look.

"Huh, well, could my boyfriend join us for Thanksgiving dinner?"

Phillip and I looked at each other as if to say, *Did we miss a conversation?* I looked back at Jeff. He looked thinner than I remembered as he stood staring at the floor with his hands folded in front of him. I slammed my jaw shut when I realized it had been hanging open. Jeff sheepishly lifted his head to look at us both and softly said, "Is this really a surprise to you?"

"No Jeff, it's not a surprise," Phillip said. "However, assuming is not the same as knowing."

Way to go, Dr. Phil! I nodded in agreement. Jeff sat down, looking somewhat relieved, colour and animation returning to his face. He had spoken his secret and he lived. I knew this feeling well.

"You're right. Point taken, Dad, you're right."

There was silence that I'm sure was not as long as it felt.

"Is there anything you want to ask me … or say to me?"

How adult of him, I thought. I looked at Phillip and he at me. We shook heads to each other.

"Not right now, dear," I said for both of us.

"Oh, I do have a question."

Oh no, here we go.

"What's your boyfriend's name?"

Jeff dropped his head with relief. "Tyler." Then, looking at his macho Dad with a teary-eyed smile, he said, "His name is Tyler, Dad." Phillip stood and gestured for Jeff to come for a hug and I joined.

"A group hug," Phillip said teasingly as we lovingly hugged our son.

Later that night once safely in bed, Phillip and I desperately held each other and cried hard. It wasn't a surprise that Jeff was gay, but my overwhelming emotional state was. I felt a love for my husband I hadn't felt in, well, I couldn't remember how long.

"Why am I crying?" I said to him as I nestled into his chest. "It's not like we didn't see this coming."

"Maybe relief?" Phillip said with a big exhale, his arms pulling me closer.

Relief was part of it. Relief that Jeff had the courage to speak his truth and also had faith in us. But there was more to it than that.

"Are you worried for him, you know — how difficult his life might be?"

There, I said it; the big scary truth.

"Yup, I'm terrified for him. If he's targeted in any way ... or hurt ..."

"Yes, that's it, that's it ..." I said through my tears.

Even though same sex marriage had been legalized in Canada years ago, hate crimes of different intensities occurred weekly, if not daily or even hourly. For the first time in many years, we fell asleep in each other's arms.

As it turned out, James had been encouraging Jeff to "come out" for years, offering him support if it didn't go well. Jeff's response was to pat James on the back with a jovial laugh as if to say, "You're crazy man, I'm not gay." It was James that told Jeff to ask us if we had questions or wanted to say anything to him when he told us. "Thanks for the advice, bro," Jeff would scoff, but he never showed any signs of anger or defensiveness with James. Eventually he was able to genuinely thank his bro for his support and guidance. All this information came out in many conversations over the weeks. Jeff looked happier than I'd ever seen him. The weight of a secret now out of his way.

Grace and I talked every day, and she soon became a pleasant constant at Sunday dinner. Within six weeks after she lost her beloved Jack, Trish fell and broke a hip, lost her driver's licence, gave up her apartment and moved into assisted living. Grace and I take her out every Saturday for tea, and sometimes she joins us for a Sunday dinner. She almost needs a booster seat at the table. Throughout the years, she remained close to her brother, Ted, and his children, and eventually Ted's new wife. Everyone loved and cared for Trish, it couldn't be helped.

When reminiscing, my sister and I spoke of our lives as either before Mum died or after. This, we discovered, is what people do when they've experienced a major event in their lives. "Do you remember when ..." stories seemed endless, like using imaginary clay to create a real past long forgotten. As we unfolded each story, our parents came into focus, like we'd only seen them through a steamed-up window. They had their own dreams and their own suffering, independent of us. We also talked about Joyce and Brian, seeing them in a new light. How brave and supportive they were. Of course, they did the best they could. We'd visit them soon. They were now both elderly but still on their feet and, thanks to Dave and Joy living close and taking care of things, they remain in the family home. Joyce claims tea is the best health food ever.

Attending therapy with Grace was a godsend. Fran, the therapist, was in her late fifties, divorced, four grown children scattered all over the country. In our first session, I admitted being afraid I would be seen as the "big bad wolf who'd done my sister wrong." The hearty laugh that comment elicited from the two of them put me at ease right away.

"That's my role — I'm the shit disturber," said Grace with a laugh.

"Well, this makes my job easy," Fran said, "both of you taking full responsibility. Let's hear all about it."

It became clear that Grace was extremely dependent on me as a child. I knew this, of course, but not to the degree she described. Through her recovery work, she dealt with her childhood as best she could with the information she had. Not knowing Mum had taken her own life was one missing piece. Her feelings of being unlovable was the worst of it all. Moving to Toronto felt as if her whole family had died. I lapped up all her stories like she was filling in missing body parts. With every detail shared, the dry, cracked earth of our lost childhood was watered.

Our desire to learn more about Dad grew as we cleaned out the closet of our extended family. A trip to Visby was tossed around as a possibility; we were curious, as we always were, about Dad. But first, Phillip treated Grace and me to an August trip to Nova Scotia. He said he needed a break from the

Holm sisters' chatter, belly laughing, crying, singing, hooting and general carry on. This is not to say that we were conflict free, however, we had tools that helped us through those times and we respected each other's healing process and timeline.

We were all set to stay in the Big House, and Lacy, to whom we had become quite attached, would be joining us. Lacy's husband, Mike, was a golf nut and could hardly wait to spend two uninterrupted weeks hitting balls. Lacy married Mike later in life; he was divorced with one son, and Lacy said that was the best kind of kid to have — one that's not yours. I was heartened to hear that Joyce had kept the nature of Mum's death from her children.

"I knew something was weird about it," Lacy said to us once, "but us kids weren't told. And that's a good thing because if I did know, I'd have told you, Grace, even if just to piss off Mum!"

Pretty funny because it was true.

. . .

The wedding room dripped in winter white linens and roses. Large silver hearts dangled from the ceiling. At the bride's request, every female in the room adorned white so there were "brides" everywhere. I confess that the result was magically effective. The spirits of all in attendance had been lifted by the deeply sincere exchange of vows, a smattering of traditional mixed with personal anecdotes that brought a tear to the eyes of all brides in the room, including yours truly.

Head tables were a thing of the past. DJ and Jenna sat alone at their own table under a crystal chandelier. They sparkled, I really do believe, with love. The kind of love that gave flight to romantic notions to all that gazed upon them. I secretly wondered, though, if they had memorized jokes to tell each other at the table. They laughed a lot, just the two of them sitting there enjoying each other's company. Believing that this affection was real would not have been possible for me at one time. Yet there I was not only witnessing it but absolutely loving it.

"Check it out, over there," Phillip said, pointing to Grace who was chatting with a man.

"Who's that?" I asked, seeing a drink in the man's hand.

"Tom Cummings. He teaches with Peter — PE and team sports. They'll have fitness in common."

Phillip smiled and nodded at me. I'd been encouraging Grace to branch out, try online dating, join singles groups, but she showed no interest.

"I've had enough men in my life for two lifetimes," she said.

"They're definitely attracted to each other," I said to Phillip. *This is what I want for her so don't start worrying. What's in front of me?* I turned to Phillip. "You look ever so handsome in your wedding attire — good enough to marry all over again."

He smiled and said, "I do," then kissed me.

There were as many grooms as there were brides. Everyone was made to feel special that night — a well-orchestrated plan by the head couple. Was

I really feeling this relaxed? With a genuine smile, I breathed in deeply as I gazed around the room, inhaling the sight of my family laughing and talking together. My eyes rested on Grace chatting with Tom. She looked stunning in the dress we unanimously agreed upon.

Since the Great Reveal, as we fondly refer to the occasion of me disclosing the truth of Mum's death, we practice tenderness. Our skin is thin, sensitive; PTSD resides in us both, something to share and care for in each other. The two of us are equally committed to healing our past so our new relationship remains healthy and strong. We will continue to see Fran until she fires us, we never miss our Women's Group, and now both of us have regular visit to Fiona's hypnotherapist. Trish turned us on to her gurus and most recently A Course in Miracles. Dr. Beth's methods are second nature to me now, as she said they would be with practice.

Grace looked in my direction, sensing my gaze. A slow smile emerged, and soon we were beaming at each other, a bit teary-eyed. My sister and I are living in the present while shaping a loving future.

"Please everyone, gather round to watch the next Ginger Rogers and Fred Astaire take your breath away as DJ and his bride Jenna perform their first dance together as husband and wife!"

Jenna adorned a short, white, softly flowing empire-waist dress that gave the impression she was a delicate, virginal hot house flower. The long and sexy bridal gown was now draped on a hanger somewhere in the building. Every groom in the room fell in love with her right then and there. Hell, all the brides fell in love with her! The happy couple stood facing each other, holding hands. With a smile and nod, "Happy" by Pharrell Williams jolted the couple into action. One could tell they had rehearsed for months, as they laughed and counted their way through the routine flawlessly. It was a splendid moment when I gave Barb a warm hug and congratulated her on her lovely son and his beautiful bride. The best part was that I meant it, therefore I could say it with a clear mind and loving heart.

"Thank you, isn't it fun?" she said, beaming and taking it all in as if she, too, was surprised by the splendour. "I had no idea about the dance".

Had Barb changed as well or was she always ready to be a friend? Someone grabbed me around the waist from behind. I knew his touch like it was a part of me.

"Come on, woman, lets boogie!"

There we were, Fiona, Dave, Phillip, me, Trish, Grace, Tom, Lacy, Peter, Barb, DJ, Jenna, Brian, Katie, James, Jeff and Tyler — all of us brides and grooms, dancing happily ever after, in the present moment.

THE END